A SHAMELESS LITTLE CON

MELI RAINE

Join my New Releases and Sales newsletter at: http://eepurl.com/beV0gf

Author's note: I also write romantic comedy as Julia Kent and paranormal shifter romance as one-half of the writing duo Diana Seere. Check out those books as well. ;)

❦ Created with Vellum

A SHAMELESS LITTLE CON

BY MELI RAINE

I didn't do it.

I never betrayed my friend.

Last year, I was kidnapped along with presidential candidate's daughter Lindsay Bosworth, forced to help her assailants, my mother implicated in one of the biggest political scandals in American history.

I've been cleared of any wrongdoing, but that doesn't matter. Once you're tried by the media, you're guilty as sin. The truth doesn't get the public's attention.

But shame? Shame *sells*.

And everyone assumes you're tainted.

Now I have my own personal security team, courtesy of the United States government. Not the one you learned about in civics class, though.

I'm being tracked by the deep state. The shadow government. They've assigned Silas Gentian to be with me 24/7. He thinks he knows everything about me–all of it bad–and he does.

On paper.

Like everyone else, he assumes I'm a traitor. A backstabber. A betrayer. Someone who helped a group of violent psychopaths, puppets of powerful men in Washington who made me into a tool.

Yet I see how he looks at me. True desire can't be faked.
Or hidden.
And that goes both ways.
He assumes I'm trying to fool him.
And he might be right.
But not for the reasons he thinks.

A Shameless Little Con is the first book in the Shameless trilogy by *USA Today* bestselling author Meli Raine.

CHAPTER 1

I didn't do it.

I never betrayed my friend.

Of course, that's what I'm supposed to say. *Expected* to say. For the last six months, it feels like *all* I've said. When you're Jane Borokov, *persona non grata*, shamed by the media for your role in aiding and abetting three rapists who kidnapped and tortured Senator Harwell Bosworth's daughter, every word you utter in public is repeated.

Ad nauseum.

Just because the press repeats what you say, though, doesn't mean anyone *believes* you.

I'm sitting in a coffee shop in Santa Barbara, hiding out on the patio. I have a new haircut and color, a frame of layers around my face that glitters in the sunlight. Highlights and lowlights for a redhead make me look older than I am. *Long* gone is my long hair. I had to shed it, along with my dignity, six months ago.

Along with everything I knew about my life.

If you didn't know any details about me and you observed me right here, right now, you'd see a twenty-three-year-old woman sipping from a small white coffee mug, sitting at a black wrought iron table in an uncomfortable metal chair, watching the surf come in. You'd see a woman in a billowing white shirt over a long jersey maxidress with diagonal stripes, red and white and blue, the colors of the flag.

The colors of true patriots. Of people who defend our government from all enemies, foreign–and *domestic*.

You'd see she was wearing silver sandals on her feet and big silver hoops in her pierced ears. She'd sip slowly, gazing at the horizon, and you'd think she was the picture of California cool, relaxed and casual, waiting for the next good thing in life to roll on in.

You would be wrong.

You would also miss the guy sitting two tables over, wearing chinos that hug his body just right, a casual, long-sleeved grey lycra half-zip shirt over a tight white t-shirt. The cloth that covers his muscular, athletic body is just loose enough to hide his weapon, and his dark brown hair is longer than most guys like him would wear it.

He's tan, with an almost too upright posture, the kind that screams Mormon missionary or former military. At a glance, he has a slight sunburn on his cheeks, just the tops, like he was playing at the beach yesterday and got a little too much sun.

He looks like an ambitious go-getter, one of the tens of thousands of guys who live on the Coasts, starting companies, managing other people's money, working at corporations in LA and San Diego.

But that hair. It doesn't fit the image.

It's just long enough around the ears to hide his earpiece.

You might think he's on Bluetooth, taking a conference call. Maybe you'd assume he's working for a start-up in Silicon Valley, multitasking while drinking a Red Bull or a trendy Bulletproof coffee.

You would be wrong again.

Appearances are deceiving.

So are people.

My phone buzzes, vibrating in my pocket. I never turn the ringer on now. *Never.* Anything that draws attention to me has been weeded out of my life. My wardrobe is carefully selected to blend in. Even my coffee order–a small latte–doesn't have any of the extras I used to ask for.

Before.

Back *then*.

Life is about blending in now, an impossible task for someone who has more notoriety than Monica Lewinsky. Shame is a booming industry, one with capital and debt, profit and loss sheets, one that trades in the hard currency of humiliation and intrigue. My ringing phone would be a constant reminder of my ongoing debasement, so I turn it off. Pretend there is no sound.

Pretend in order to function, because if I let myself receive a notification every time someone mentioned me, I'd be buried in cacophony, shattered by so much noise I would dissipate, particles of Jane Borokov in the air everyone breathes, and we can't have that.

If I did that, I wouldn't exist, and right now my best defense *is* just existing.

I'm innocent.

No one believes me.

And as time passes, I see that what people actually believe doesn't matter.

It's what you can manipulate them into *feeling* that counts. Media reports about my so-called heinous actions last year are all about stoking the furious fire of public anger. Get them outraged. Get them frothing. Pitchforks and torches are *so* twentieth century.

Now you tar and feather people with a Share button and a Like. It's so easy. Read the words, feel something, then tap. *Click.*

Move on to the next scandal.

It's all part of your life, right?

Until *you* are the shame sacrifice of the day. Week. Month. *Year.*

We're trained to seek high rewards, but the internet lets us do it with low effort. Got to get that dopamine fix some-where, right?

"Jane."

I start, spilling a bit of the crema from my latte on my hand. The perfect heart at the center of the foamy milk on the surface of my coffee turns into a mangled, jagged mess.

"Jesus! You scared me." I keep my voice to a low hiss, mortified by all of the layers this interruption is breaching. I refuse to look at him, because if I look at Silas Gentian, my newly assigned bodyguard and babysitter, I'll see disgust.

And while I've gotten used to it from everyone else, I still can't stomach seeing it reflected back at me from *him*.

"Sorry." He's clearly not. "We need to go." His eyes dart left and right, evaluative as he scans the patio.

"You can't tell me what to do. My schedule. My life. My choice." Being blunt isn't in my nature. But nothing about my life is natural anymore, so while it's changed, so have I.

Blunt it is.

"We need to go now."

"No."

His sigh is impatient. It's the sound you make when you really can't stand someone. It's the sound you make when you're barely holding it together for the sake of decency. The sound you make when your least favorite roommate is eating crackers on the sofa and you hate them for no reason.

"There's a credible report that you've been targeted by another internet site. Specific plans for physical acts against you discussed in their forums," he says, the diplomacy jarring. What he really means is that anonymous people on the internet are talking about all the ways to rape and torture me, focusing specifically on actual, actionable plans.

"Another one? Are you kidding me? Of course there is. Have you seen my defunct Twitter account, Silas? I was getting a hundred threats a day. Come on." My voice has more snap than normal. I do it to hide the shakes.

His revulsion ripples off him like a shockwave. I can't be around someone who hates me so much. While I'm used to bathing in the scum of internet chatter, it's different in person.

"This one is specific. They've been following you. And it's not from Twitter." He says as few words as possible. Silas has

4

been following me for three days, assigned to my security detail. He said more words in those three sentences than in all the time he's been assigned to me.

All other communication has been printed instructions. *That's* how much he can't stand me. Why did anyone assign him to me, then? Could I at least have a bodyguard who doesn't view me with disdain? Is that too much to ask?

Apparently so.

I look at his hand, the one resting straight at his side. It's a strong hand, the nails neatly trimmed, the knuckles thick and callused. Those are hands accustomed to hard work, clean and ready, trained well to manage violence.

And to deliver it right back in order to protect and serve.

Serve. Who exactly does Silas serve? I know who he protects. Me.

Yet in protecting me, he's protecting others.

Who?

A chill floats across my skin, like the inverse of a ray of sunshine. He's protecting others. At what point do *I* become expendable? I know plenty of people want me dead. Trust me. I know it. I'm not being paranoid. They killed my mother, so I'm not just speculating.

What if this is all a trap?

His hand moves, going up to his ear, and as he turns slightly to the right, toward the ocean, I stand. A swift breeze whips my skirt up. I gasp and shove my hands down, fast, like Marilyn Monroe over a street grate. The feeling of my long jersey skirt against my thighs is seductive, arousing and luxurious, like a lover's touch.

As the salty air licks my face, I expect my hair to wrap around my neck, but it doesn't. You spend more than a decade with waist-length hair and your body comes to know it, view it as an extension of yourself.

And now it's gone.

Tears pinprick behind my eyelids at the thought. The shell I've built to keep in my pain isn't easy to crack but for some reason I start to cry, mourning my hair. It was my choice to cut and color it. One of the few choices I've had in this crazy mess.

But *mine*.

I widen my eyes and look straight into the wind, creating an excuse for my tears. Silas will not see me crack, will not watch me weep. I do that alone, where it's safe, where I can let all the shame drain out of me in sobs and hitches.

Never, *ever* in public.

Silas is on the phone, watching me, his voice hushed, sky-blue eyes cold and on guard. When they–the mysterious *they*–appointed him to protect me, I took the assignment at face value. Now I'm starting to wonder if I've been a fool.

Scratch that. Not *if*.

How *much* of a fool.

I went along with being offered–*ordered*–to let Silas "protect" me because at this point, most of the fight in me is gone. No longer under official investigation, my case is closed, even if the public humiliation is far from over. Senator Bosworth told me in confidence that letting his team offer me protection would be smart. Too many rogue elements, too much media frenzy.

I'm still the scandal *du jour*, and if keeping me in the spotlight sells newspapers and gets websites more eyeballs for their ad revenue, then Jane Borokov is going to be hawked until the website clicks die down.

Given that my mother is dead, I don't exactly have a trusted adult I can turn to. Senator Bosworth is it.

As Silas becomes increasingly cagey, though, I'm rethinking my whole understanding of how this all operates. Maybe I put my confidence in the wrong person. After all, why should the senator be nice to me? In everyone else's mind, I helped his daughter's abusers and worst of all, my mother handed his daughter Lindsay off to them like a UPS driver delivering a box of shoes from Zappos.

Cold terror floods my veins. Is that why Silas is being so mean to me?

Because he's *allowed*? Did I misjudge the senator?

Have I misjudged *everyone*?

That's it. I'm done. I need to get away from all of this and just think.

As I walk toward the small alleyway that leads to the parking lot, Silas grabs my arm, hard. It's the grasp of a man who views me as an object to be controlled.

I wrench my arm free.

"Don't go out there. It's not safe," he barks.

People start to watch us, whispering in huddles of two and three, all of them the overdone women of our town, the kind my best friend–make that *ex*-best-friend–Lindsay was supposed to grow up to be.

"You're making a scene," I hiss. "I'm trying to blend in and you're making it impossible."

"Blend in?" His eyes rake over my body, pausing at the swell of my hips, locking on my lips. "You're long past that, Jane." If we were in any other situation, I'd assume his words were a double entendre, that he was admiring my body rather than insulting my pride.

I know better.

"No thanks to you, asshole," I mutter as I stalk off, Silas on my heels.

"Now who's the one making a scene?" he says so quietly, but the wind pushes his words to me. He doesn't try to touch me again, though.

I'll take my victories where I can get them.

The alleyway is cavelike, with a high arch to the adobe ceiling. It's cool, a relief from the sun, but I scurry as fast as I can, unnerved by being in such a dark, enclosed space. After spending much of the last six months in small offices and interrogation rooms, my tolerance has been pushed to the limit.

Sunlight floods my face as I emerge, Silas behind me, his pace picking up.

"Jane!" he bellows, voice tinged with a tone that makes me slow–but not halt.

I flip him the bird. He grabs my wrist, suddenly there. How did he move so fast? Hot breath, smelling like coffee and mint, fills the air as he leans in, impossibly big and terrifyingly attractive.

"Don't run away from me. Ever. That's not how this works."

"You're making it very, very hard for me to be invisible."

"Invisible? Good luck with that. You lost the right to be invisible the day you betrayed Lindsay. How long ago was it, Jane? Were you part of the entire attack from the very beginning?" None of his words surprise me, even as the verbal knife digs in deep, flaying me to the bone. I've been waiting for three days for Silas to finally speak his mind.

Here we go.

"I didn't do it. I told you."

"You mean you *lied* to me. Lied to everyone."

"Believe what you want to believe."

"I believe the truth."

Electricity shoots up my back, the pinpricks of outrage finding their way to the surface of my skin. After months of literally being spat at, having photoshopped pictures of me giving head spread far and wide on the internet, finding dead animals on my front step, and of being refused service, taxis, and apartment rentals because of my face, my name, my notoriety, you would think I'd be immune to what Silas is dishing out.

But it's Silas. Long gone is the sweet do-gooder who came with Lindsay to meet me for coffee seven months ago. Long gone is the man who blushed when I made a sex joke at a bar.

Back then–before.

"I *am* telling the truth," I hiss back.

"Your truth is a lie, then, and you're too stupid to realize it."

"No, Silas. It's the other way around. You're too blinded by loyalty to Drew to see that you're all hurting everyone more by believing I'm a monster."

His hands go up in the air, like a man surrendering. No–like a man so disgusted by an animal in front of him that he's given up on it, deeming it a hopeless case.

That's me. Hopeless. Shameless and hopeless. Why fight it? The world assumes they know I'm one way. Maybe I need to give up resisting and just go with it.

"Go, then. I'm done trying to talk sense into you."

"I already have more than enough common sense, so quit wasting your time."

"You confuse stubbornness with common sense."

"And you confuse truth and lies. Leave me alone and stop following me. You make me stand out!" More passersby watch us, eagle-eyed, and paranoia rises in me. I stare back at them hard, moving one step closer to Silas as if this is just a lovers' spat, nothing to see here, move along folks.

Except he moves away from me, recoiling.

"Leave me *alone*," I whisper through tears.

He ignores me, pressing his fingers against his ear, listening, frowning.

I break into a light jog, slowing down as I see it just makes people look at me more. I take a deep breath and pretend to jolt, grabbing my phone out of my purse as if it had vibrated. Joining the masses, I stare at my phone, acting like I'm reading important business on it.

Just blending in.

I look up to see my little silver car, the back rear light cover cracked, the remnants of bumper stickers littering the bumper. I carefully scraped them off right after I was allowed to go home, deeply grateful to my past self for choosing a boring silver car back when I bought my little hybrid. Talk about fitting in here along the California coast. I look like a million other people on the I-5, and that's a good thing.

Boring is safe.

Blending in means survival.

Something darts from the front of my car. Looks like a bird, but bigger. Weird. As I tilt my head and narrow my eyes to get a better look, two things happen.

One: a boulder made of muscle and pure sizzle collides with me from behind, my name a breathless growl on Silas's lips as he slams me to the ground, knocking the wind out of me, making me freeze in pain. I can't breathe, and as I buck

9

underneath his immobile body, all rolling strength and steel-boned flesh, I look up.

Two: a wave of heat sears my face as I look at my car, which is now engulfed in flames that shoot ten feet in the air, like someone poured brandy all over it and set it on fire for entertainment.

Except I'm supposed to be *in* that car.

All thoughts fade as my vision pinpoints, something hard on Silas's chest digging into my shoulder blade. I'd scream if I could, but there's no air. No air at all as I float off, my body spasming and thrashing under him, trying to breathe so the grey crowding my vision will stop.

He rolls to the side, arm and leg over me, muttering into his earpiece, words and numbers in code. A great whoosh of air crushes my diaphragm, making me cough, the fire's glow growing bigger. Silas's mouth is against my ear, his breath hotter than any burning car, and he whispers:

"Invisible. Blend in. Right. Doing a great job, Jane." He huffs. "It's like you don't even exist."

CHAPTER 2

J'm yanked roughly to my feet and half dragged to an SUV that pulls up with a screech, blocking the front entrance to the small strip of quaint little stores, covering a giant No Parking sign. Silas picks me up like I weigh nothing, like I'm a rag doll he can toss into a child's toy chest. The car door snaps shut and I jerk to the right as we peel out, my body flopping into Silas, face-planting directly into his lap.

I don't exist, huh?

"Get your face off my dick," he says, lifting me by the arm.

"Get your dick out of my face," I shoot back, a thousand percent done with being treated so poorly. "And where do you think you're taking me?"

"Somewhere far away from the burning coffin you used to call your car."

I sit up and grab the seat belt so hard, it catches, forcing me to be patient as I reel it all the way back in, hear a click, then slowly pull the belt out, securing myself in place. The SUV is roomy, but it feels like we're in an interrogation cell, stale, humid air filling my senses.

Except I wish the air were stale. Instead, Silas's scent dominates. There is something about a man in charge, a tingling mix of aftershave and nerves that makes breathing hard. Not unpleasant. Quite the opposite. I'm so angry.

I don't have room in my body to be turned on, too.

Tamping *that* emotion down, I turn and look out the back window. We're already so far away that all I see is a tall line of black smoke rising up, like a puppet's string leading up to whoever's in control.

"My car," I groan, the sound more like a wail.

"You're welcome," Silas says tersely.

"I'm *what*?"

"You're welcome."

"I'm supposed to thank you? For what?"

"For stopping you before you got turned into a human Pop-Tart in a Toyota toaster."

I gape at him, my hands pressed hard against the tops of my thighs. If I don't, I might strangle him. "You follow me everywhere. I can't fade into the woodwork and try to pick up some semblance of a normal life. I have some shadow intelligence agency tracking my every move, my car just got flame roasted, and I'm supposed to be *grateful*?" The air reeks of burnt gasoline and hair.

He shrugs. "Wouldn't hurt."

"Fuck you."

"Not in a million years, Jane. Not in a million years," he says with a laugh that feels like rusty nails being dragged over sandpaper.

"You used to be nice," I spit out, hating my hurt tone.

"And you used to be decent. Or at least you fooled everyone into thinking you were."

"I *am* decent!"

He makes that sound again. The one that feels like a knife against my heart. Disgust radiates off him. Maybe that's what I really smell in the SUV. The scent of my own rejection.

My phone buzzes again. I ignore it. I'm being monitored by every government agency you can imagine, and my mother's dead. Most of my texts are from sleazy newspapers offering me money for insider info. For nude pictures. Being falsely accused and turned into the villain in the biggest government scandal since Watergate means people offer you seven figures to take off your clothes.

If I were as indecent as Silas thinks I am, I'd take the deal.

As it stands, though, I'm stuck being naked in other ways.

"Take me home," I say, but without conviction. I know he'll tell me no. Besides, where is "home"? My mom's house is a crime scene. My landlord evicted me from my apartment as soon as the scandal erupted. I've been living in safe houses and government-paid-for hotels since all the investigations ended.

Ended.

Nothing's ended. Just the dog-and-pony show for the public. All of the nastiness is still present in my life. Every last pungent drop.

"We're taking you somewhere safe."

"You mean to Oz?"

He frowns. "Australia?"

I snort, the sound coming with a strange lump in my throat that I can't handle right now. I will not cry. I will not cry.

I will not cry in front of *him*.

"No. The Wonderful World of Oz. You know, that magical safe place that doesn't exist?"

"You're ranting."

"I have every right to rant."

His eyes take me in, gaze piercing. For once, he's looking at me. Really looking, as if studying me matters. As if *I* matter. No one has looked at me like this in six months. For half a year, I've been arrested, detained, accused, advised, pitied, hated, and most of all–shamed.

But I haven't *mattered*.

It feels like I can breathe again when Silas looks at me like this.

His face is broad and skin clear, eyes the color of a placid Caribbean bay. With wide shoulders and perfect posture, he carries himself with purpose. No movement is wasted. No action is lost.

At the same time, he is gentle and polite. I cannot judge

him by his outer shell. Thick hair, a strong brow, a carefully shaven jaw... none of these tell me a single, solitary detail about Silas's inner world.

Turning toward me, his knee brushes against mine, the gesture so intimate, my body warms suddenly. I'm already nervous and edgy–who wouldn't be, after that?

This is different. I can't stop staring back.

"You do have a right to rant. You have lots of rights."

"Like what?"

"You have the right to remain silent," he starts, one corner of his mouth twisting with a sick cynicism I can't stomach.

So I turn away.

And invoke that very right.

"Gentian?" Drew Foster's voice crackles on some sort of communication device. The driver hands Silas a two-way radio, big and bulky, like something from a 1990s television show.

"Yes, sir?" Silas knows how to use it.

"Secured?"

Silas doesn't bother to give me a glance. "Yes, sir."

"Looks like the firebombing of the subject's car was just some internet trolls who took it from mom's basement to the real world."

The subject? Now I'm *the subject*?

I groan. I can't help it. The sound comes out more emotional than I want. It's more like a whimper.

No. I can't have that. My feelings are the only privacy I have left. I can't reveal them.

Silas turns away from me, his muscled body large yet graceful. When he was guarding my friend Lindsay, seven months ago, he always wore a suit. But Lindsay is Senator Harwell Bosworth's daughter. People expect to see suited bodyguards surrounding her. For me, the men who follow my every move seem to dress in business casual wear.

Which makes Silas even more attractive, for some reason.

"Shitlords? Jane's car was set on fire by *shitlords*?" Silas's use of internet-speak for online trolls, vicious commentators who threaten people online for the sake of attention, surprises me. Maybe he knows more than I give him credit for. I've been dealing with shitlords online for a very long time.

"Affirmative," Drew barks. "Which makes this easier."

"Easier," I mutter. Whatever that means. Nothing about my life has been easy. You know someone's a hardened former special-ops high-level security person when they refer to any part of a firebombing as easy.

"Not an inside job?" Silas asks, more as confirmation than inquiry.

"No. Too messy. If they want to take her out, a public display of pyrotechnics definitely won't be it," Drew says.

The clinical way they're talking about methods people might use to *murder* me is fascinating. And terrifying.

Mostly terrifying.

"Tracked them down yet?"

"Close. Looks like your average group of angry online guys who think John, Stellan, and Blaine got a bad rap."

I lose the ability to listen after that. A small minority of shitlords on the internet consider Lindsay's attackers–correction, *my* attackers, too–to be the victims of a conspiracy designed to bring good men down. The video of Lindsay stabbing Stellan point blank in the crotch has been shown nearly as many times online as the most-watched cat video in internet history.

And the comments on every copy of it? Don't read them.

Don't. Save yourself the agony.

My skin is a live wire as the implications of what just happened start to sink in. While fighting with Silas is a perfectly fine way for me to manage my panic, in the long run it won't stop my body from reacting to the fact that someone just torched my car.

Seconds before I was *in* it.

"Was it a bomb?" I ask, feeling stupid.

For once, Silas doesn't treat me like I am. "A timed bomb. Yes."

"Why did it go off before I was in the car?"

"Because shitlords aren't exactly known for their technical prowess." He shrugs, a muscle at his temple twitching in anger. "They spend more time perfecting their Photoshop skills on cartoon frogs than on the finer art of explosives." The planes of his face change as emotion radiates out paradoxically, his controlled demeanor contrasting with the tells his body is giving.

His anger is directed at *them*. Not me.

It's a nice change.

"You mean it was a fluke that the bomb went off before I got in the car?"

"Looks like it."

I sag against the window, bile rising in my throat. My hair feels like a wave of stone against my forehead. I push it off, feeling a dry grit in it. I peel whatever's stuck in my hair out and look at my fingers.

It's like dust, but not.

Silas watches, then frowns. "It's singed."

"Singed?" The word doesn't make sense. Nothing makes sense.

"Your hair. The ends of it." He reaches up and touches his own. "Looks like you were closer, so the heat got you and burned the ends."

"I was that close?"

His face goes blank. "Yes."

My tongue feels big in my mouth, closing off my throat. I know what it means when security guys go blank.

It means I was a lot closer to death than I thought.

The shakes set in, making my knees knock together. Even my long maxidress can't hide that. My thighs rub together under the long diagonal stripes. I cross my legs and arms, curling up into myself like a potato bug. If I roll into a tiny little ball, can I disappear?

That's the part I don't understand. People don't want me to exist. If they don't want me to exist, why hound me? Why talk about me and follow me and torment me? Wouldn't the path of least resistance be to ignore me into oblivion?

Which is what Silas appears to be doing right now as he turns away. I get a cold shoulder after a hot car. Perfect.

Just perfect.

The driver turns on some music, the sound of 1970s rock filling the small space as we zig and zag our way out of Santa Barbara and into an old neighborhood I don't know. Silas is murmuring into the walkie-talkie. I reach into my purse, pull out earbuds, shove them into my phone and open a music app.

I mute it.

I pretend to zone out.

Pretending is the cornerstone of civilized society.

It's also the only way to survive this mess I've lived through for the past year.

Longer, actually. I've been pretending since the night I found Lindsay naked, hog-tied, bruised and bloody, left by our three friends after they raped her. I wasn't faking my outrage and horror that night. Definitely wasn't pretending to feel compassion or empathy.

But from the moment they took her away in an ambulance, I knew I had to shelter my knowledge. Put it deep inside me, in a place no one could ever reach.

Because knowledge will kill you in politics. When you're the child of people involved in a high-stakes governance game, you learn that by kindergarten.

Exhibit A: my burning car.

"She swears, Drew," I hear Silas say. "I believe her. I don't want to, but my gut says *yes*."

I know he isn't talking about me. My heart wishes he were, but he's not. My chest starts to cave in, the space where my soul resides a sinkhole. My belly curls, navel stretching back as if it's trying to touch my tailbone. It makes breathing difficult, but that's to be expected when I'm trying not to sob.

A thousand feelings cry out inside me, like people in a large crowd screaming to be heard above the white noise of everyone just being. No single voice makes sense, even when some feelings are louder than others. It's all crazymaking. As

I sit here feeling like I barely escaped becoming a flambéed Jane, my skin wants to peel off me and run off to join the circus.

People think the hardest part about being shamed is the feeling itself, but it's not. People think that being in the media spotlight 24/7 is unbearable because of the constant intrusion into your life, but it's not.

All of that sucks, yes.

The single hardest part is being inside your own body, your mind trapped in place, and living second by second without a chance to pause. Think. Breathe.

Be.

I fiddle with my phone as Silas continues talking. I pick up a few phrases, like "the senator" and "investigations confirm she's not guilty" and "surveillance shows she's not on Tor." I know now that he *is* talking about me.

The radio cuts to voices, the tone jarring as the '70s rock turns to the intro of a famous radio show, one where a host picks a topic and various people do short segments about the topic.

"Tonight, our focus is on a universally experienced emotion, one that crosses all cultures: shame."

Silas's glance cuts to me. I see him out of the corner of my eye. I do not meet his gaze.

"Internet shaming, to be specific. The convergence of hyper-modern technology and old-fashioned values makes the topic of shame uniquely fascinating. We all fear being shamed. It's rooted in our DNA, for to be shamed means to be excommunicated–physically and/or emotionally–from others. It's the whole point. When someone is called shameless, it's always an insult, one driven by social horror. To be without shame is to be not quite human."

I almost throw up.

I don't imagine the choked, derisive sound Silas makes. I pretend to fiddle with my earbuds as if I'm not listening.

"The internet gives humankind unprecedented access to instant communication with perfect strangers, leaving us with a sense of intimacy that is evolutionarily misplaced. We think we're closer than we are to people when we Tweet, leave a Facebook comment, send an

email. It's as if technology allows us a shortcut, the brain equating the push of a button to Submit, Send, or Follow with the shake of a hand, the eye contact of introductions, the smile of an understood joke."

The skin around Silas's eyes turns down, his brow lowering as he makes an expression of listening. I feel my breath tickle my hand as I hold the palm toward my mouth, elbow on the SUV's armrest, turning away from Silas.

I can't look at him right now.

I'm also not sure where we're going and what's about to happen to me.

"Tonight, we're going to look at three instances of modern-day shaming, and how technology plays a role. First, we'll look at the most famous scandal in politics–"

No.

"–in US history with a report from our correspondent, Prakesh Mahti. Second, we'll examine the internet campaign against Dr. Roberta Goundin..."

The voice drowns out as a strange, airy silence fills my head.

See? Shame sells.

Literally.

CHAPTER 3

"Could you change the station?" I call out to the driver.

"Don't," Silas says, cutting me off. He doesn't look at me, staring straight ahead. "I'd like to listen to this. Besides, you have your earbuds in, right?" His smirk makes it clear he knows they're a ruse. He's calling me out on my own fakery, damn it.

"Fine. Suit yourself," I grumble, shoving the earbud back in and really turning on the music.

Except... I'm curious.

Stupid, right? Why would I marinate myself in popular culture's interpretation of what I did or didn't–mostly *didn't*–do when it came to a senator's daughter being gang raped by our friends?

Because I can't help myself.

I *can't*.

Just like some part of me can't help wishing Silas would validate me. Be nice to me. *Believe* me.

If I could tune it all out, turn it all off, make it all go away, I would. Sometimes I envy sociopaths. Narcissists. People with character disorders who have no consciences. It must be so easy to live without an inner voice. Can you imagine? Going through life without tracking other people's emotions.

21

Spending time without beating yourself up, or worrying about how your actions make other people feel.

Not caring that the world thinks you're a traitor, a betrayer, a woman who helped three men gang rape and nearly murder your friend.

Twice.

How do I turn off all these feelings that crawl along the inside of my skin like termites, eating me from the inside out?

Seriously–how? Tell me the secret.

Instead, I listen. My music volume gets lower and lower as my resolve disappears.

"Two words. Lindsay Bosworth. What comes to mind when I say her name? If you're like most Americans, you recall the live-streaming television and video that circulated nearly five years ago, in which Senator Harwell Bosworth's daughter was captured on camera having sex with three men. After the fact, her friends came forward to claim Ms. Bosworth's actions were intentional and consensual, leading to an internet shaming campaign that lasted for years."

Oh, God. I'm not sure I can listen to any of this. I glance at Silas.

His face is a mask.

"But if that's all you know, then you've been living under a rock for the last six months. Because just as Senator Bosworth announced his run for the presidency, a new scandal rocked the senior senator from California, as the men in the original video turned out to be more than they seemed–much, much more."

"Isn't everyone?" Silas says in a cold voice. "No one is ever what they seem."

I ignore him. I can't ignore the gut punch his words create, but I try.

"It turns out those three friends of Lindsay Bosworth lied about the original incident, and Ms. Bosworth was drugged. The sex was never consensual, her reputation ruined for reasons that are still opaque. Thousands of hours of testimony before lawyers, Senate and House inquiries, intelligence community investigations, and still all we know is this: Lindsay Bosworth was a victim. And she was victimized twice. Once by those men, and once by her friends."

"Friends," Silas sputters. "Right."

Shut up! I scream in my head.

"Then it happened again. Targeted by the very same men who brutally attacked her before, Lindsay Bosworth was the focus of a campaign to destroy her father. She was a pawn. He was the king. And a man Senator Bosworth had known for decades–Senator Nolan Corning–was aiming for checkmate. At any price."

"How's your old buddy Nolan, Jane?" Silas asks, finally turning and looking at me.

I point to my earbuds and give him a twisted, fake smile. "What? I can't hear you."

His eyebrows twitch, a strange gesture of doubt that gives me a weird electric bolt of hope. Maybe he'll at least stop being mean to me if I pretend I'm not listening.

"Records found by intelligence agencies investigating the Bosworth matter found evidence of communications between Senator Corning and the three attackers, major league baseball player John Gainsborough, television celebrity Stellan Asgarth, and California state representative Blaine Maisri.

"In a shocking development, emails and texts between the group of men and Corning and sent through privacy channels designed to make the communications untraceable show a careful, calculated plan to harm the senator's daughter."

This time, Silas says nothing. I let my shoulders relax.

"The twist: all three men who assaulted Lindsay Bosworth are now dead, two killed by her security team, one at her own hand. The heroic rescue, captured on live-streaming video under bizarre circumstances involving noted pornography star Tiffany Marquis, left Gainsborough, Asgarth, and Maisri dead. Untangling the full story has taken six months. We have twenty minutes. We'll do our best."

Great. Hurry up, journalists. Get in as much shaming as you can. Bring out the bad guys.

And by bad guys, I don't just mean John, Stellan, and Blaine.

I mean *me*.

"Central to this brutal story is the role of Jane Borokov, Lindsay Bosworth's friend, who found her beaten and bound nearly five years ago in the first event. Lindsay's childhood friend and daughter of

Senator Bosworth's executive assistant, Jane Borokov called 911 immediately and administered basic first aid at the time, explaining that she had left the house party by accident, intending to be there. She went back to the house to use the bathroom and discovered Ms. Bosworth alone, naked and tied up, covered in blood, with numerous broken bones. Borokov's testimony at the time was contradicted by their mutual friends, Amanda Witherspoon, Jenna Marquez, and Tara Holdstrom, who claimed that Ms. Bosworth had asked for drugs and had told them that she wanted to experience having sex with all three men."

And then.

And then Tara's voice, breathy and panicked, fills the SUV.

"I never meant to lie! I swear! We were threatened that if we didn't lie and tell everyone that Lindsay got high on her own, that if we didn't tell the police that Lindsay set it all up and wanted a gang ba–um, an orgy, then we'd be ruined."

Even Silas winces, pinching the bridge of his nose in an expression of pain.

"That was Tara Holdstrom, in sworn testimony before a House inquiry committee. As the story unfolded, security teams and private investigators, prosecutors, and FBI officials all interviewed the six surviving people at the heart of the matter–Lindsay Bosworth, Andrew Foster, Jane Borokov, Amanda Witherspoon, Jenna Marquez, and Tara Holdstrom–to piece together a comprehensive whole. The bottom line: we now know the original story to be a lie."

I've been holding my breath without realizing it. With that last line, I exhale. Silas turns and looks at me. I see him out of the corner of my eye, but don't look back.

"Lots of stories told back then were lies," he says smoothly. "Especially yours."

"I'm the only one telling the truth," I mutter, unable to keep up the pretense. "Aside from Lindsay."

"Or you're the only one capable of continuing to manipulate people for longer than most people could endure."

"You tell me, Silas. You're a military intelligence specialist. Am I really lying? Are you *sure?*" My voice goes up, turning bitter, like overripe fruit about to drop, long past the point of remaining attached.

For a brief second, a flicker of authentic emotion comes into those blue eyes, dark now, the color of stormy skies over a giant lake in August, so blue, they're almost gunpowder grey. Maybe I'm deluding myself, but I swear what I see is uncertainty, a crack in the armor of his anger that comes from assuming I'm as bad as the media says I am.

And, unless I'm seriously and truly inventing my own little world, I am pretty sure I saw a spark of desire in there, too, setting my skin ablaze. It can't be. I'm so desperate for any validation that I'm human that I've reached a point where I am inventing this.

I'm sick.

I'm sick in the head.

Sick in the heart, too.

"I know what you did."

"You know what people want you to think."

"And you're one of those people, Jane. You're trying to manipulate me. The difference between you and them is that they're not backstabbing little–"

The radio crackles, the next words cutting through our argument:

"...the three assailants went on to become stars in their respective fields, high flyers who rose up the ranks a little too quickly to call it merit. A major league baseball player. A television acting star. A state rep on his way to a national Senate seat before the age of thirty. It was too good to be true.

"Because it was."

"Lindsay Bosworth spent four years in a private 'meditation retreat' known more for its medical mental health services than for its yoga and spa treatments, slut-shamed and portrayed as a woman who asked for it."

"They got it wrong with Lindsay, and they got it wrong with me," I snap.

"When Harwell Bosworth, the senior senator from California, decided to announce his candidacy for president of the United States, Lindsay Bosworth re-emerged into public view. Present at his

announcement in Sacramento, her head of security was none other than Andrew Foster, her ex-boyfriend who sat by and did nothing during the attack four years earlier. No one knew that the faceless man in the video was him—or, at least, the media didn't know."

Silas makes a little noise, almost an acknowledgment of Drew's suffering. Even without the guy here, Silas shows compassion.

I'm blindly jealous, suddenly and intensely. He's so tight with Drew. There's no way the guy is just a boss. They're friends, their bond forged by years in the military, by a deep trust that I've only ever had with one person.

My mom.

Who handed one of my best friends over to torturers.

An ache inside me threatens to split my body in two, my skin fragile and tissue thin, as if it'll tear if I even think about anything for too long. The world is full of topics too fraught with emotion. I understand now why people drink to black out, take drugs until they go unconscious, eat themselves to half a ton, watch television for days in a haze.

Every second inside my own head is misery. Getting a break from the never-ending racing thoughts would be nice, and by "nice" I mean heavenly. Living is hard enough.

Living under so much scrutiny, with the self-critical voice inside me amplified by millions of external critics all cranking out their opinions to get attention on social media and in the news makes me wish for an escape.

Pray for connection.

Beg the universe for a break.

"Here's the biggest question in the Lindsay Bosworth scandal: what, exactly, was Jane Borokov's role?"

My stomach drops and turns to ice at the same minute. I will my finger to move to the window button, knowing I have seconds before I throw up.

The window doesn't move. Of course it doesn't.

They've locked me in.

"Borokov is the daughter of longtime executive assistant to Senator Bosworth, Anya Borokov. By all accounts, Lindsay and Jane were friends. Maybe not best friends, but good friends. They ran in the

same circles as John, Blaine, Stellan, and Drew Foster. Hung out with Jenna, Tara, and Amanda, who goes by Mandy. Imagine, if you will, a social group made up mostly of the rich children of high achievers. The crème de la crème. And Jane was low man on the totem pole."

"Unlock my window!" I rasp, feeling the cold dread as it pinpricks through my blood, rising up from my belly through my throat, the acid burning up into the back of my mouth, choking me. This is what they do to you. They talk about you. They talk and talk and provoke and speculate until all the lies and all the truths blend together into a tornado of attention.

The truth doesn't matter. People aren't held to account.

All that counts is *attention*.

I use every ounce of energy left in me as my eyebrows go numb, the force of gagging too much. In the nick of time, the window lowers and a big burst of fresh air hits my face. It's an antidote, a balm, a quick fix.

Maybe not a cure. But it's something. And it stops me from emptying that lovely latte all over the side of the SUV.

The wind from the open window obscures the radio, so I can't hear the lengthy section where the announcer talks about me, but I know what they're saying.

Jane Borokov has Russian connections.

Jane Borokov allegedly found Lindsay tied up, raped, and beaten five years ago.

Jane Borokov may have been in on the original attack from the beginning.

Jane Borokov was feeding false information to Lindsay while she was in a mental hospital.

Jane Borokov colluded with her mother to bring down Senator Bosworth in an alliance with Nolan Corning.

I know every word they're saying.

I have to.

It's not like I've had a choice.

And every word of it is wrong. No one believes me.

Especially Silas.

"Close the window," he says softly. "You're at risk."

"And so are you."

He gives me a nonplussed look.

"At risk of getting a lapful of my mouth."

FROM. I mean to say "from my mouth," but the look on his face combined with my own internal horror render me speechless just as the radio announcer says:

"...despite so much evidence showing Borokov had extended contact with the men who harmed Lindsay Bosworth, from Nolan Corning to the three men who did his dirty work, she remains at large, thoroughly investigated but never charged. Her mother, Anya Borokov–"

I close my eyes and start to shake, the wind blowing the tears in the corners of my eyes into the curl of my outer ears. My stomach curdles, the sensation like a hot piece of metal inside, searing me, making my blood warm. All of the regulation in my skin is gone, pieces of me alternating between hot and cold, relaxed and tense, my body a machine that is malfunctioning, firing at will.

And yet I inhale. I exhale. I ignore Silas. I ignore the radio.

Until I can't.

"...questions remain, though. Jane Borokov claims she is innocent, used as an unwitting tool by the attackers. Five years ago, she says, she was supposed to stay at the party, her departure with friends an accident, her return a simple act of fate. When her mother handed Lindsay Bosworth off to her attackers in broad daylight on the helipad at the Bosworth compound, Jane claims she, too, was kidnapped, forced to act as an errand girl for John, Blaine, and Stellan, unaware that Nolan Corning was the mastermind. She maintains to this day that she never worked with them. While the court of public opinion has virtually tarred and feathered her, with her name one of the most hashtagged worldwide for the last six months, others believe her."

Silas makes a noise that shows he's *not* one of the "others."

"A member of the intelligence community who agreed to be interviewed for this report on condition of anonymity says that Jane–and possibly her mother, Anya–were set up by Nolan Corning and others. While no one has pieced together a single cohesive story to explain all of the byzantine details, our source says the following is possible."

Silas leans in slightly, eyes narrowing.

A different man's voice, clearly from a recording, comes over the car's speakers.

"No one should take what they see at face value," the anonymous source says, his voice like sandpaper dragged against the inside of my eyelids, my tongue, my beating heart.

I know that voice.

Oh, God, do I know that voice. The light Irish lilt.

It's the man who told me how to "help" Lindsay all those years she was stuck on the Island. The man with the light stutter that always made me feel more nervous.

That's my informant. My source.

And ultimately, he's the person who betrayed me. I don't know his name. I've never seen his face. Yet I spent four years trusting that he was helping me help Lindsay.

And here I am, paying all the prices for my mistakes.

"Jane Borokov is as much a victim in this web of deceit as Lindsay Bosworth and Drew Foster were."

Silas sits up. "He called him Drew."

I just look at him.

"Only people who know him call him Drew. The media use his full name."

A thousand sharp needles are running fast through my blood. It's impossible to concentrate on what Silas is saying. The words coming out of the speakers feel like burning coals being poked at me.

"The level of backstabbing, corruption, lies, and scandal in this mess is so much greater than the public could ever imagine. People you think are the villains are innocent, and people the public reveres are tainted. The truth will come out in time. It always does."

As he listens intently, Silas looks troubled, his throat tightening. He blinks rapidly, then runs a hand through his hair, clearly struggling to control his thoughts.

Or maybe his emotions.

"Our anonymous source paints a wildly different picture of the mother-and-daughter team the Borokovs created. His opinion dissents greatly from the crowd, yet he is not alone."

I work on breathing, reaching up to touch my hair, finding

it crinkled. I frown, then remember in a wave of panic that just twenty minutes ago someone blew up my car. They tried to kill me. I'm a wanted woman.

Wanted *dead*.

Life happens at whirlwind speed these days. Nothing unfolds in a calm, orderly fashion. It's all shouts and whispers, screams and taunting, an endless line of provocation and reaction.

I never, ever get time to think. To recharge. To relax.

To *exist*.

"'He is not alone,'" I whisper, letting the tears come as fat drops fill until they are impossibly big, so close to breaking I can't stand it, the pressure of so much salty despair concentrated on my eyeballs like being trapped alive in my own coffin.

As the tears break, the water runs over my cheeks, pouring out.

Silas ignores me. I ignore him. We're sitting three feet from each other.

This is how people die from shame.

So many questions remain about the Bosworth affair. Why did Nolan Corning set up such a high-profile, extraordinarily violent scheme to bring down Harwell Bosworth? What were his motives, and why did he use an innocent young woman as the proxy for hurting the senator? How did Gainsborough, Asgarth, and Maisri drug Lindsay and, allegedly, Andrew Foster and get away with it? Why did Lindsay's best friends from school turn on her in such a public, cold manner? Motive is always the key to solving any mystery, but in this web of deceit, untangling motives is like trying to find the head of a two-headed snake in a Gordian knot. Just when you think you've found it, you're wrong. And it has a deadly bite."

Silas's eyes dart sharply to look at me after that last line.

There aren't enough tears in the world right now to deal with his look.

Shame has a deadly bite, too.

It feels like Silas's gaze.

CHAPTER 4

"*H*ere we are, six months later, with fewer answers than we had at the beginning and more questions than ever. As the—"

A few beeps from the radio, then a second of silence before a live broadcaster's voice cuts in.

"We interrupt this scheduled program with a breaking news alert. Jane Borokov narrowly escaped another attempt on her life as a firebomb—"

Click.

"Oh, sure. *Now* you turn off the radio?" I cry out, incredulous, shooting daggers with my eyes at the driver. "Turn it back on so I can hear!" I demand of him.

"You have enough information. All they're going to do is spin," Silas interrupts.

"You think I don't know that?"

"Then why listen?"

"Because if I don't know how they're portraying me, how can I defend myself?"

"You think there's a way to defend yourself against the media machine?" His turn to be incredulous, the look on his face making me want to smack him.

"Truth is an absolute defense."

His eye roll is epic.

"Has it ever occurred to you that maybe, just maybe, if you thought it through, there might be a completely different angle on every part of this mess? That maybe I'm telling the truth?" I taunt him. That's how this feels–like nothing but a nasty game. The push-pull of wanting him to treat me like a human being and wanting to lash out and hurt him is infuriating, but it is better than sitting here and taking his negativity like a passive little doormat.

"Of course I have."

"And you've rejected that. Completely."

"Yes."

"Then you're really bad at your job, Silas," I say, letting all the bitterness and contempt come through my voice.

"You've wounded me, Jane." Turns out he can do contempt, too. Better than I can.

"I mean it. Anyone whose job is to protect people can't be such an absolutist. It makes you weak. Gives other people an easy shot at you."

"'Other people'? Do you mean people like you?"

"No. I mean people like the ones who attacked Lindsay."

"Right. People like you."

I shake my head slowly, the waves of panic flowing through me, giving in to them. Letting them come because what choice do I have?

And guess what?

You can feel all of that panic, let the anxiety overwhelm you, nearly black out from the incongruity of being shamed, driving toward an unknown destination where you have no control–

–and still stand up for yourself.

"I have nothing left to lose, Silas. My mom is dead, my reputation's beyond salvageable, I don't have a job or a place to live, and everywhere I go someone's trying to kill me. Even my online world is nothing but garbage and threats from shitlords. So, as a simple thought exercise, can you *try*? You're protecting me. Someone assigned you to me. Give me the courtesy of doing your job completely. If I'm stuck with you–and I know I am–I, at least, want you to do your best."

I've struck a nerve.

Finally.

"You think you can tell me how to do my job?"

"Someone needs to. Looks like Drew's not doing it."

"Don't you *dare* criticize Drew," he growls, sitting up taller, curling toward me like a predator.

"I absolutely *will* dare. No one is immune from being analyzed. No one is so perfect that they don't have flaws. No one is one hundred percent bad or one hundred percent good. We're all a mixture."

He smirks. "Like fifty shades of grey?"

"You brought up sex. Not me."

His eyes flash with a smoldering look, combing up and down my body.

"Who said anything about sex?"

"You did. Mentioning the title of the biggest-selling erotic romance novel in history implies it."

The tips of his ears turn pink, the only hint that talking about sex is having a physical effect on him. I try so hard not to squirm.

I can't show him it's having an effect on me, either.

"How did we get from absolutism to sex?" I say, trying to cut the tension, trying to scramble backwards from the arousal that floods me suddenly. Dormant parts of my mind and body call themselves to attention, making it damn near impossible to hold onto the all the shaking parts of me that were working together just long enough to defend myself.

"I am not an absolutist," he says, carefully avoiding the second half of my question. "I take in every single detail." His eyes sure do, looking me over.

"And yet you take all that information, form a judgment, and then religiously follow it."

"No. In the face of new evidence, I'll change my approach."

"I've given you new evidence!"

"No, you haven't, Jane. You've protested. You've proclaimed. You've pleaded and you've bitched. You've lawyered up and you've gone silent. You've done everything–everything–*but* give us new evidence." He runs a shaking hand over the top of his head, his lips curling with anger, eyes staring ahead, avoiding me.

"I–"

He jolts, digging into his pocket to pull out a phone. Before he turns the screen away from me, I see his backdrop. It's of a small dark-haired child on a beach, the picture taken from behind, her skirt flying around her legs, the little girl in motion, the blue skies over the green water idyllic.

Does he have a child? Who is the little girl? As Silas reads his screen, his shoulders slump slightly–in defeat.

What the hell is in that text he's reading?

He leans his elbow against the door, setting the phone face down on his thigh, his expression troubled. I want to ask him if he's okay. I want to ask him about the little girl. I want to ask him so many questions.

Most of all, I want to ask him to be kind to me.

I need someone to be kind to me.

Anyone.

Because you can live for a very long time in isolation.

But you can't live among people for very long without needing kindness. It's as essential as oxygen, as water, as food.

While you might not technically die without kindness, the existence you're left with is worse than dying.

We turn down a familiar road. I realize I haven't paid a bit of attention to where we're going. I can feel Silas pull away from me as he ponders his personal cell phone, frowning. I scoot as far away from him as I can and lean my forehead against the bottom of the cool window glass, sighing.

Firebomb.

Silas saved me.

He's right.

I should be grateful. I should be grateful because I should be dead right now, by all rights. Dead like my mother.

Dead like John, Stellan, and Blaine.

No, I was never part of their horrible, violent, evil plans. Ever.

Not willingly, at least.

But I am keeping secrets from everyone. I have to. If I tell the truth, then people will die.

Lying is the only way to arrange all the fractured pieces of this strange mess I'm in and feel like there is some semblance of a whole.

Evidence? Silas wants me to produce evidence that will change his mind about me. I have that evidence. Or at least, I did. A long time ago, long before everything exploded.

Here's the problem: the same evidence that exonerates me, implicates me. After a while, it all blurs together. Who is good? Who is bad? Who has pure motives?

As Silas sighs and puts his phone back in his pocket, the walkie-talkie squawks.

"Get her to The Grove. Bosworth wants to talk to her."

Silas nods, as if Drew can see him.

Wait a minute. He probably can. I'm sure this vehicle is under surveillance.

Nothing I do isn't being recorded. Nothing I do isn't being watched. I cannot pee without assuming someone, somewhere, is documenting and observing, working to find the one tidbit of information that will give them a strategic advantage.

I am nothing but someone's leverage.

I'm being summoned to The Grove, the home of Senator Harwell Bosworth and his wife, Monica. My mother was the senator's right-hand woman for decades. She was fired in disgrace for handing their daughter Lindsay off to the same men who gang raped her four years before.

The Grove is the last place on earth I want to visit.

I have no choice, though. No say. If Senator Bosworth, a man who is running for president of the United States, wants an audience with me, he gets it.

Without question.

I can't prepare myself. I can't defend myself. The familiar

steel-edged butterflies start to stir in my stomach. My mother worked for Harry–I can't call him that in person, but in my mind, he's Harry–for so many years. She lived for her job. Gave him her best years, rising up the ranks with him as he went from state office to national prominence. When Harry announced his run for president, she came close to quitting for reasons I never understood.

Behind the scenes, my mother was devoted to Harry's well-being. Not just his political career, but how he was as a person. As a man.

And in the end, everyone thinks she betrayed him.

Maybe that's the lesson I need to take from all of this. I glance at Silas, who is a rigid, six-foot line of tension, his fingers absentmindedly twitching, his attention split.

"Everything okay?" I ask, the words out before I can pull them back in. It's a reflex. I care, apparently. I can't help it.

The look on his face overwhelms me. His brow is tight over judgmental eyes that are also disconcertingly capable of compassion. "I'm fine."

"I'm not. And neither are you. But if you need to lie, go ahead."

"I don't need your permission, Jane."

"No, you don't. I was just offering a little kindness. Whatever's going on, I hope it gets better. You don't look happy."

"What does happiness have to do with anything?"

I laugh, the sound sharper than I intend. "That is an excellent question." The words turn sour in my mouth.

He stares at me. *Hard*. I can sense more than anger and contempt toward me. Dehumanizing someone you view as an enemy makes it easier to think of conflict as a chess game. Black and white, the only nuances those that help you strategically. Compassion is the first victim of absolutism.

And if I am anything these days, it's a victim.

"Well, anyhow," I say, deciding that I might as well give up on being believed and just be authentic. "I hope it all turns out fine."

He nods, staring straight ahead. Then he sighs. "It won't."

"I'm sorry."

"Thank you."

We ride the rest of the way to The Grove in silence.

A silence that is no longer empty.

CHAPTER 5

*W*hen the entire world seems to hate you, the framework of your life disappears, leaving you floating in an endless place where there is no edge, no boundary, no line.

First I was fired from my job.

Then I was evicted from my apartment.

My credit cards and bank account were frozen because of investigations into criminal activity. I had to give up my phone when they took me into custody, even though technically I wasn't arrested.

Every electronic item in my apartment was taken by the feds.

Later, when I finally got access to a computer, I tried to log into my email account.

Wrong password.

Facebook?

Wrong password.

Amazon?

Wrong password.

You get the idea.

I owned my clothes, my personal belongings, and a little bit of furniture in my apartment. My original car was seized along with my computer and all the other items that could have plausibly–or not so plausibly–been used to commit a crime.

And then the attacks began.

One of the few mercies in those early days after John, Stellan, and Blaine kidnapped me and used me to get to Lindsay was that I didn't have my electronics. While I'd been pissed when they were taken away and my accounts accessed, all my activity downloaded and combed over by investigators, it was a blessing.

Because I never saw all the death threats. The messages urging me to kill myself. The rape promises.

And worse.

Oh, yes. There are worse things people can say to you. Especially when they do it with attached pictures, GIFs, and videos.

It took about a week before Senator Bosworth, of all people, came to my rescue. He gave me money privately. Offered me a smartphone. I knew it was being tracked, but I didn't care. It was literally a lifeline.

I still couldn't access my own accounts, but I could start new ones. New accounts that I made sure were scrubbed clean of any hint of activity that could get me in trouble.

I had Senator Bosworth to thank for giving me some peace.

The Grove is like something out of a documentary about the wealthy, a sprawling, oceanside estate that makes it very clear Senator Bosworth had money long before he rose to become a presidential candidate. I've been here hundreds of times since I was little. While my mother worked here, it was open to me. Lindsay and I forged a friendship in elementary school–a weird one, but a good one. How do you become best friends when your mother works for her father? The balance of power was awkward.

We managed.

Silas shakes his head slightly, as if ridding himself of unwanted thoughts, then turns to me. "This won't be a typical meeting. Bosworth's entire PR team is there."

"Again?" This isn't the first time I've been forced to sit in the senator's office and be talked about like I'm a potted plant. I don't understand why they make me go to these meetings. I'm basically forced to sit through hours of being talked about like I'm a problem, and then I'm handed marching orders.

It's not a choice. It's a blueprint.

When we were still friends, Lindsay used to complain about being treated this way. I never understood.

Now I do.

More than I ever wanted to.

"Yes. The firebombing complicates matters."

"You think?"

He cracks, just a little, his mouth turning up with an aggrieved sigh. "You are a complicated woman, Jane."

"Me? I'm simple. It's the rest of the world that makes me complicated."

He does a double take and drops the topic, turning away.

What does that mean?

We pull up to the back door, a modest side entrance off the south wing of the house that I know has more security than the president himself receives. After Lindsay's kidnapping–which happened right here, on the helicopter pad behind us–The Grove went through massive lockdown, security tripled, the place more a fortress than a home.

The SUV comes to a halt, the driver's precision in pulling up between two thick sets of bushes not an accident. It's all carefully calibrated to provide cover, for the agents stationed around the grounds to be able to handle an attacker, a bomb, every move calculated to maximize the safety of the people they're assigned to protect.

The memory of Silas's body against mine less than an hour ago as he shielded me from my car's explosion floods my senses. It's as if I can smell him again, feel his nose pressed into my neck, sense those big calloused hands on my ribs, my shoulders, my head. I swoon, pausing as he waves to me to slide across the bench seat and exit the SUV on his side.

He turns from solid to waves, my vision swimming, but I push through.

I always push through.

When I stand, I wobble, my legs like rubber bands. His hand goes to my elbow, holding tight, the other at the small of my back, assured and instinctive.

"Are you okay?" he asks, mirroring my own words from a few moments ago back to me.

"No. How about we stop asking each other that question?" I ask, catching his eye, trying to let him know I'm half joking but also coming from a place where I get it. I really do.

"What do you suggest instead?" His hands move off my body, leaving me more unsure than before. The withdrawal of his touch is a disturbing sensation. Silas only held me steady for a few moments, yet it felt so good. So right.

I need to stop doing this.

I need to turn whatever I'm feeling off, because as I look up at him to answer, I see his mask is back on.

Whatever I thought I just felt from him, I'm clearly wrong.

He's only doing his job.

And right now his job is to deliver me straight into the middle of a hornet's nest, without a suit.

"Joe," he says, nodding at one of the security people. He's wearing mirrored sunglasses, my own image reflected back at me for a split second, just long enough to realize I look like a sooty, grass-stained mess.

"Wait!" I cry out, unable to stop the impulse. My hands fly up to my hair, my right eyebrow, my cheek. I turn back to confirm what I saw in the mirrored glasses, seeking the SUV's window.

"What?" Silas asks, impassive.

"Why didn't you tell me I look like this?" Frantic, I touch my face. Part of my layered bangs rest against my eyebrow like a tangled piece of burnt yarn. A long green streak might as well be blush on my cheekbone, and when I look down at my right arm, I see more grass stains along the forearm.

"Look like what?"

"Like I've been playing flag football in a bonfire, Silas."

Joe's eyebrow goes up. Silas's eyes fill with mirth for a second, then fade out.

"It's not my job to comment on your appearance, Jane. It's my job to keep you safe."

I look him over, pausing in the space between the car and the door, feeling the push from all the security guys to move, to take myself out of the transition space where so much of the danger resides.

Too bad.

I'll take control where I can get it, even if it's table scraps.

My visual inspection of Silas makes him uncomfortable, but he doesn't back down. His pants have grass stains at the knees, a long smear running down one shinbone in a ragged pattern. He doesn't have any other obvious signs of the dramatic rescue on the landscaped grounds of the small shopping center.

I took the hit.

"Why don't you look like me?" I blurt out.

He takes one step closer to me, his hand on my back again, this time making it clear I *will* move to the building, I *will* go through the door, I *will* do as he says.

As I take one halting step, he leans in and whispers, "Because I am a man."

Oh, my.

He sure is.

"That's not what I mean–"

"*Shhhh.*"

"Are you shushing me?"

"I'm helping you."

"Helping me what?"

"To get ready for what's next."

"You mean for *who* is next. Monica Bosworth is in this meeting, isn't she?"

"I'm not privy to that information." I know I'm right. I can tell.

"Why do you care whether I'm warned?"

He stops touching me again, his pace speeding up. I'm slightly behind him, trying to match his stride.

"I don't know," he says, sending my blood rushing fast through me, making me wish he'd just shut me down instead.

Walking into the office of any high-ranking government official is an intimidating experience. I'm used to it. It's all I knew from childhood. Still fraught with protocol, every person on staff is in constant vigilance mode. Every part of the staff, from the janitor to the head of security, is paid to make the machine work properly and perpetually. They're paid to remove every obstacle in the boss's way.

I'm a *big* obstacle.

So why am I here?

"Why does Senator Bosworth care about my car being bombed?" I ask Silas. He looks around the hall with his eyes only, neck not moving.

He ignores me until we turn a corner to a section where no one is visible.

"I don't know. I assumed you could tell me," he replies, leaning closer than he needs to.

"But you never asked me." I try to keep my breath steady. It takes all of my energy.

"I was debating whether it was worth bothering."

"Bothering?"

A door opens. Marshall Josephs appears. He's super tall, a middle-aged man who has the body of a former athlete, all the muscle that used to be in his chest now residing as a paunch around his waist. His eyes are keen, eager, watchful.

I know those eyes.

Everyone in my life has them.

"Silas. Jane," he says, the words clipped, his body language pushing us to come into the room, the message clear: *get in here*.

We're holding him up.

As he turns, I see he's wearing a patterned tie with his blue shirt, something cartoony. In a world of grey suits and red ties, he's a rebel.

Don't mistake rebellion for mercy, though.

I walk into the office I've seen plenty of times over the years. This time it's different. Since my mother died, it's as if I have to relive everything through a new lens. Mom's place, where I grew up, became a graveyard of lost hope.

My apartment became a house of horrors, my eviction brutal and unfair.

And now, Mom's workplace: a place I have to visit without choice or input.

Being invited to do something from a place of inclusion is a very different experience from being told to report to a meeting where not attending isn't an option. We forget so quickly when we're not embroiled in high-level scandals that our freedom to opt out is precious.

And taken for granted.

The floors are all highly polished blond wood, the walls painted in earth tones. A bubbling fountain, zen-like with an Asian decorating influence, percolates quietly, the sound intended to be soothing. The wing is carefully decorated, updated in the last year or so.

My mother chose some of the paint for the senator's office. His wife doesn't know. Mom often fielded whatever questions he didn't want to deal with from Monica. The two of them had an agreement.

Remember–it's the job of staff to remove obstacles.

Even if the obstacle is the wife.

I brace myself as we walk into the senator's office, all of us herded to the enormous conference table on one side of the room. I am scanning carefully without making eye contact.

My sigh of relief almost escapes me, but I hold back.

No Monica.

Whew.

Monica Bosworth is not just the senator's wife. She's Lindsay's mother. She's trying to become the First Lady of the United States.

She's also a stone-cold narcissist.

Am I biased? Yes. Openly. I know so much about her from

my mother and my friendship with Lindsay. And for years, I told myself not to judge, because everyone has different facets of themselves that they show to different people, right? We can't be *all* bad.

Like I told Silas in the car on the way here–no one is one hundred percent good or one hundred percent bad.

That doesn't mean Monica Bosworth isn't one hundred percent bitch.

Silas beat me to it, reading the room faster than me, already picking a seat across the room between two women I don't know. There are two empty chairs right next to me.

Message received: he doesn't want to sit next to me.

When you are in combat mode–and make no mistake about it, I sure am–you notice *everything*. I'm not being picky or overly sensitive. No such thing exists when the world is an all-out assault on you.

I can't turn off the noticing.

And I especially can't turn it off when it comes to Silas.

"Jane," says one of the women, who stands, extending her hand for a shake. I'm caught off guard, because people generally avoid me.

Shun me.

"I'm Marcy Boorstein, a member of the PR team. This is Victoria Ahlmann." Both women shake my hand and smile kindly. They're almost carbon copies of each other, like someone hit Copy and Paste in a cloning program and made Marcy and Victoria. They're not sisters. Just similar.

And they blend in. They look like any boring old soccer mom you'd find in a well-off suburb.

Which means the idea that they are really PR people is ludicrous.

These are agents. NSA, FBI, CIA–pick your alphabet. Their friendliness is a cover. I'll take it.

This is a far cry from the last time I was here, when everyone looked like an angry ice sculpture.

"Would you like a moment to freshen up?" Victoria asks me, her lipstick more red than plum. That's how I can mentally mark her. How she's different from Marcy.

I play along. I've forgotten my looks already. I wince. "Yes, please."

Silas walks to the doorway and extends his arm for me to leave again. I follow as he escorts me to the bathroom.

"I know where it is," I tell him. "No need to–"

"I'm not showing you where it is."

I'm confused. "Then why are you–"

"It's my job."

"It's your job to escort me to the bathroom? Like a kindergarten teacher?"

"Like someone who is in the home of a presidential candidate, Jane," he says, halting outside the door to the bathroom.

"Because you think I'm a danger to Harry?" I slip and call him by his first name.

Silas quirks one eyebrow. "Harry?"

I turn away and go into the bathroom, locking the door behind me.

I take a deep breath, inhaling the fresh scent of lilacs, a bunch of them in two or three vases sprinkled around the room, on the counter and also on a small wooden stand that holds towels.

Privacy.

For the first time in hours, I am alone.

Bathrooms are the one holdout when it comes to having bodyguards assigned. Most of the people who are on my detail are men. I do get the occasional woman, but even then the bathroom is sacrosanct. In the near future, even that will be breached, likely by technology before they start sending humans in to monitor people in the most private space, but for now–

I'm truly alone.

You cannot underestimate the body's physiological response when it's under constant tension and gets a brief respite. You would think that the momentary relief would be helpful. That systems could adapt and use the break in a beneficial manner. Basic systems theory would say so.

Bodies are systems, after all.

But emotions most definitely aren't.

I taste the tears before I feel them.

Breaking down isn't new. Doing it in the bathroom at a presidential candidate's house is a bit much. I don't care. If I ever cared, that ship sailed so long ago. I brace myself against the sink and grab a washcloth, shoving it into my mouth and turning on the water full blast.

And then I scream.

I scream until I start to cough, the back of my throat raw, the pain a relief. It's a relief because I can finally fixate on something I caused. Something I *did*. Something I had control over. Screaming like this is the lamest form of stress relief, but it's *mine*.

My chest starts to heave, the emotions all rising up layer by layer through my body like the rings of a tree that mark the years. My layers mark months of shame, a varnish poured over me in endless buckets, the shame seeping into every nook and cranny until I *am* the shame.

No amount of stripping will ever get me back to my core. "Jane" is no more. I don't get to be a person any more.

I am just "Jane Borokov."

The enemy.

Victoria and Marcy's friendliness in there is part of a scheme. Maybe Silas is, too. They all have an agenda, and as my body starts to shake, my stomach burning like someone's stabbing a poker into my duodenum, I realize I'm going mad.

Crazy.

Insane.

I can't stop it.

Maybe that's the problem. I've been fighting it all. My mind won't give over, give *in*. I keep thinking that the truth matters. That if I can find the right person to tell, then this will go away.

All of it.

Especially the shame.

I've told eighty percent of the truth. The other twenty percent can't be revealed until the time is right, but when it is, I'll be exonerated in the court of public opinion, right?

Because that's all I have left.

Tap tap tap.

"Jane? The senator is ready."

I look up into my own face in the mirror. My hair is singed, the green streak covers the right side of my face, and mascara runs in long tendrils down my face, bleeding into the white washcloth.

I look like a horror book cover model.

Feel like one, too.

"Just a minute," I lie, stretching out time. I sit on the toilet and try to pee, but I can't. Stress does funny things to the body, and mine has decided that relaxing all my muscles is too high a price to pay for being vigilant. You can't spend almost every waking hour in combat mode and expect your body to downshift suddenly.

Even for something as basic as bathroom functions.

No one talked about this in my psychology classes. No one mentioned that a moth flying close to my head would feel like a scud missile coming for me. I'm getting a doctoral education in the undocumented effects of being a constant target.

Only I don't just have one attacker.

I have *society*.

And on a lower level, I have every single person in the senator's office right now all wanting to find another way to tell me I'm a horrible person who needs to be managed.

Downplayed.

Made small.

I clean my face, washing away the grime. I wish I could wash off the shame, but that's impossible. It's etched into me like a tattoo I never asked for.

As I center myself, I look in the mirror, radiating compassion to my reflection. I don't have a way to fill my own battery. My source keeps getting depleted. Soon I'll have nothing left.

I can't think about that right now.

I slowly open the door to find Silas there, leaning against the wall, glaring at his personal smartphone screen. Without a word, he deftly slips the phone in his pants pocket and turns, pivoting on his right foot, soundlessly leading me back.

Back to face whatever's coming next.

"You okay?" he asks softly.

"I thought we weren't going to ask each other that."

"I slipped up."

"Isn't your entire job predicated on never slipping up?"

"Yes."

"You're undermining my confidence in you." But I smile, pressing my lips together, biting them.

"I'm hurt."

"You have a feeling!"

He lets out a light laugh. "Don't tell anyone. Wouldn't want it getting around. People might think I'm weak."

"I can't imagine anyone thinking you're weak, Silas."

He pauses. I don't look away from his body.

And then Senator Harwell Bosworth appears, turning a corner, his stature erect, eyes on us.

"Hello, Jane," he says, not smiling.

And away we go.

CHAPTER 6

"*Y*ou're unharmed?" he asks, but he already knows the answer. People do this all the time. They ask me questions when they already know the answer. I notice it more now because I'm struck by it. They don't do it to be malicious.

They do it because admitting that they have already been briefed about my every move is impolite. We're still pretending there's a layer of decency here.

There isn't.

But if there is, the senator is part of it, because he helped me when no one else would.

"I'm fine. A little bruised and my hair was turned into a roasted marshmallow by the blast, but otherwise I'm okay." Reflexively, I smile.

He puts one hand on my right shoulder, looking deep into my eyes, the seconds ticking by. Ever since my mother died, he's been so *nice*. Helpful. Involved. I know he's the reason Drew's team is my security detail. Why Silas is my bodyguard.

But… why? After what my mother allegedly did to Lindsay, why would he care? And… does he care? Or is this just another way to control me?

"Thank you again for the new phone," I say, genuinely grateful.

"It's nothing. You know you're being monitored," he says gravely. "It's for your own good."

"I know."

"But you also need a connection to the world." He says this with a strange mixture of compassion and authority. It's hard to read him. I spent my entire life hearing stories about Harry, going to work events and hiding in a back room, Harry coming in and talking to me in small conversations. Occasionally, when work was light and I went with Mom to the office, we'd eat dinner together, Harry asking me about school, dance class, my flute lessons.

It was nice.

It was like having a father. I guess.

Not that I know what that's like, because my father died before I was born, but it was the closest I knew.

"Jane?" Harry's question makes me realize I've gone blank, stuck in the past.

"Oh! Sorry," I say, following his lead to move.

Once we're all in the office, I realize there's a young woman, a few years older than me, flitting in and out of the room but always speaking with the senator for brief sentences.

"Ah, Glen! Let me introduce you two," he says, gesturing toward me and the woman. "Jane, this is Glen, my new assistant. Glen, this is Jane Borokov, Anya's daughter."

New assistant?

New assistant.

Glen gives me an eager, speculative look, the kind that says she has so many questions to ask me, all of them juicy and lurid. Only basic decency and self-preservation stop her.

Maybe just self-preservation. Who knows?

"Jane," she says fluidly, in a voice that is lower, more cultured and confident than I expect to hear. "I've heard so much about you."

"How could you not?" I joke, but it's not really a joke. She knows that. I know that.

We laugh anyhow. It sounds like someone holding a coffee can full of buttons and shaking it violently.

Even Silas seems to be able to spare a modicum of sympathy for me. I'm standing in my mother's ex-boss's office, talking to her replacement. A replacement who is close in age to me, and who carries no baggage as the senator works his way toward the White House. She's a blank slate, a clean whiteboard, a remedy to my mother's horrid stain of betrayal.

"Can I get you coffee? Tea? Juice?" she asks, her question smooth and easy. I've noticed that the younger female staffers in politics tend to hate this part of the job, finding it demeaning. Mom always rolled with it, saying it was a reflection on other people if they viewed her as a servant.

No negativity comes from Glen, though. She is the consummate pro.

"Coffee would be great. I could use the liquid adrenaline," I say, smiling. She leaves, and Marshall looks at me.

"Not enough in your system after the near miss?" he asks, a barb in his voice.

"Different kind of adrenaline," I reply, trying to stop the conversation.

"We ready?" the senator says to Marshall, the words in question form but it's not an inquiry.

It's a command.

"Yes. Everyone," Marshall says, the rest of us settling down. Drew Foster comes in at the last second and takes a seat next to me. If Silas has contempt for me, Drew hates my guts. He's an order of magnitude worse.

And his knee is inches from mine, clenched hand angrily writing on a legal pad with a ballpoint pen, his body radiating heat from a simmer that makes me glad *he's* not my full-time bodyguard.

Lindsay ran off with him to Vegas six months ago in a clever maneuver to get her out from under her mom and dad's control. They eloped. It was all over the news, the one bright spot in the media onslaught after everything went down.

Drew married her so he would become her next of kin and her parents couldn't keep shuffling her away to a mental institution to manage their reputations.

Not the most romantic start to a marriage. Then again, they didn't have the most conventional relationship, either. You don't go from being wildly in love to being drugged and raped by your buddies without a few bumps in the road.

Like, mountain-sized bumps.

But I'm so happy they're back together, even if they both hate my guts now.

I look around the room. Drew is to my right, then on his right sits Marshall, then Victoria. Between her and Silas is the screen for presentations, followed by the senator, then Marcy to my left. There are plenty of empty chairs.

Lots of time for Monica to appear.

I shiver. I pretend I'm cold and rub my forearms.

"Jane's car was firebombed ninety minutes ago," Marshall begins.

Ninety minutes. Less time than a major motion picture.

"And while our tech team is figuring out the specific culprits, we're certain it's an online hate group and not political opponents." Marshall grabs a clicker and turns on the video presentation screen. A short film of my burning car displays instantly, the wail of emergency service sirens in the video filling the air. He hastily punches the volume button and turns it down.

"Which opponents would those be, Marshall?" Drew asks. "Corning, or someone else?"

Marshall's eyes dart to me. "We were hoping Jane could give us some insight into that topic."

I groan. "I've told you a million times before–I don't know!"

"You know more than you're letting on," Drew says, turning to me with an aggression that makes me flinch. "You were Lindsay's darknet informant for years. You fed her information. You're more skilled than anyone in the room at hacking and accessing networks and information."

"You're not hearing me."

"Oh, we've heard you. We've heard what you've selectively told us, the FBI, the NSA, the CIA, congressional subcommittees, intelligence community experts... we've heard. But we haven't heard everything."

I sigh. Marcy and Victoria share a quick look. The senator watches Drew but doesn't interrupt.

To my surprise, it's Silas who speaks next. "I thought we were here to brief the group on Jane's car bomb incident today, Drew."

"We are."

"Shouldn't we address that first?"

Silas is calm. Deferential. But something has changed in him, and I'm not the only person in the room who notices. If I didn't know Silas can't stand me, I'd almost think this was a very covert form of defending me.

"Jane, why don't you tell us what happened?" the senator orders, threading his fingers before him in his folded hands, his face placid.

Drew gives him a sharp look but says nothing.

"I, uh... Silas knows more than I do," I say, giving him a half-panicked look.

"I didn't ask Silas," the senator says. "I asked *you*."

"Well, we–I was at a coffee shop," I start.

"For what?" Drew interrupts.

"For coffee," I say slowly.

Drew gives me a sour look.

"I wanted to drink coffee. You know, in public. Like a normal person. I wanted to sit with my drink at a table and stare at the ocean until some of the tension from being the worst shitstain in the history of the United States dissipated. It's a hard job, but someone's got to do it."

Drew doesn't react.

Normally, I'd never curse in front of anyone except friends, but I'm all out of those.

And patience. My patience is gone, too.

"And?" the senator asks.

"And Silas tried to tell me I had to leave."

"You refused?"

55

"He didn't tell me why."

Drew, Marshall, and Senator Bosworth look at Silas, who glares at me.

"I was about to, but Jane was being difficult," he explains.

My turn to stare back. "I was being human."

"Like I said."

"When a 'subject' wants to have a tiny shred of control over her day, she's 'difficult'? Are the men you protect 'difficult' when they object to being moved around like an object?"

"Don't try to turn this into some anti-woman rant," Marshall demands.

"I'm not trying. It's Silas who–"

"I'd consider any subject in your position to be difficult, Jane. It's not a gendered complaint," Silas says in a robotic voice, the lack of emotion a tip-off.

Marcy and Victoria share a look I know all too well. It's the look women give each other when they're in a room filled with powerful men. I'd join in, but they don't look at me. I'm not in the club.

"Let's get back to the story," Drew says drolly. "Silas didn't tell you why you needed to leave, and…"

"And I walked to my car. He grabbed my arm and told me not to. I argued with him. He was drawing attention to us, and I didn't like that."

"Then why did you fight him?" Marshall asks in an accusatory voice.

Did Marcy just roll her eyes? Huh.

"Maybe because Jane is a sentient human being who has the right to preferences?" Victoria comments, scribbling on a notepad. She does not look up.

My opinion of Victoria just improved.

"Go on," Drew says, giving me more attention suddenly.

"I was walking to my car and saw something dart out from in front of it. I thought it was a bird, or a Canadian goose, or just some little animal."

"Did you see it, Gentian?" Drew asks, the question making it clear he was supposed to.

"No, sir. I was busy listening to the intel on the threat, then ran to protect her."

"And how did he 'protect' you?" Senator Bosworth asks, frowning.

"I–he was just on me, from behind. I was flat on my stomach, grass in my face, just as the car exploded." I reach up and touch my bangs. "The heat singed my hair."

Silas scrubs his dark hair with an absent-minded hand.

"Good save," Drew says to Silas, who just shrugs as if it were nothing. No big deal. All in the line of duty.

The senator takes it all in, peering at me for a long time, searching my face. Inventorying me.

And then:

"I think the safest course at this point is to hide Jane at an undisclosed location." He looks at Marshall. "You got the PR on this?"

"We're making sure it doesn't affect you, sir."

"Great. Poll numbers are stronger than ever and we want to keep them that way."

"Actually," Marcy said, interrupting, "we're discovering a sympathy effect every time you're associated with Jane, Senator."

"A what?" Harry is perplexed.

"Women over sixty-five seem to have a small bump to your advantage whenever a news story is about Jane."

Before I can react, Silas asks, "Where do I take her?"

"I think she should stay here," the senator says, to my surprise. "We have a guest house by the pool. Security's tighter here than anywhere else. Might as well have Jane spend the night at The Grove."

"Like hell that's going to happen," says someone from behind me.

I don't even need to turn around.

I know exactly who it is.

CHAPTER 7

"*M*onica," the senator says in a judgmental tone. "I told you this meeting is–"

"One I should attend," she says smoothly. "Looks like I got here just in time." She examines everyone but me. "You were about to make a decision you would later regret."

"I was executing a plan designed to maximize safety."

"Whose safety? Hers?" She flops a limp-wristed hand toward me, as if she isn't even going to bother to use enough energy to condemn me. "I think we've had more than our share of Jane, anyhow. We don't need more."

"Her car was firebombed, Monica. Less than two hours ago."

"*Mmmm.*"

"We need a safehouse for her. We're still unwinding what happened."

"Maybe Jane rigged her own car and set up the car bomb herself."

Just when I think I can't be more horrified, I am.

"What?" I squeak, wondering how she made *that* leap of logic.

"If it wasn't her, it was one of the people she works with." Her eyes narrow. "In fact, it's a clever way to simultaneously draw attention away from what you're really doing and get sympathy. I didn't peg you for being that clever, Jane." She gives a slow golf clap, two quiet claps, letting the silence scream at me along with her eyes.

How can someone use silence like a sword? Yet she does.

"I never–I didn't–"

"We confirmed the identities of the car bombers. They were shitlords on a pro-state secession forum," Drew tells her.

"A pro *what*?" Monica asks coolly, eyebrows as high as Botox allows.

"They want to create their own U.S. state and then secede."

"Oh, good Lord," Monica declares. "What does that have to do with Jane and her scheming?" Before Silas or Drew or anyone can answer, she turns to the senator. "Good grief, Harry, how can you let her come here? Especially when Lindsay is visiting?"

"I'm well aware that Lindsay's here. In fact–"

The door opens smoothly and in she walks. First, her eyes seek out Drew's. He's tense, clearly in protective mode, but emotion fills his eyes.

I wish a guy would look at me like that.

Without thinking, I glance at Silas, who is watching Monica with a raw intensity, like he thinks she might make a violent move.

Not really, but that's how he looks.

"Speak of the devil," the senator says, giving me a tight smile without making eye contact. I know the smile is for me, because I hear Lindsay make a small gasp when she sees me.

"Daddy," she says softly. "You didn't tell me Jane would be here."

"See, Harry? You're upsetting her," Monica admonishes.

Lindsay turns on her mother. "Since when have *you* cared about my emotional state at any given time?"

"Lindsay, sit down," the senator and Drew say at the same time, but in completely different tones.

Lindsay remains standing.

I almost applaud.

"Actually," she says with a sigh, turning to me, "I'm glad you're here."

"You are?" It's an echo chamber in the office as every single person at the meeting says the same two words.

"I am." She looks down, then right at me. "I'm so sorry about your mother's death."

"Oh, Christ," Monica groans. "*You're* offering sympathy to *Jane* about the woman who delivered you to those monsters? Right in front of your father, in his office? The woman betrayed him in every fundamental way!"

"That's enough, Monica!" The senator stands up and walks around the conference room. I expect him to grab her arm but he doesn't, standing next to her, saying a short sentence in her ear. She turns a sickly shade of pink.

Her eyes dart to look at me.

I'm trapped. Triangulated. Caught in yet another one of these crazy dynamics between real live human beings who don't view me as fully one of them. It's the cornerstone of the last six months:

I am an enemy.

I am a target.

I am guilty by association.

My blood is tainted by my mother.

"Thank you, Lindsay," I say, the only words I can summon through the buzz of all the nonverbal activity flying through the room. "I really appreciate it."

Empathy, compassion, plain old *niceness* comes through the look she gives me–for less than a second.

Then the frozen mask comes back.

"Why are you here?" She doesn't make eye contact.

"Because your father called a meeting."

"I heard about the car bomb."

"You mean the one Jane set up?" Monica snaps.

Lindsay's eyebrows drop in confusion. Drew's jaw tightens, his sigh obvious. Monica is all hard edges, her words a whirl of sharp knives, but Drew has bested her.

"Jane *what?*" Lindsay asks her mother.

"Oh, please, Lindsay. If you want to gain sympathy for yourself, what do you do? Create a diversion."

"You think Jane rigged her own car and set it on fire at a shopping center in Santa Barbara to gain sympathy, Mom?"

"It's not out of the realm of possibility."

"Just like I cut my own brake lines last year?"

Monica goes pale under her makeup.

"I never said you did."

"You didn't have to. My fingerprints were all over the brake lines, right? You and Daddy assumed. It was all part of Nolan Corning and his plan. Set me up to look like the unstable one. Set me... up," she says haltingly, looking at me.

Silas watches her with a dawning expression, one that shows layers of rapid thought. He blinks furiously, then looks at me, swallowing hard, intelligent eyes reflective and alert.

"When bad people are after what they want, they'll do whatever it takes to make innocent people look bad," I say quietly.

"That's exactly what manipulators say to throw people off their tracks," Monica huffs. "Just because you weren't convicted doesn't mean you didn't do it, dear."

That *dear* might as well be a curse word.

"Monica," the senator says in warning.

"You make it sound like I have so much power that I can somehow hide true evidence that implicates me. As if I have some insider protecting me. If I had that kind of power, I wouldn't be in this crazy position in the first place!"

Monica's eyes go even colder as she looks at Harry, then me. "The apple doesn't fall far from the tree, does it?" she says to him with a glare that feels deadlier than it should.

Now she's talking about my mother.

"I've told you everything I know about what happened with John, Blaine, and Stellan. And yes, I was Lindsay's informant when she was on the Island, but I was only feeding her information that someone else gave me. I don't have the technical skills to go into the darknet and do what he did."

"Who is *he*?" Monica demands. "You refuse to tell everyone."

"I don't know." It's true. I don't know. I have my suspicions, but I don't have evidence.

"You know damn well how this looks to everyone in this room. Just as Lindsay's mess–"

"Quit calling it that, Mom! It's not *my* mess." Lindsay reaches for Drew's shoulder. His hand comes up, clasping hers. "It's Nolan Corning's mess."

Monica starts to speak but bites her lower lip, eyes narrowing as she looks at her daughter. "Semantics don't matter."

"They do when you're naming the scandal after the victim," Drew interjects, his voice full of venom.

"Fine. We'll just call it Anya's mess, then. Or Jane's mess. Let's call it what it is–you two colluded with someone to bring down Harry and his entire political career."

"I told you, I–"

"Shut up."

I do.

"And now you're here because your car got bombed? Do you have any idea how much PR work it's going to take to distance this from Harry's campaign?" Her tongue moves between her upper teeth and skin, flaring her full red lip.

"That's why we're here," Marshall says, the undertones of his words not subtle at all. "This is a briefing meeting for how to accomplish that."

"Do a better job this time than you have for the last six months," she says softly.

"We're done," the senator announces, using his body to herd Monica out of the room.

Everyone starts to stand except for Drew, who watches the scene calmly, eyes calculating. Lindsay shakes her head, her mouth tight.

"Stay," Drew says to Silas, who starts to stand. "The meeting's not over."

"But–"

"You can't just usher me out and–" Monica's objections to the senator are cut off as he closes the door behind them. Low growls of anger come through the door as vibration, the two arguing. In less than ten seconds he returns, resolute.

Without his wife.

"Do you really think I rigged my car with a firebomb?" I ask the senator.

He freezes, halfway to sitting, but doesn't look away. "No."

"Because you think I'm telling the truth?"

"Because Silas was with you the entire time and there was no room for error."

No room for error. Everything I do, then, has a potential for error.

I am an error.

But at least they don't seriously believe I bombed my own car.

"It would be easier, frankly, if you had," Marshall comments matter-of-factly.

"Excuse me?" His words aren't getting through. I start to shake, unable to control it.

"Your reputation is already shredded. People will believe anything negative about you. If you'd really planted the explosives yourself, you'd be portrayed as even more mentally unstable."

"I don't think that's possible," I say sadly.

Lindsay gives me a sharp look. Drew rolls his eyes.

"Enough speculation. We need to act."

I can't stop shivering. I don't even try to pretend I'm cold. When was the last time I ate? Had water? My only private moment was a washcloth scream a few minutes ago.

I need a remote log cabin, no internet, and a month to do nothing but sleep.

"It's decided, then. Jane will take the guest house by the pool. Marshall, downplay this and point the finger at the unstable fringe. Don't make it political–nothing left wing or right wing. Just pump up the idea that internet culture and violence have reached a fevered point. Maybe get the news shows to broaden coverage to other unstable elements online. Dilute the message."

"Yes, sir."

"And watch poll numbers."

"Always."

"Jane, you can move your belongings into the guest house, and–"

I hold up my phone and purse. "What belongings?"

The senator looks shocked. "What do you mean?"

"Everything I own was in my car."

That shuts everyone up for half a minute.

"Everything?" Lindsay looks at me.

"The rest is still seized as evidence, or if it's free for me to take, no one knows where it is. So many agencies and committees have reviewed it..."

"That's not fair," she replies, looking at her father, who doesn't return the favor.

"None of this is fair, Lindsay. Not one bit of it," I whisper.

Drew stares me down. I turn away and shut up.

"All you own is what you're wearing, your phone, and your purse?" the senator asks, his breath slow and steady, his gaze filled with concern.

"Yes."

He nods his head. "Good."

"Good?" I squeak.

"Not good that you're left with no belongings, but good in that you'll be easier to move from place to place."

Losing every item I own has now become a logistical benefit to the powers that be.

I stand. I'm shaking so hard, I see strange dots in my vision. I have never fainted in my life. Not once. As I get to my feet, my hand brushes against a manila folder, pushing it off the edge of the table. It's the lightest of touches but it does the trick.

Sometimes that's all it takes.

One last tiny, insignificant act can tip the scales.

"No," I say, not sure what my *no* means. No, I can't faint? No, I won't be moved like a chess piece, an object in other people's game?

No, this isn't happening?

No.

Just... *no*.

"No, what?" Marshall asks.

"No, I won't continue to be moved from place to place. Do you realize I've been homeless for more than six months? I've lost everything–everything! My mother is dead. All her belongings are considered evidence. All my money and hers is considered government property now, and I know I'll never get it. I have nothing. *Nothing!*" I shout, looking straight at the senator.

I've tipped.

My phone buzzes at that exact moment, the sensation so unexpected, I let out a high-pitched scream, all the stress centers in my brain being pushed at the same time, in unison, until I become nothing but a million live nerves. My body isn't under my own control anymore, so it shakes and jerks, my throat tight and all awareness beginning to fade.

I am not fainting.

I am just disappearing.

My brain stops linking me to the other people in the room. I don't know how else to describe it. Their words are spoken. Their muscles stretch, their lungs draw air in and blow air out. They move in angles and lines, waves and particles, as we share the same air, the same planes of existence, the same layers of the room.

But I am not quite there.

"You can't," I gasp, pressing my palms into the oak conference table so hard because I want to leave a mark, to do *something* with so much pressure that it relieves some of what was inside me, "take away every part of my life and expect me to comply. You can't expect me to do whatever you say just to preserve my life. If the only reason you're protecting me is because you think I am a danger to you or someone else you care about, then," I say, pointing to Silas's firearm, "just take out the gun and shoot me. Now. You can do it, you know. You're all powerful enough. Silas could kill me right here, right now, and you'd all make up some story about how unhinged I am. How I attacked the senator."

He recoils.

"Even better!" I shout. "Marshall and Marcy and Victoria could spin it so that I attacked Lindsay. Yes–let's go with that." I whirl on her. "In a fit of rage, I turned unpredictable and your security team had to take defensive measures. What a great story. It fits so many narratives, doesn't it?"

"Jane, that's not what we're doing here," the senator says, looking at Marshall with an expression that is clear: *Fix this*.

"You might need medical attention," Marshall says. "The firebomb obviously caused physical damage, but there could be head trauma."

"Oh, stop. *STOP!* You're just finding more ways to control me. I'm not a thing! I can't continue to live like this. It's bad enough being shamed in public. But you've kept me on the run, hidden away, and for what purpose? I have no life. It's been systematically stripped from me."

"Because of your own actions," Drew reminds me.

"Because someone has made it *look* like those were my actions!"

"Not this again. The whole innocent act," he replies.

"It's not an act! I would think that you, of all people, would understand what it's like to be set up by forces beyond your control and unfairly accused of doing something you didn't do, Drew!"

Lindsay gasps, giving me an open look that makes me feel human again.

"Don't you dare compare yourself to me," he says with contempt dripping from every pore.

"You can't stand the idea because it introduces doubt, doesn't it? And when you have doubt, it might make you wrong. Quit taking everything at face value. You know what it's like to be a victim of that," I shoot back.

Drew rears on me, his body an angry system designed to shut me down. He's smart enough to know I have a point, but stubborn enough to decide that it doesn't matter, because his one and only calling is to protect Lindsay.

Who is watching me with a critical, evaluative expression.

"Calm down," the senator snaps. "Both of you."

"I am about as calm as you can get, sir," Drew insists.

"You're inflaming her. And she has a point."

"Sir?" Drew's incredulous look is matched by Silas's.

"There are people who believe Jane is innocent."

I wonder if he's becoming one of them.

CHAPTER 8

*O*hile Drew and the senator argue, my phone buzzes again in my hand. I open the email app, ignoring the cracks in the screen. It must have gotten damaged in the blast, earlier.

Silas is watching me instead of Drew, who is going toe to toe with Harry over the question of my innocence while Lindsay stands closer to Drew, her ever-stalwart shadow.

I look at my phone screen, eyes blurring. It's an email from a very, very welcome friend.

My *only* friend, at this point.

DEAR JANE,

I know your email is heavily monitored, so I'll just say this:

Dear NSA, fuck you. Leave poor Jane alone.

And Jane—come see me. I'll provide you with companionship, a place out of the spotlight, and some good steaks and my special lemonade. Let us catch up. It has been too long.

Yours,

Alice

WHAT A BLAST FROM THE PAST. The near past, but still.

Alice Mogrett was my oil painting professor in college. I needed an elective, something that didn't involve math or coding, and her painting class fit into my schedule at the time. It wasn't love of art that drove me into her studio. It was pure pragmatics.

But fate has a funny way of being pragmatic, too.

Alice had taught at Yates University, my alma mater, for more years than anyone remembered. She was famous, not for her art but for one very dramatic reason:

She was the only daughter of a beloved vice president from the 1950s.

And she was the epitome of a *character*.

"I know where I would like to go next," I announce, emboldened by Alice's words.

"Do you, now?" Marshall's tone makes my teeth ache.

We're interrupted by the senator and Drew's voices, which are rising.

"Come on, Har–Senator. You don't think those crackpots are anything but attention seekers. If we investigated every anonymous tip from wackos, we'd never get the really dangerous ones."

"I think it has merit."

"We've determined it doesn't."

"And have you never been wrong, Drew?"

"I have, and I get the feeling I'm about to be, whether I like it or not."

"What makes you think you're not wrong on this?"

Drew pinches the bridge of his nose. "You really want me to investigate the person we presume to be Jane's informant? An anonymous call telling us who is responsible for what's happened to Lindsay, to you, to everyone?"

"Yes."

"Jesus."

"If he can help us, throw him in the mix, too."

"Gentian," Drew barks. "Go down the rabbit hole."

Silas looks like Drew just told him to have sex with a porcupine on live television. "What?"

"Do it. I'm assigning you. You're the most familiar with it."

"But that rumor is crazy. Impossible."

Drew gives Harry a look that says he agrees.

"Regardless," the senator declares, "I want it investigated. Because if it's true, we need to be on top of it."

"If it's true, sir, you'll be in more trouble than anyone ever imagined," Silas interjects.

"What are you all talking about?" Lindsay asks, looking as perplexed as I feel.

"Nothing," Silas, Drew, and the senator say at the same time.

"It's confidential," the senator adds.

"You always say that when you just don't want to tell me something," Lindsay prods.

"This time," Drew responds, "it's true. We've already said too much."

"You're saying that someone has been feeding you information about me? About information that proves I'm innocent?" I ask.

"Crackpots," Drew mutters, but it's clear he wants everyone to hear.

"And you never investigated it?" I am agog.

"We did. *Thoroughly*. With as much time and attention as it deserved."

"Which wasn't much?" I accuse.

"How many resources are we supposed to devote to the thousands of stupid tips we get? People call the senator's office to report alien prostate probes, Jane. Those are about as credible as the tip Harry–the senator–is talking about." Drew unbuttons his suit jacket and lifts his arms, stretching his shoulders. It's a dominance approach, body language designed to claim space.

It works.

"Glad to be lumped in with prostates," I mutter.

Silas bites the inside of one cheek. Is he trying not to laugh? It feels too good to be true. The senator is making

Drew investigate leads about my being innocent, and Silas is showing emotion toward me.

It's like Christmas and my birthday rolled up in one.

"Do it," Senator Bosworth orders.

"We are," Drew responds.

"Let's get Jane in the guest house–"

"No, Senator," I say quietly, politely, but firmly. "I would like to be taken somewhere else."

"Where?" He's clearly surprised.

"To Alice Mogrett's ranch in Silverton, Texas."

Every set of eyebrows goes up.

"Alice Mogrett?" Marshall asks. "*The* Alice Mogrett?"

"The former vice president's daughter?" the senator asks, folding his arms over his chest as he leans back, clearly intrigued.

"Yes," I confirm. "She was my art professor in college and has reached out to me. I have an invitation from her, personally, to come to her ranch and be her guest."

"She's a fruit loop," Marshall declares. "That woman has been part of every crazy scandal you can imagine since the 1950s. The rumors about her are still circulating among the Secret Service. I can't believe she's still alive. How old is she now? A hundred?"

"Ninety-two," I say, correcting him. "And she is my friend." I lower my chin and look up at him, my face designed to imply that he's being an offensive asshole.

"Of course she is," Marshall says, unaffected by my look. "You would, somehow, be allied with a woman who was the epitome of sex scandal back in her day."

"I'm hardly at the center of a sex scandal," I protest.

"Aren't you? Look at what they did to Lindsay," Marshall argues.

Every woman in the room freezes.

"What those bastards did to Lindsay wasn't about sex, you idiot," Drew speaks up. "It was about violence. Control. Domination."

"Shame," I whisper.

He does a double take. "Right."

"Alice Mogrett is a terrible move," Marshall says, ignoring Drew's acid tone.

"It's where we're going," I say, taking a deep breath to continue. I'll need to dig in to get what I want.

Silas stands and leaves the room. Great. So much for any thought that he might help me. Not that I held out much hope, but...

"Sir, it's best if she stays here," Marshall turns to the senator to appeal to him. I'm reduced to "she" again. An object. I'm not even worthy of a direct comment.

"Alice Mogrett, huh?" the senator says with a nostalgic smile on his face. He shakes his head slowly. "I remember when Rupert Mogrett was appointed to the Supreme Court. Shocked everyone. Right after he and Paulton timed out of office. Paulton was able to appoint him in his final months in the presidency and Mogrett resigned as VP, then became a justice. Served for twelve more years."

"And meanwhile, his daughter made headlines," Marshall says tightly. "Didn't she found a commune in the late 1950s, for God's sake?" He acts as if communes are equivalent to ISIS terrorism compounds.

"She was part of the naked protest movement of the 1960s," Victoria adds, reading from her phone. "On the vanguard of the second-wave women's feminism movement."

"See?" Marshall declares. "Bad PR for us."

Silas returns, not sitting, standing at the doorway. He says nothing.

"If you've been invited, I think it's worth considering," the senator says. Lindsay suddenly breaks away from Drew and leaves the room, walking past Silas, who just nods.

"Harry," Marshall addresses him in a low voice. "This is a really inconvenient time for–"

"Security's already set up," Silas announces, deliberately interrupting Marshall in what can only be considered a challenge. "I've notified the Secret Service at her ranch that we're escalating."

"You? You did that without orders?" Marshall barks.

"Nothing's set in stone. I'm making sure we're prepared

in case *the senator* makes a decision to send Jane there," Silas smoothly answers.

"*I* have made a decision to go there, so..." I stand and move toward the door, walking past Silas, who turns smoothly to follow me as Marshall calls out for me to return. I ignore him.

I am *so* done.

Until Lindsay appears, staring me down.

CHAPTER 9

"*H*ere." She thrusts a small soft bag into my hands. It's silklike, with a zipper and two small handles, designed with a geometric pattern that is heavy on earth tones.

"What's this?"

"Some old clothes of mine. I was setting them aside to donate, and you said you have no clothes other than what you're wearing." She eyes me up and down. "We were always the same size growing up, and you look like you've dropped weight, but so have I."

"Stress," I say reflexively. She didn't ask for an explanation, but I give her one.

"Yeah. Being in the spotlight when you don't want the attention is the best diet ever, isn't it?"

"Why?" I blurt out.

"Why… what?"

"Why are you being nice to me?"

"I don't know. Don't push it."

"I'm not. I'm really not." Tears fill my eyes.

"It's a change of clothing, Jane, not a new car. You're not Dobby being set free by a sock."

"It's not *what* you're giving me. It's the kindness," I explain, wiping the corners of my eyes. "Thank you."

"Drew thinks you really did it. *All* of it," she says sharply. "That finding me tied up and... well, that back then, you 'found' me because it was all part of the plan. A performance. That you were in on it from the beginning."

"Does he really?"

She nods. "He does."

"And do you?"

"I want to."

"You want to believe I'm guilty?"

"Yes."

"Why?"

"Because if Drew's wrong, then we've been as bad to you as all those assholes were to us."

"No. Never that bad."

"But bad."

"I didn't do it, Lindsay. I swear. And I'm so, so sorry for what you went through, both times."

"You've said that before."

"Because it's true."

"Your mom delivered me into their hands. Right here, at my childhood home. She tainted this place. It used to be a sanctuary. Now it's just another prison, like everywhere else that touches my dad."

I go silent. I don't know what to say about my mother.

It's so complicated, and I wish I could ask her why she did what she did, but I can't.

Because she's dead.

The look on Lindsay's face makes it clear this conversation is stirring up old emotions, her fists tight at her sides, her eyes glistening, throat tight.

"I don't know why my mother did what she did," I try to explain. "If she were alive, then I could–"

"If your mother were alive, she would just be a liability. At least she spared taxpayers the expense of letting her rot in jail," Monica interjects, one manicured hand going on Lindsay's shoulder. She gives her daughter an expression of deep concern, leaning in. "Is Anya–I mean *Jane*–bothering you?"

"No, Mom. It's fine."

"Remember everything that has happened, Lindsay. Don't let your guard down. From the night of the original attack to the online information Jane was feeding you to the kidnapping, she's at the heart of everything. Ask yourself how someone can be connected to so many parts of this mess and not be implicated?"

Just then, Silas appears next to me, his presence much appreciated.

"Good question," he says to Monica, who smiles at him.

"You ready?" I ask him. "Because we're going."

"We are?" one corner of his mouth twitches with a smile.

"*I* am."

"Wherever you go, I go."

I ignore him. "Thank you, Lindsay," I say sincerely, motioning toward the bag that now hangs on my shoulder. "I really appreciate it."

"Just stay safe." She looks at Silas.

Monica glares at me.

"She'll be safe," he says, pointedly not looking at Monica.

"Good," Lindsay says before Silas leads me out. "Because I think we need to talk more."

I want to respond, but she's pulled aside by a hissing Monica before I can, Silas tugging firmly at my elbow. "We need to go," he says, the words redundant as his body moves me to the door that takes us to the SUV again.

"Don't I need to say goodbye to the senator?"

"Not unless you really want to go back into that conference room and face everyone you just walked out on." His look says I'd be crazy to do just that.

"Then no."

He lets out a huff of amusement and into the SUV we go, ready for my trip to Alice's home.

A haven.

A sanctuary *I* have now made happen.

This time, being in the backseat with Silas has a completely different feel. How in the heck did that meeting somehow clear the air between us?

"Lindsay was nice to you back there," he says, making me

startle in my seat. I turn and look at him in surprise. He's initiating a conversation with me? Like I'm a real person?

"Um, yeah." I pat the bag she gave me, which is on the floor between my feet. "She gave me some clothes."

"She didn't have to do that. You have funding to buy whatever you need."

"I know. But it was a really sweet gesture."

"She's a good person."

"And I'm not?"

"I didn't say that."

"You implied it."

"No, Jane, I didn't. You inferred it. Big difference."

I take a deep breath and steady myself, getting my bearings. He's right. I'm living in a cloud of reaction, my nerves on edge all the time because I don't know who is a threat and who is safe. When everyone around you questions your motives, the only sane reaction is to question theirs.

His words are coming at a time when I thought he was angry with me, disgusted and barely tolerating my presence.

Did Senator Bosworth's order to investigate the "wacko" lead Drew talked about change Silas's opinion?

I'm about to ask him that very question when he jolts, then reaches for his phone. It's the personal one, with the picture of the girl on the screen.

"Gentian," he says softly. "Mom? What?"

Now I know his mother is alive.

Something we don't have in common.

"Is she okay?" he murmurs, turning away. "Can I call you back later?"

I reach for my earbuds and push them in, trying to signal to him that I am respecting his need for some privacy.

I don't actually turn on my music, though.

"She is? Again? Damn," he mutters. Real anguish is in that voice. I suspect if I turn and look at him, I'll see it in his face, too.

Who is "she"? His sister? Niece?

Girlfriend?

Wife?

It's suddenly hard for me to breathe, those last two ideas shoving my lungs aside. Silas's personal life is none of my business, but it's not like I have an easy way to distract myself right now. I have no apartment. No home. No job. I'm not in school, and my entire world has telescoped down to what I'm wearing, my phone, my purse, and Lindsay's gifted clothing.

We're primed to notice our surroundings. To read people around us.

It's built into me to listen.

Let's just say it's not my fault I'm eavesdropping, then.

"And Kelly's okay? Day care has her?"

Hmmm. Kelly must be the little girl. Is she his little girl?

"Good, good. Um, go ahead and get Tricia settled. I'll handle the money. Just don't give her any directly. I'll make sure it's done behind the scenes."

Is Tricia his wife? Ex-wife? Why doesn't he want people to give her money directly? This sounds bad, whatever it is.

"No, Mom, it's fine. Really. Look, I can't talk now. You know how work is." He pauses, blinking rapidly. "Uh huh. Right. Ok. You too. Bye."

Awww. How sweet. His mom still tells him she loves him. And he says it back, man style. It's a lovely gesture and makes me more interested in how Mr. Silas Gentian works on the inside. Nothing about him adds up. All the pieces don't typically go together to make this kind of whole.

He was a sweet, almost naive guy when I met him the first time. Security guys normally aren't so fresh faced and nice.

He was stone-faced and cold when he began working with me a few days ago.

And now he's... well, *this*. Whatever you call it, he's a chameleon, changing as I learn more about him.

Do we really ever know anyone, though? Especially in this crazy political world. I don't seriously think he would ever harm me, but one thing I've learned over the last six months is this: people have agendas.

And some people will do anything–including murder–to

see their agenda through.

He hangs up and switches phones, clearly talking to Drew now. I look out my window and try to relax my muscles. My foot jiggles, an old nervous habit from when I was a kid. Mom used to tell me to stop, that it drove her nuts, and I smile sadly at the memory.

And then my brain hijacks me by remembering her in the morgue, dead, the marks on her neck plain as day.

I gasp, the image so brutally fresh, it might as well be on a billboard as we drive down the highway.

"What's wrong?" Silas asks, tensing as he sits up and looks at me, eyes already scanning the area outside the moving car.

"I was about to ask you the same question." I really don't want to talk about my dead mom, so I deflect. "Your phone call sounded like something's going on? Everyone at home safe and sound?"

He scowls. "It's fine."

Interesting. He's lying. "That's better than the alternative."

He makes a dismissive sound and settles back in his seat.

The SUV turns onto a small airstrip, one that is so private, it's only used by the government and people so wealthy, they might as well run a small nation. I've flown via private aircraft before, and I know how easy it is versus the commercial cattle call most of us only ever experience.

The difference is night and day.

As the SUV comes to a halt, Silas climbs out and walks away. I admire him from behind, his broad shoulders ramrod straight, his legs long and thick. Silas has a body that is just big all over, nothing but muscle, a body made for tailored clothing and aggression.

He talks to people in Air Force uniforms, men with more fruit salad on their lapels than hair on their heads. A salute, a handshake, a smile, and then he jogs back, just as our driver opens my door and I climb out clutching Lindsay's cloth bag.

"Ready?" He motions toward a small jet on the tarmac.

"Yes. But we never let Alice know I'm coming."

He smirks as he puts on sunglasses, the fading light of the day marking the passage of time. Silas turns to me and starts walking toward the jet, expecting me to keep up with him. "She knows. She definitely knows."

The private jet is exactly like the others I've been flying on for the last few months. Stately without being ostentatious. Functional and sophisticated but not gaudy. It's just us as we enter the plane. Silas takes a seat in the far back. There are four clusters of four seats, spread out. I stand at the entrance, uncertain. Do I sit with Silas? Find my own spot? Are we sharing the plane with other people?

Scratch that. How many people are going to Alice Mogrett's house right now? Not fourteen other random government-affiliated people.

Tentative, constantly questioning myself, I move to the first cluster on the left and settle in, facing forward. I sink into the seat and take a deep breath.

Ew.

I need a shower.

Sweat coats my arms, the underside of my shirt a wet mess at the armpits. I'm still wearing the white shirt and maxidress I had on when my car was bombed. Lindsay's bag beckons to me, so I open it. Inside, I find a lovely long dress with no sleeves, a flowing wrap to go over it, and simple slip-on sandals.

My eyes fill up yet again as I stare at the clothing. The one person in this complex web of deceit who has the most right to hate me–correctly or not–is the one who has shown me the most kindness.

"Jane?" I look up and twist in my seat to find Silas right behind me, holding a small pink shopping bag.

"*Mmm*?" I don't want him to see that I am crying.

"The senator had this delivered here." He hands it to me. I see something silky, lace-edged, inside.

My blood turns cold.

Why would Senator Harwell Bosworth buy me *lingerie*?

"Lindsay insisted you needed some, uh, private clothing." Silas's ears turn pink and he goes back to his seat. From there he adds, "The bathroom is behind me. Once we're in the air, you can shower. Lindsay assumed you'd want to freshen up for your visit with Ms. Mogrett."

Oh.

That makes much more sense. It was Lindsay.

"Why is she being so nice to me?" I mutter to myself, pulling out the items in the bag. A simple sports bra and basic women's underwear with a little lace on them greet me, both in generic-enough sizes to fit me. Given my sweat-soaked, stained clothing, this will be a major step up.

I stare at the bag as the pilot starts to give instructions, his voice warm and friendly as he recites it all in a routine I've come to embrace. The takeoff instructions aren't just an FAA requirement. They aren't given simply to make sure passengers have an inkling of what to do in case of a true emergency.

They are also a ritual, designed to help calm you. My mom told me this a long time ago as she explained the theory of human behavior in crowds and how processes are designed to meet different needs.

"Don't take what you see at face value, Jane," she had said to me on one of our flights to D.C. "Every process, every system has a shadow purpose beneath it. The more you understand all the layers, the better."

As the pilot drones on, Mom's words make me think.

Why would Silas agree so easily to take me to Alice's place?

To the point of clearing the path before permission was granted.

Nothing about Alice screams treachery. She's so out of the mainstream. All of the character traits that Marshall derided are the very qualities that appealed to me when I was her student.

She doesn't give a single whit what anyone else thinks.

And while she was born with a spirit few possess, she was also forged by her experience as a child of a rising politician.

Lindsay would like Alice, I think to myself as I snap off the tags for the bra and underwear, folding the garments neatly into the little cloth bag that holds the clothes from Lindsay. It's too bad they won't meet.

I set the plastic and cardboard tags aside as the airplane starts to move, taxiing down the small airstrip. We're up and in the air within minutes, all the preliminaries so much easier with a private jet. Once the pilot announces we're at cruising altitude, I unclip my seatbelt, pass Silas, whose eyes are closed, seatbelt on, and find the bathroom.

It's big.

I've learned not to be surprised by how extravagant government-provided services can feel. This isn't Air Force One, of course, but it's clearly used for people at the highest levels. As I close and lock the bathroom door, I take a long look around.

Airplanes aren't supposed to have bathrooms the size of my childhood bedroom, but then again, I'm not supposed to be here, either.

Not if life made sense.

The bright white tiles and gold trim make the room look like a piece of china, all polished porcelain. The room is lined with mirrors, a toilet against the side wall, the glass-enclosed shower taking up most of the room. A soaker tub with low-set jacuzzi nozzles takes up the remaining space.

I mean, it's not enough to have a soaker tub in your private jet, right? Got to add that shower, too.

Stripping down turns into a show for myself, all the mirrors angled just so. I get an all-too-good look at myself as I open the shower door, bend to turn on the hot water, and wait.

I pause. I stare. I scrutinize, because that's what I've been trained by society to do.

Look for the flaws.

We all have them, but a mirrored bathroom magnifies them. I'm not uncomfortable being naked in front of the mirrors, but as I look and notice my bruise, my cut, how my knees are pale, the tan line at my neck, I realize it has been a very, very long time since I've wondered how a man who wanted me would gaze at my body.

Would he search incessantly for flaws? Would he be tentative and careful or dominant and aggressive in his assessment of my features? Would he overflow with innuendos and compliments, want me all the time, devour me with his eyes?

Silas comes to mind, my normal resistance draining away as I step in the shower and begin to wash off the day. He shouldn't invade my personal sexual thoughts. He is a handful of meters away.

And yet he does.

The shower feels so good, the water hot and lush. I'll bet the showerhead is NASA-invented, refined and calibrated to some sensory precision that makes the rich and powerful feel that taking a shower is somehow better for people who deserve the best.

Lavender soap, shampoo, and conditioner greet my senses as I fumble, eyes closed, water in them. Washing the day off my body is a relief, one I took for granted until six months ago. My preferred bath scent is orange. If I were in my own apartment, I would have citrus soap and orange shampoo and lemon conditioner, all of those scents hand-chosen and carefully selected to please *me*.

When you're essentially homeless, living where the government tells you to live, you get whatever other people provide you.

Lavender is really, really popular these days.

I position myself so the wall of water slides over my hair and down my back. I pause, asking my mind to trace the sensation of a single drop as I try to focus, pull myself together, make myself centered.

I don't need it. Not where I'm going. But I'm taking my recharge time where I can get it.

A sudden jerk to the left leaves me hacking and coughing, my knee cracking against the edge of the now-open shower door, which slams back and nearly traps my fingertips. I move just in time, the floor slippery as hell, making me fall on my bare ass.

I get a big mouthful of shower spray, too, and choke my way through that.

"Just a little turbulence," the pilot announces.

If this is a little, what's a lot?

The floor seems even again, so I grab the shower door handle and pull myself up, hoping for no more injuries. My hip throbs, the long red streak from my ass to my knee clearly a scrape from slamming into the glass door.

Tap tap tap.

"You okay?" Silas shouts.

"Get back in your seat!" I call back.

"I'm not worried about me."

"I'm fine."

"You might want to hurry up in case we have more weather problems. Looks like we're flying into a storm."

Great. With my luck we'll get caught in a tornado, crash, and people will find my bones after Silas and the crew eat me to stay alive.

What the hell is wrong with me? I laugh to myself as I get under the spray and finish shampooing my hair, rinsing it, then applying conditioner. My hands keep grabbing air long after my hair ends. I cut so much of it off in order to hide myself.

To blend in.

Really helped, huh?

Tap tap tap.

"Seriously, Jane. You need to stop the shower. Pilot says we're–"

I don't hear his next words because the shower goes sideways and all the soaps and shampoo bottles come flying at me like missiles thrown by an angry god.

My shoulder whacks into the soap dish and the shower's hand-held nozzle points up at me, the arc of water strong, nailing me between the legs for a deeply erotic and highly disconcerting two seconds. I start to roll as the airplane rights itself, my leg bending, knee catching on the shower door as I fall, my body out of my control, wet and slippery, as much an object as the shampoo bottle, the soap, my washcloth.

I'm being tossed around like a toy.

"JANE!" Silas's voice is powerful even through the door's muting. "Say something!"

I open my mouth to do just that, but the wind is completely knocked out of me.

By the toilet bowl.

The round curve of it slams into my ribs, which bend in a sick, wet way as I rebound off it, the shower door opening again, my leg jerking out, the foot pointed and sliding into an opening between the glass shower wall and the hinged door.

And then the door slams shut on my ankle.

I scream.

BAM! BAM! BAM!

"JANE!" Silas bellows from the other side. "I'M COMING IN THERE!"

Oh, my God.

"No!" I cry out as the main bathroom door smashes open, Silas leading with his shoulder.

To find me naked, legs parted, ankle jammed in the shower door, my face smushed against the toilet's edge.

He's breathing hard, eyes wide and focused, taking in the scene so he knows how to act with rapid-fire precision because that's what bodyguards do.

They save your body.

Mine happens to be right in front of him, nude and trapped.

Who knew shower doors could be so dangerous?

"I, uh..." I say, my eloquence long gone.

From the top of my wet, conditioner-covered head to the ankle trapped between two pieces of glass, Silas takes me in. Under any other circumstances, I'd find this embarrassingly amusing, or humiliatingly erotic, but the sheer pain radiating out from my ankle is sending waves of nausea and ice-pick bone pain through me.

Before I have to say a word, he's on his knees before me.

Between my legs.

CHAPTER 10

"*L*et me alleviate the pressure on that ankle," he says, carefully avoiding eye contact, one hand on the shower door handle and the other on my calf, as he finds a way to bend down and hold his position. He must have core strength that is out of this world. The firm but tender touch of his palm as he removes the source of pain makes me tear up.

And my nipples turn to pearls.

No. No, no, no. I will not be aroused by Silas in this position. Oh, no.

Hell, no.

My body doesn't listen to me, though.

My body is a *yes* woman tonight.

It's not the being naked part. I'm comfortable with that. Trust me. I have no problem being nude in front of people.

But people aren't *Silas*.

Choked up, still in shock, and very, very aware of my naked inner thighs (and everything above them), I can't speak.

"I have to get your ankle out of there," he explains. Still holding the door in place, Silas lunges slightly and tugs on my calf.

I scream. The ankle bone is so wedged in there that it can't make it through.

Silas readjusts the shower door.

"That's as wide as I can make it," he says. "Will it fit?"

I try not to giggle.

"They always say it won't fit," I murmur.

He laughs, a sound of shock.

"Point your toe," he orders, composing himself with remarkable speed, eyes firmly on mine, unwavering. His focus is so precise, I can tell it comes from a place of extraordinary restraint. He *wants* to look. He's holding back. Not because of basic decency.

Because if he looks, he'll be aroused.

I try to follow his command. "I can't. My toe won't do that."

"If you keep the foot in there for much longer, your ankle will swell and block it. We need to get it out *now*." He suddenly searches the room, looking for something.

"What are you looking for?"

"Conditioner."

"My split ends aren't a priority right now, Silas."

"I'm going to use it to lube you up."

I giggle again.

This time he sighs, but a smile makes his mouth look lush and friendly. Grabbing the conditioner bottle from behind the toilet–mercifully on the other side of me–he squirts a huge amount all over my bare ankle, then uses his free hand to massage it in.

Oh, those fingers. The absolute *last* feeling I should be having is this–being turned on by Silas's fingers massaging my injured ankle while I'm naked and hugging a toilet.

I don't have any control of my external world. Apparently, my internal emotional control center has gone bananas, too. Warmth pours over my body like a waterfall. I stifle a moan.

"Ok," he says, his touch featherlight and sweet. "I didn't dig in, just got the important parts."

Other important parts of me disagree.

"Pull out before it's too late."

I snort but do as he says. It comes free. I pull my foot in to my body and groan with the pain. Without looking back, Silas grabs a towel that magically stayed on a heated towel rack and hands it to me, his hand dangling the plush terry cloth.

"Here."

"Thanks."

Without another word he leaves, closing the door, which has a long strip of trim hanging off it from when he broke into the room. The handle doesn't quite catch, but it stays closed just enough.

His laughter from the other side of the closed door makes me smile. Not that I plan to go out of my way to have him find me like that again, but if it makes him chortle like that, a sound of happy hilarity, I might be worth the sacrifice.

I think about that for precisely two seconds, until I put weight on my foot and pain shoots up through me like a current. It's nerve pain, the kind that makes you feel like a bulldozer is rolling over a nerve cluster. The pain radiates up into my thigh and I gasp, grabbing a towel rack for stability.

Gingerly, I put a little more weight on it. Better.

I still have conditioner coating my hair, so I give the shower a resigned look. It doesn't look back.

I need to get in there and rinse, don't I?

Eyeing the shower door gap with a healthy dose of respect, I limp in and direct the water spray to my head. My fingers flow through the thick, wet lump until I can tell I've rinsed thoroughly. The hair around my brow is shorter, but not too short. Thankfully, that heat blast from the car bomb wasn't a few inches closer, or I'd have a perpetually surprised look on my face after having my eyebrows burned off.

Even in my shitty life, I can find small mercies to be grateful for.

As I wash off the extra conditioner from my ankle, I relive Silas's touch. Shame turns my insides into fire, but there's so much more than embarrassment.

Being touched by him makes my pulse race, tempts me to

lick my lips, makes me feel alive and real in ways I haven't felt in, well–*forever*.

I laugh to myself. I laugh *at* myself. I'm being ridiculous. Silas has made his feelings about me well known. I'm not alive and real to him.

I'm just a client.

Toweling off, as the plane bumps up and down slightly with just a little turbulence, gets me dry. I grab the bag of clothes from Lindsay with the new panties and bra tucked in there. I slip on the new underwear. The bra is a close fit–a little tight, but that's ok. I slip into her sleeveless dress and sigh.

That's better. I'm not naked any more.

The imprint of Silas's hands on me won't fade. It's as if he's still holding my ankle, fingers slick and slippery, touching me so I can feel better. I close my eyes and force myself to feel the present. My wet hair is soaking the thin dress I put on. My ankle throbs from pain. My skin fluctuates between warm and cold, a weird series of shifts that finally even out as my heart slows down.

The airplane is level. No more turbulence.

Like any surprise, living through it is hard, but the aftereffects require more energy to process than you ever expect.

I'm still shaking on the inside. I need to figure out how to go out into the main cabin, take my seat, and not melt into the plane's floor and ooze out into the atmosphere.

I just got myself trapped, naked, in a shower.

On a plane.

And a man who cannot *stand* me was my rescuer.

I hang the towel back on the rack, take a deep breath, and reach for the broken door. Squaring my shoulders, I open it, head high, and walk back to my seat. As I pass Silas, I see his eyes are closed, head against his seatback.

He's pretending to sleep.

Cool operator.

I settle into my seat and mimic him.

By the time we land in Texas, I still have my eyes closed, but never fell asleep.

You can repeat a lot of memories that way, but the one that keeps looping through me is the tactile sense of Silas's hands, providing more direct comfort and help than anyone has offered me in ages.

And Alice represents even more.

But her comfort comes with conditions.

Conditions I'm starting to think about.

CHAPTER 11

*Y*ou cannot spend days on end around someone, endless hours bleeding into each other, and not get to know them on some level. Even the most stone-faced Secret Service agent gives off little clues, signals about who he is. We all do. It's unavoidable. You would have to be a robot to be able to keep every nonverbal tip about yourself completely secured, safely compartmentalized, hidden from the world.

Silas doesn't even come close.

His humanity radiates out from his pores, his face showing emotion even if it's just in little flashes that give me insight. Some personal issue is distracting him. Not in the sense that he's not protecting me, but more on an internal level.

People have lives that connect them to others. It's one of the fundamental tenets of being human. We don't necessarily define ourselves in terms of others–though some people do– but we are defined by connections of some type.

Which is why losing my links to other people, one by one, is so damaging.

We're social animals by nature. All of us, even the most introverted person you know. On some level, we need to engage in circles of communication. We check in with others to see where the boundaries lie, to make sure we're functioning and contributing, to be nurtured and to nurture right back.

I have none of that.

And the empty silence as the SUV takes us to Alice's home heightens my sense of isolation.

Being teased about the shower situation would be a relief. Humiliation, even, would be welcome. It was funny. Truly.

Not joking about it makes me feel less human.

While I can't go around being naked and needing help all the time to break the ice, my stupid predicament in the bathroom seemed to crack the layer between us. It's back up, that thick barrier demarcating our space. As we drive down endless highways, marked off by cattle fencing and oil fields, I feel like we're moving faster and faster away from any real connection.

Back to client and bodyguard.

Self and other.

The SUV slows, so much dust kicked up that it's hard to see as we turn sharply at a corner. No other traffic can be seen for miles. I've never been to Alice's home before. She lived near the campus when I was in college, though I knew she kept the family ranch here in Texas.

It's an honor to be invited.

It's also got me on edge.

Alice is a character. And that makes her unpredictable. When the invitation came through, I jumped at it. Now that we're driving down a tree-lined driveway in the middle of a flatland oasis, I'm starting to get nervous.

Because Alice is a very demanding woman.

What, exactly, will she demand of me today?

The tires start to make a loud crunching sound, the SUV slowing as the unpaved road becomes rockier. A large, sprawling white mansion greets my eyes, though it's hard to see through the dust-caked windows.

At first glance, the house is almost colonial, a white peak in the middle, black shutters, rectangles for windows all spaced evenly. Your standard clapboard New England-style home.

But then there are the wings. To the right, a single-story wing stretches out, as long as the main house. To the left, a double-storied section has a huge open-air-but-covered porch on the second floor, a solarium beneath it. Large trees, willowy yet full in a strange contradiction, reside in a crooked line along the entire front of the house, some close, some far away.

I can imagine Alice climbing out of a bedroom window onto a tree branch, her youthful indiscretions legendary for her time in the 1940s, 50s, and 60s.

I expected perfectly manicured, lush, rolling grass, the kind of lawn that is out of place where water needs to be conserved but wealthy people insist on having anyway. Instead the house is surrounded by blinding-white rock gardens, the trees surrounded by rocks, too. Small succulents dot the edge, carefully planted to look accidental.

Silas isn't looking outside, his attention all for his phone. As we pull up to the front and stop, I'm slightly irritated. Aren't bodyguards supposed to be constantly aware of their client's surroundings?

And then I see all the Secret Service agents.

Ah. That's right. This is the daughter of a vice president. She needs to be protected.

"Wait," I mumble. "That's not right. She wouldn't get a Secret Service detail, would she?"

"Huh?" Silas's acknowledgment that I've spoken is progress.

"Why are Secret Service here?"

"First, I can't confirm or deny that those are Secret Service agents, Jane, but if they are, it's because you're here."

"I don't need a Secret Service detail. You know as well as I do they don't protect private citizens."

He shrugs. "Someone, somewhere, decided to send these guys. I don't write the orders. I just execute them."

"Is that why you're ignoring the environment? Because you know it's all safe and covered?"

"Ignoring?" He's distracted, looking at his phone.

"Never mind." I open my door and start to climb out. Before my first foot is on the ground, an agent is holding the handle, hand extended to help me out.

"Thank you," I say to a pair of dark sunglass lenses with a human wall behind them.

He just nods.

Silas sighs behind me, then gets out on his side, immediately huddling with another agent, their conversations clearly an exchange of details necessary for protection. Emotionless faces attached to moving mouths lob words back and forth. I watch Silas, how he moves his hands carefully, the gestures precise and efficient. A curt nod from him, then one from the other agent, and Silas breaks away, walking toward me with a determined gait that is suddenly so commanding, I have to look away.

My throat tightens and my ankle feels like he's stroking it again.

"Hot," I gasp as he walks up to me.

He frowns as I struggle to cover for my weird lapse. "It's Texas. Comes with the territory. You want hot, try Afghanistan in the summer." His smirk isn't unkind. Pointing, he guides me around the left side of the house, along a flagstone path that doesn't have a single weed or blade of grass poking between the stones.

He's a gentleman, walking behind me. "To the right, under the pergola," he directs. I make a turn and see where we're headed.

"A separate house?"

"It's her studio. This is mostly where she lives, too. She comes to the main house maybe once a week, mostly to look at old photographs or entertain."

"Good for her," I reply. "Alice deserves to live by her own rules. When I'm ninety-two I hope I can do that, too."

Silas mumbles something that gets caught in a short blast of wind. I stop, his hand brushing against my hip as he continues walking, not seeing I've halted. While he doesn't plow into me, those reflexes of his aren't quite sharp enough to stop without touching me.

"What did you say?" I ask, pretty sure I heard him but wondering why he said it. I turn around fully and look up at him, inches away, his sunglasses blocking his eyes.

That strong mouth tightens, his chin jutting and head tilting slightly. "I said, 'Let's hope you live that long.'"

"Is that a commentary on my current situation? You think I'm in so much danger, I'll die young?"

He lifts the sunglasses and props them on his head, brow turning down over those bright blue eyes that are like mirrors of the sky. His dark hair contrasts and makes it very hard not to watch him.

"You're being followed 24/7 by a bodyguard who isn't permitted to have you out of his sight, bathroom excluded." A smirk lifts one corner of his mouth. "And even then, you manage to get yourself into a serious scrape."

I feel my face flush. My skin ripples with heat, none of it from the weather.

"And?" It's all I can think to say.

"And you wouldn't have a security team assigned to you if your life weren't in grave danger." Concern mixed with a fierce protectiveness floods his face. "Do you really not understand that?"

"I understand that I don't have control over anything in my life anymore."

He makes a sound, low and quiet, like he's suddenly getting the point at the same time he doesn't like what he's hearing.

"You're here, aren't you? You stuck to your guns for this one." Sweeping his hand toward Alice's studio, he cocks one eyebrow, his whole demeanor more congenial.

I just stand there and blink.

"You think I made the wrong choice?"

"I think you needed to be given a choice, Jane."

"What?"

"You said you've had everything stripped from you. Dignity. Respect. The benefit of the doubt." He pauses, then adds, "Your mother. And you're being told what to do and where to go, so it makes sense that you need to be given some choices. Humans are wired for free will. Not being able to exercise it creates a kind of madness."

I gape at him.

"Why are you suddenly being so nice?"

"I'm not. I'm just stating the facts."

"You are."

"I am."

"And you're being nice."

"Your bar is very, very low if this meets your definition of *nice*."

"Yes. It is."

He jolts, my words hitting a nerve.

Before he can reply, a commotion near the front door of Alice's studio makes us both turn.

A man in a black jacket and jeans is running away from Alice's studio, his long legs fast, dust puffing up in little clouds as each footstep stirs up the dirt. He's holding some kind of black electronic thing in his hands. As Silas takes off after him, I start to follow, my skirt wrapping around my shins enough to bother me.

I bunch the fabric in my fists and run.

Silas turns around and shouts, "Stay back! Get behind something!"

Oh, I'm behind something, all right.

Him.

No way am I going to be the good little obedient client who does whatever the big bad bodyguard says. Alice has some creep who has just run away from where she is. I need to help her.

Silas has taken off to the left after the guy, and as I sprint to the front door of Alice's place, I reach the small paved path before her porch steps and halt.

Alice has a rifle in her hands and it's pointed right at the running man, who now has about eight agents in hot pursuit, all shouting, all with handguns drawn.

One eye is closed as Alice sets the sight level and–

CRACK!

She shoots.

She misses.

The guy cries out as two agents tackle him. I am watching Alice with a morbid fascination. Her hair is loose, flowing halfway down her back, a shock of white against a patterned silk jacket that looks more like a warlock's robe than anything else. Her eyes are narrowed, mouth pursed, and I swear she's ready to–

Another gunshot.

"HALT!" Alice shouts, the voice confident, almost serene. I guess when you're holding a gun in Texas on your own property, you can use that voice.

And then I look to see Silas holding his gun, aimed straight for Alice Mogrett's head.

"Oh my GOD!" I scream. "Put down the gun!"

"I'll lower my weapon when she does," he barks, hands steady, gun pointed right at her face, full on.

"Then you'd better have a strong arm, young man, because I'll lower mine when I'm dead," Alice retorts, her hands a little shakier than Silas's, but not much.

"Don't test me, ma'am. Lower your weapon. We have the trespasser situation under control."

"Clearly you don't, or he'd have never gotten on my land in the first place! You Secret Service men have really gone downhill since the early 1980s. You used to be sharper."

"I wasn't even born then, ma'am."

"See? Proving my point."

"Ma'am, you're pointing your weapon at a member of a presidential candidate's security detail."

"And you're pointing your gun at the last remaining living daughter of a famous vice president. We're even, young man."

I know Alice. She isn't kidding, and she isn't budging.

I don't know Silas as well, though. I know one thing: he doesn't care about my opinion.

I have to try anyhow.

"Put down the gun, Silas. Once you do, Alice will drop hers," I say in a determined voice.

"That's not how this works, Jane," he answers, jaw tight, line of sight clear and focused. He has one eye shut, the other on his gun, the sight level. I've seen plenty of men holding guns over the last year, and I know the look of someone who is ready to fire.

One step. I move closer to Silas, who glances at me, his eyes barely moving but darting left, then right.

"Jane! Stay put!"

"You love ordering women around, don't you?" Alice cracks, giving me confidence to move suddenly until I am between them, blocking both of their shots.

"Jesus, Jane!" Silas shouts. "Don't do this!"

"You've given me no choice!" I thunder, nerves bouncing like pennies on a trampoline.

"Well played," Alice says, lowering hers first with a long sigh. Her grin is electric. "Tea or lemonade this time?"

"Lavender lemonade?" I ask, hopeful.

"With fresh mint?"

"Yes, ma'am."

Silas is lowering his gun, watching us like we are insane.

"You can't do that!" he shouts, moving in, gun still in hand, safety off.

"Now you want to tell me how to use my own home-grown mint?" Alice objects. "You can pull a gun on me on my own land, young man, but I draw the line at being told how to make refreshments for my guests."

He's not playing our harmless little game. "I could have you arrested for what you just did."

"Try it." Alice's wrinkled face rises up as she smiles, her skin moving a half second later than the expression. "Arrest a ninety-two-year-old beloved American icon because you people couldn't do your job and keep a wacko stalker off my land? Here in Texas you'd be rolled in barbecue sauce and thrown on the grill as a primer for the real beef, sweetums."

Silas stares her down.

Alice stares back.

"Here's the difference between us, young man. You still give a fuck. I don't. Jane, get in here and let's add some vodka to those lavender mint lemonades you love so much. We have a lot of catching up to do, now that you're Public Enemy Number One. Who the hell did you piss off so much that you got stuck with *him* on your security detail?"

She points at Silas as we walk into her house.

"I, uh–"

"I mean, he's pretty on the eyes and all, but a few cows short of a herd on common sense."

Silas ignores her and climbs up the stairs, blowing past us, standing in the living room facing Alice, who pats her gun like it is an obedient dog.

"I'm here to protect her," he said, pointing to me. "You were a presumed threat. Put the rifle away for the duration of our visit."

"No." Alice watches him with that professor's gaze I knew well, the slightly amused twist of her lips below eyes that evaluate him.

"Do it or I'll tip off the local sheriff and the press that your antique guns aren't registered." He cocks an eyebrow as he eyes the rifle. "That's a beautiful Winchester 94."

"Thank you. Been in the family for generations."

"Would be a shame to lose it."

"The only way I'd lose this gun, young man, is up your ass after shoving it there."

"Can't shove what you don't possess, ma'am. Kindly put the rifle away in a secured gun safe, unloaded, and we can just pretend this never happened."

"Or, I can keep it with me for protection. Who was that crazy photographer? How did he get on my land? Ask all these Secret Service agents I don't want in the first place. Make them do their job."

"I don't know the answers to your questions, ma'am. I just know Jane is here at your invitation and I cannot let her spend time in a room with someone holding a gun."

"*You're* holding a gun," I point out.

"I'm your bodyguard," he says slowly, as if I'm being belligerent.

"And?"

"I need a gun. It's part of the job."

"I need my gun," Alice says with a sniff. "Because people like you *aren't* doing your job. That trespasser could have attacked me!"

"He was looking for pictures."

"Of what? My saggy old ass?"

Silas reddens. "Probably of Jane."

"Jane's ass is a much better target for a photographer," Alice concedes.

"Stop talking about asses!" I interject.

Alice thumbs toward Silas. "Bet his is nice."

"Alice!" I gasp.

She pulls me in for a hug, her deep, open laugh so strong, it vibrates through my chest as she embraces me. "Oh, Jane. It's good to see you again."

Silas pries the rifle out of her hands, carefully unloading it, shoving the ammo in his front right pocket. He sets the rifle against the wall next to Alice and wordlessly stands next to us, typing furiously on his phone.

Alice wraps one silk-covered arm around my shoulders. "Come in! Sit. You must be exhausted from the trip."

"I am."

She pauses, peering at me. I have seen pictures of Alice when she was younger, with jet-black hair and big piercing eyes. She was a classic beauty back in the 1940s and 1950s, likened to Elizabeth Taylor.

But wild.

"You're exhausted by much more than your trip, Jane," she says with kindness, leading me up the stairs to the front door.

"No kidding." It's no use trying to lie to Alice, or shave a little something off the truth to keep the peace. She's a straight talker, no bullshit, and the sooner you just get to the truth with her, the better. In art classes, she was exactly the same. Never be pretentious with Alice, and never lie.

Both end badly for anyone who tries.

The studio is a large, lodge-like building with an enormous high-ceilinged great room, a small kitchen without walls along one side. Paintings are everywhere, on easels large and small, most angled toward the large glass windows in specific locations.

Some painters are more into composition, color, white space–but for Alice, it is all about the light. Sunlight and moonlight, dusk and dawn, the in between that changes faces without movement–that is her tool. It doesn't matter the subject. If she can play with light, using the different saturations and shadows to explain anew, it is enough.

Alice's style is a combination of Georgia O'Keeffe and Maxfield Parrish, with a little Warhol thrown in. You never know what her vision will look like, but she paints exclusively women, most as nudes, and they are breathtaking. She sees into your soul and turns it into brushstrokes, deconstructing emotion and flesh, migrating it to canvas.

"Come in! I can't believe you've never been here. I've hosted a few students over the years," she says, turning to the left, where there is an open-plan kitchen with counters covered in old Formica, filled with appliances that look like they are out of a 1980s sitcom. Big spider plants hang from enormous exposed beams, the tendrils of the plants woven like nature planned it all.

"I wasn't one of your protégés, Alice."

"You were my best subject, though."

Silas came into the house uninvited, but is unobtrusive. Alice casts an amused glance his way. "You want some lavender lemonade?"

"Yes, ma'am, as long as there's no alcohol."

"You like it virgin, do you?" Her eyes twinkle as she asks him the question.

He doesn't take the bait. "Can't drink on the job. Besides, I get the impression I need to keep every wit about me and on standby when I'm around you, Ms. Mogrett."

"Alice! Call me Alice."

"Will do, Ms. Mogrett."

Alice rolls her eyes and says to me, "He's a fun one, isn't he?"

"Don't be too hard on him. He rescued me today in an embarrassing bathroom incident on the plane."

"Got sick?"

"Got stuck." Too late, I realize I've brought up the awkward moment, my mouth moving faster than my brain. In a way, I can't help myself, loosening up the longer we're here, in spite of the gun moment.

"Stuck in a bathroom?" She looks behind me. "Your ass isn't that big!"

"Now we're back to asses again?" I joke as she opens the fridge and takes out a pitcher of lemonade. From the freezer she retrieves a bottle of vodka, putting the two on the counter next to each other.

"You can never talk about asses too much, Jane. Get used to it. When you're my age, all people want to talk about is what comes out of them."

I'm speechless as Alice laughs, pouring liberal amounts of vodka into two tall iced tea glasses, then adding lemonade. She reaches for a small pile of greens in a little clear glass. As she crushes some leaves between her fingers and tosses them on top, the cool scent of mint tickles my nose.

"Voilà!" she declares, handing me mine. Then she pulls out another glass, fills it with lemonade and mint, and offers it to Silas. He takes it.

"Thank you, Ms. Mogrett."

"You're welcome, Mr. Formal."

He turns away, admiring the paintings, his back to me and Alice.

"See? Asses. Can't stop, can we?" she says with a laugh.

I watch his face in profile. He's really paying attention, taking in all the canvases, looking at the exits and entrances, observing.

Silas is an aware person. Nothing gets past him, and while it's his job, there's more to it.

He is just this way.

Some people are dull. Boring. Uninteresting. They're dry

and bland because they lack curiosity. You can see it in their faces. Alice talked about that a lot in the art classes I took with her, and at the time I thought she was exaggerating.

Time has shown me she was right.

Silas, though, is someone who is constantly aware, constantly learning, always interested. I get the sense that the job hasn't made him this way–if anything, maybe the reverse.

He chose a job that requires constantly paying attention because he was *already* always paying attention.

A ray of sunlight catches a small prism hanging from a hook off one of the main support beams, the blue and green light distracting me. Silas turns, and as he does, we both see the wall to the right of the kitchen. The painting.

Oh, boy.

It's *me*.

Naked.

CHAPTER 12

*E*ver see a spit take in real life? I never have.
Until now.

Silas pulls the glass away from his mouth and sprays the small table in the kitchen, his eyes going big as he looks at the enormous canvas, life-sized, about seven feet tall and four feet wide. I remember the painting, the pose one of me standing, drying off from a bath with a terrycloth towel, the side view the focus, my breasts dipping down, gravity making them look like grapes waiting to be plucked.

"Excuse me," he says in a tight voice, grabbing a kitchen towel from a small towel rack next to the sink before Alice or I can react. As he cleans, he can't help himself, staring at the painting. "Is that–is the model–"

"That's Jane, all right," Alice says, reading his mind.

He lets out a low whistle.

Now I blush.

"Pardon me," he immediately says, regret filling his voice. "I shouldn't have reacted that way."

"What way? Like a straight human male who sees a beautiful, artistic rendition of a woman?" Alice asks.

"Uh, yes," he replies, flustered. It's adorable and hot at the same time. Silas is the only man I've ever met who can manage both.

Or maybe he's the only man I've ever *noticed* being both.

He finishes cleaning and Alice takes the towel from him, grinning.

"I was offered seven figures for that painting," she tells him, watching his reaction as he looks at it, spellbound.

"I don't doubt it," he says, not breaking away, his face fixed on looking.

"I refused."

"That's a lot of money," I say.

"Money? I don't need any more money. What I need is more beauty."

"You have quite the talent, Ms. Mogrett."

"I don't need validation from you, Mr. Formal, but thank you."

We take our drinks and move into the center of the studio. Painters have a way of creating a unique scene with their art. I didn't understand that until I took my first painting class.

"Have you considered posing again?" Alice asks. Oh, she's direct, all right.

"What?"

"Posing." Alice sweeps her arm around the room, her hand resting in a position pointed straight at the wall of paintings featuring me. "You're an exceptional subject, Jane. Always have been."

"I just know how to sit still." Silas remains standing, looking at his phone in one hand, holding the lemonade in the other. His eyes dance between his phone screen and my portrait, the painting winning.

"No. You know far more than that. If just sitting still were the sole criterion for being a subject, then door jambs and stones would be painted by the millions."

I give a half shrug.

"You have the ability to turn stillness into emotion."

"No, Alice–*you* have that ability."

"I translate that emotion into a visual trigger. But I cannot paint what is not there."

I can feel Silas listening.

I don't care.

"You came to college an open, curious child. Yes, *child*–all eighteen-year-olds are children when you are my age. Hell, fifty-year-olds are, too."

I laugh.

"And your sophomore year you changed."

I stop laughing.

"It was like someone had taken all the light in you and dimmed it. You came back timid. Unsure. Fearful. You had a shadow following you everywhere that wasn't yours. It co-opted you. That is why I reached out to you at school."

"Huh?"

"When you are a painter, you see things no one else sees. It's a gift and a curse. It's like being the child of a politician," she adds, her laugh bitter. "You spend every waking second trying to understand all the connections between people, events, and ideas so that you can see the whole picture, and then beyond."

"Beyond?"

"Nothing in life is ever what appears on the surface. Shallow people like to pretend that the first layer is all that matters, but it's only pretend. Child's play. Very few people are that dim. They know deep inside that their obsession with the surface is a falsehood, a story they tell themselves to avoid the depth. In the deep, we have no control. In the deep, we're at the whim and mercy of forces beyond our under-standing."

"Now you sound like you're talking about religion."

"Is religion really different from politics? No," she says, answering her own rhetorical question. "Everything converges given enough time, Jane. Make it to ninety-two and you'll understand."

"I'm just trying to make it to twenty-five."

Her sharp gaze unnerves me. "Which is why you're here."

"I'm here because you invited me. And thank you." I down my drink. The vodka burns, but the mint soothes.

"You're also here because you insisted. I know how controlling those bastards in Washington can be. You had to make this happen. Your persistence shows." Clear eyes catch mine.

"I guess?" My uncertainty tears me to shreds.

"Embrace it, Jane. You're stronger than you think. Look at what they've put you through."

I just sigh.

"Now," she says, walking to the kitchen and pouring me another glass of lemonade. The first one has loosened me up, the tension in my hunched shoulders and neck receding as the minutes pass. My muscles still burn, but I can feel the shoulders lowering.

I'm finally safe.

Alice pours a generous shot of vodka into my lemonade and hands it to me, smiling. Her eyes are curious, her look piercingly clear.

"Talk. I have all day. And tomorrow. The entire weekend for you, Jane. I want to hear everything, from the start."

"You–but you already know it."

"I know what the press has told me, which means it's half true, half lies, and figuring out who is lying is a full-time job. I know you. I believe you. Give me your story, right here, in front of these insufferable blowhards disguised as bodyguard babysitters."

Silas doesn't react.

"And if there's anything confidential you don't want them to hear, we can fix that, too."

Silas cocks an eyebrow.

"You want me to start from the beginning?" I ask with a pained laugh.

"That's generally how stories are told, Jane."

"What if I don't want to start there?"

"Then start where it makes the most sense."

"None of it makes sense."

She nods. "Those are the hardest stories to tell."

"Yes."

"But they're also the stories with the most meaning."

"I have more than enough meaning in my life. It's just that none of it is mine."

"By telling your story, your way, you make it yours. You own it. Be fierce in your ownership of your life, Jane. No one else will make it easy."

"How did you get so wise, Alice?"

"By telling a lot of hard stories. Mostly with paint."

Silas looks at my painting and holds his breath.

I lick my lips, leaning forward to sip from my refreshed lemonade. Vodka spikes my taste buds. It's refreshing. Nourishing. I guzzle half my tall drink and close my eyes, the cool glass, wet and full, giving my hand something to focus on. As I swallow, I'm aware of Silas's eyes on me. I know that if I open mine, we'll lock on each other.

So I don't.

Because I need something that is all *me* right now.

"You know about what happened to Lindsay Bosworth almost five years ago," I start.

"Yes. You told me."

Silas's head turns sharply in my direction. "You did?" he asks.

Alice waves him away. "Go on."

"And I told you that it was an accident that I was there. That I found her. I needed to pee and ran back into the house while our other friends took off."

"Yes."

"After the police and ambulance came and took Lindsay to the hospital, my mother arrived. Took me home. None of our friends ever reached out. Not one. As soon as Lindsay was stabilized, I asked to see her in the hospital. Her dad agreed but her mother fought it. Was suspicious I had something to do with it."

"I remember," Alice says kindly. "It always bothered you, how Monica Bosworth treated you."

Silas is listening openly. He says nothing.

"When my mom told me the senator and his wife were putting Lindsay in a mental institution, I was so mad. I knew Lindsay. She wouldn't want that. But I also knew from my mom that they were doing it to hide her. Shield her from the press. And it was an election year, so..."

"When votes are your only currency, you protect them," Alice says in a cynical tone.

"Exactly."

"Wasn't she in that mental institution for four years?"

"Yes."

"That's brutal." Disapproval bounces off Alice's face like sunbeams on a prism, blinding and predictable but still catching me by surprise..

"Yes."

"Not a single friend contacted her?"

I almost drop my lemonade. Alice is sharp. "I did."

Silas stops breathing.

"I sent letters they censored. So then I found a way to reach her through the darknet. Someone at the Island helped her connect."

"Who?" Alice asks.

"I don't know. But then one day, I got a cryptic Snapchat. All it said was, 'I can help you with Lindsay.'"

"What's a Snapchat?"

"It's a kind of social media. You take pictures and write captions, like Facebook, but then the picture and caption fade after a short time."

"Like writing someone a note and setting it on fire after they read it?" Alice asks, incredulous and judgmental.

"Yes. Exactly."

"Sounds stupid."

"It is."

"And yet you use it?"

"Yes."

"So some anonymous person reached out to offer help."

"Exactly."

"Did you take him up on it?"

"I did. For four years, I did." After years of lying, the truth feels like shrapnel working its way out of my wounded heart.

"You *were* the informant," Silas says, setting aside any doubt about whether he was listening in, breaking the false pretense that he's just an observer.

"Of course I was. I've been open about it." It's a relief to be so direct. I blame Alice.

And the vodka in this delicious lemonade.

"But I wasn't the *only* informant."

Silas suddenly moves closer to me, enthralled.

"I tried to reach Lindsay however I could. She finally found a worker at that institution who she could pay off. Her parents didn't allow her much spending money–or maybe it was her therapist. I don't remember. But about once a month, she could get regular unmonitored internet access for fifteen or twenty minutes. And after a few times of telling her whatever she wanted to know, I got this phone call."

"From?" Alice asks, sitting up, clearly relishing the story.

"Some guy."

Silas snorts.

"I still don't know his name," I say pointedly. "But the information he gave me to tell Lindsay was interesting. And right."

"What do you mean, right?" Silas asks sharply.

"This was someone in Senator Bosworth's inner circle. Someone who knew the family really well, and who knew John, Blaine, and Stellan, too."

"You believed his info?" Silas asks, clearly doubting my intellect.

"Everything he said turned out to be right."

"Like what?"

"It was mostly about John, Stellan, and Blaine. Lindsay was obsessed with revenge. Sometimes I'd try to tell her about their meteoric rise in their respective fields, but she never cared. Would cut me off, and instead ask where they lived, how the district attorney was using the evidence against them–"

"But no one charged anyone with a crime. That was the frustrating part," Silas says, confused.

"I know. It was weird. Until I remembered how drugged they kept her at the Island."

Silas's face changes, a look of understanding replacing his confusion.

"Right. But who drugged her? Why did her parents let that happen?" Alice asks.

A slow, pleasant sense of being grounded infuses me. We're talking about horrific events, but doing it in a really normal way. Silas is asking me questions, Alice is listening, and I'm telling my story.

My story.

I'm finally being treated like I'm not a pariah.

And oh, it feels so good.

"Who was this guy?" Silas asks, giving me some very skeptical side-eye.

I decide to take a big leap and trust him.

"I never knew his name, but remember yesterday? Right after someone bombed my car?"

"He was there?"

"No. But the radio show you forced me to listen to? The one about *me*? He was one of the people interviewed."

"Jesus." Silas leans against a small end table, blinking furiously, staring right at a smaller painting of me, clearly deep in his thoughts. "Why didn't you say anything?"

I let my eyebrows rise and give him his skeptical look right back. "Why should I? Yesterday you weren't exactly friendly."

"And he is now? Jane, if you think *this* is friendly, we need to teach you the basics of psychology," Alice cracks.

"Says the woman who greeted us with a rifle," Silas says dryly.

"He's starting to grow on me," Alice says.

Me, too.

"I don't need to be friendly for you to tell me mission-critical information," Silas grouses.

"You're a ray of sunshine, aren't you?" Alice turns to him, stretching one arm over the back of the couch, giving him a regal look that could peel paint. "Who are you to demand more loyalty from Jane than she is receiving?"

"What?" Silas narrows his eyes and gives Alice an intimidating look.

It doesn't work.

"You people have spent months convinced that Jane colluded with those depraved, spineless, evil little fleshbags. All the committees searched for evidence against her and didn't find it. You know how Washington works," she said, turning back to me. "If someone hates Jane enough, they would have dug up concrete proof by now. I don't doubt someone hates Jane, but they're not powerful enough to lock her up."

"Just because they didn't find evidence of criminal activity doesn't mean Jane is innocent," Silas replies.

"Are you really that stupid, Silas? Of course it does," Alice argues.

"Jane's hiding information from everyone," he barks back."Like this new detail."

"Someone out there knows damn well about Jane's informant. You know that."

He glowers but says nothing.

"People in Washington have elevated planting fake information to an art form. It's never about the truth. It's about propping up your reputation so you can gain more power. What power do you think Jane is seeking?"

Alice's question makes Silas squirm and frown.

He looks at me then, jaw set and face filled with restrained anger. "You'll need to give me a full explanation of the informant. Dates, locations, all the ways he contacted you."

"I can provide that."

"Has he ever tried to see you? Hurt you?" Those last two words come out urgent, worried.

"No."

He nods, blinking hard, clearly glad to hear it. "Good. One less issue to worry about."

Right. I'm just a client.

"Let her finish," Alice says, showing him her hand. "Quit playing DC cowboy and rushing in to bring the cows home. Give her a say."

Silas grabs his phone and starts typing, ignoring her.

Alice pats my knee. "Tell the rest."

"The informant stopped shortly before Lindsay was sent home. I was so happy. I'd missed her, and wanted to be there for her. We were good friends and what happened to her–I've always felt guilty."

Silas makes a huffing sound.

"Not because I was part of the group who hurt her."

"Then why?" Alice asks gently.

"Because I'll always wonder–if I hadn't left with the rest of the gang to go out to eat, would Lindsay have been saved somehow? Could I have stopped it, or prevented it, or..." My voice starts to shake.

"No. Those men were determined to hurt her. You couldn't have stopped them," Alice gently reminds me.

"And even if you'd tried," Silas cuts in, his voice thick with anger, "you might have just become another victim, like Lindsay."

I shudder.

"I know. Everyone says that. *Everyone*–my mom said it, my therapist said it, even Lindsay said it, later. Before. Oh, you know."

"Later or before? Pick one," Silas says.

"Later *and* before," I stress. "Later, as in after their first attack. And before, as in before the second one."

He doesn't say a word.

"You've lived more trauma in five years than most people live in a lifetime," Alice says sympathetically.

"Lindsay's lived through far more," I reply.

"That doesn't take away your pain. And Lindsay's mother is still alive. Yours isn't."

Tears well in my eyes.

Silas watches me, clearly wanting to ask more questions but being respectful. It makes me appreciate him, being treated humanely again. His questions aren't intrusive. In fact, the more questions he asks, the more he sees me as multi-faceted, not just an evil little bitch who betrayed her friend.

"The newspapers said she died in prison," Alice prods. "I'm so sorry."

"Thank you."

Silas moves suddenly, crossing the room and returning with a box of tissues. He's a blur through my tears. I pull out a tissue and wipe my eyes, a pool of emotion poured onto my skin.

Coming here was a smart move. I need to fall apart. I'd prefer not to do it in front of Silas, but while I have a few hard-won choices, I can't expect to be given full privacy.

Yet.

"Jane, how did she die? The papers said a heart attack," Alice asks, but I can tell from her voice she's not convinced.

"That's what they say." I frown. "She died of a broken heart, I think. To the end, she swore she didn't betray anyone. Every action she took was designed to protect me. But there were strange marks on her neck." I let the implications of my words soak in. I don't need to say more.

"You don't throw another woman to the wolves and then kill yourself," Silas jumps in, overriding the emotion of the moment. "She handed Lindsay off to those assholes. That isn't what innocent people do."

"She didn't know! She didn't until the very last minute. And they threatened her life, too, when the helicopter came to The Grove."

"Your mother told him that Mark Paulson was escorting Lindsay back to the Island!" Silas is mad. "She told the senator that, and meanwhile she was handing off Lindsay to her rapists!"

Alice interrupts. "She's not telling *you* the story, Mr. Formal. She's telling me. So shut up and sit there and look pretty and just listen." Her hand touches mine. "Go on, Jane."

"There isn't much more to tell."

Silas makes a dismissive sound.

"Mom was in jail, being held on all kinds of felony charges. She spent months in there. I was barely able to see her. Meanwhile, she was vilified in the press, worse than me, depending on the news article or the slant. At least she was in jail," I said, my voice filled with bitterness. "That sounds so selfish, but she didn't have to deal with the full blast of it all."

"I should have reached out sooner,"Alice says, her voice full of self-recrimination.

"No. Really. I probably wouldn't have answered. It's been a crazy seven months. Yesterday's message from you came at the perfect time, right after the car bomb."

"I saw that in the news." She glares at Silas. "What on earth are you bodyguards good for? They bombed her car right under your nose." Shaking her head, Alice stops, reaches for her lemonade, and finishes the glass.

I'm warming up, getting loose. As I drink part of my second lemonade, I watch Silas out of the corner of my eye. His tongue is rolling in his cheek, jaw clenched.

He doesn't answer Alice's question.

"You can stay here," she declares as the ice in her glass clinks the second she sets it on the small table in front of us. "Live with me until this all settles down."

"I can what?" I ask.

"Absolutely not," Silas says at the same time.

"Who are you to tell Jane where she can live?" Alice challenges.

"I'm the contact between her and the people trying to protect her. I do have that authority."

"No," I say. "You don't. You only have control over what I do because I let you."

"Excuse me?"

The thought of giving him *actual* control over me makes me breathless.

"I mean that I could fight you and your bosses a lot harder. So far I haven't, because I don't have alternatives. Senator Bosworth gives me money to live on. Someone in the government pays for hotels and food. Maybe it's him. Maybe it's someone else. I don't know. I'm told not to ask questions. When I do, I'm ignored anyhow. I'm completely at your mercy." I look up at him, defiant and terrified at the same time. "But I could say no."

"You can," he agrees, nodding somberly, looking me in the eye and then away, frowning. "You absolutely can."

"It's settled!" Alice claps once. "Jane will stay here."

"For the weekend," I protest.

"For as long as you like," she responds with a grandmotherly smile that makes me want to cry again. "Besides," she whispers in a stage voice designed to let Silas hear. "The Secret Service hates me. I love pissing them off. You're giving an old woman some great entertainment!"

Silas rolls his eyes.

"She's not wrong," he mutters.

"And," Alice adds slyly, "you need to pose for me. I've been in an awful painting slump, and I'm not getting any younger."

"Pose?"

"She can't pose," Silas says firmly.

"Why not?"

"If word got out, the media would go nuts. Former vice president's daughter painting nudes of the current presidential candidate's daughter's turncoat friend?"

Ouch.

CHAPTER 13

A quiet stillness settles into my bones, the constant chatter in my mind fading out, like a decrescendo of an important note at the end of a symphony. It lingers long enough to do its job, to evoke emotion, and then I'm left with an eerie internal silence that makes me know.

Just *know*.

"I know what I want to do," I declare, making Alice's lips twitch, the smile tight, deep grooves in her lips a sign of age and many, many complex movements that aren't quite smiles, but designed to fool.

This one is real, though.

"I'll pose."

"No!" Silas commands, his spine stretching to full height, his body filling out in a clear stance of power and authority.

"Yes. I consent. It's my choice."

Plus, I'm pissed.

He turns to Alice. "These new paintings–will they be on display somewhere?"

"Maybe. Galleries love me."

"You're Alice Mogrett. Of course they do." He gives me a look I can't name. "As long as–"

I cut him off and address Alice. "Robe?"

She nods toward a partition. "Behind the screen."

And with that, I parade past Silas, eyes never leaving his, my mouth tight with a *fuck you* smile.

"Jane, I know you're emotional right now. The car bombing, and you've had to deal with Bosworth and his team, and then the crazy old lady with the rifle–"

"Hey!" Alice protests. "Don't call me a lady! I'm anything but."

"Fine. Crazy old *woman*. But Jane, are you sure you really want to do this?" he implores.

"Why wouldn't I?"

"If the paparazzi are stalking you here, like that guy who got on the premises, if one of them gets a photo of you naked..."

"What? I might be shamed?" I cover my mouth with my fingertips in mock outrage. "That would be so embarrassing, wouldn't it?"

He gives me a look of reluctant understanding. "Got it."

"I have nothing to lose and everything to gain."

"Gain? What do you gain from taking your clothes off?"

"If you haven't figured that out yet, buddy..." Alice says with a chuckle.

Silas interrupts with, "You know what I mean."

She props her closed fist on one hip and turns to him."No. I don't. What possible reason would Jane have for not posing as the subject of a work of art? This mess she's in now–it's scandal. It's a feeding frenzy. It's yellow journalism at best and sleazy gossip at worst." She looks at me. "But it is temporary. These jackals will go away. Some bigger, better scandal will come along. And then Jane will be a tarnished footnote in history. The painting, though... it will show her truth. Her essence. It will represent who she really is, and in one hundred years her name won't be uttered, but her temporary beauty will be gazed upon and admired."

I don't need his permission. But I don't want his contempt. Living in the space between those two is a kind of torture.

Madness, really.

I have to cross the line that separates them, so I step

forward, one step toward the screening partition. Then a second step. A third. By the time I am behind it and see the robe, my heart is beating so hard in my chest, I'm sure it's dented my ribs.

"Alice, I didn't plan for this. My hair, my–"

"You know none of that matters," she chides. "It's the authenticity that is important. Not the exterior wrapping."

Twice in the same day, then, I find myself naked in front of Silas.

Once by accident.

Once by choice.

My choice.

As I reach back to unzip the sundress, I remember his touch. Maybe that's why I'm doing this. Because it's real. Because it makes me more real. Silas is on the other side of this screen, unable to stop me, but unable to leave.

For once, I have power.

If this is what it takes to grasp some, then so be it.

I remove the bra and panties, folding them neatly on top of my sundress. A small stool behind the screen is a simple place to set my clothes. The robe is cold cotton against my heated skin. The warm air is responsible for some of the heat, but Silas is the trigger for far more.

I've never posed in a state of arousal before. I take a moment to cycle through some deep breaths, the familiar warmth between my legs now a curse. A deep acceptance comes when I pose, all the judgmental voices inside me quieting.

Expectations come from the outside, but also from our inside self. We find our boundaries by failing. Sometimes, though, the boundaries are imposed by the most critical expectation-setter of all.

Self-doubt.

And that is a prison. The only way to break free is to face all your fears. It's a kind of courage so terrifying, people would rather lie to themselves than be real.

You can't be unreal when you're naked, on display for the sake of the gaze. The artist's expectations are simple:

Just be.

Move when told. Angle your body a certain way to achieve a certain effect. And then–relax. Or not. Pose. Freeze. Smile. Move that leg. Look contemplative.

Be an object.

Do you know what a relief it is to just be an object sometimes?

Not someone else's object.

My own.

I step out from behind the screen and walk to the staged area where Alice wants me to pose. A simple woven shawl, some flowers, and a small pitcher rest on a table.

"Whenever you're ready, Jane," she says, all business, all kindness.

Like Band-Aids, the best way to disrobe in public is to do it quickly, suffer through a few seconds of pain, and then sigh with relief.

I get ready. My hands play with the sash, suddenly bashful.

I look at Silas's baby blue eyes the entire time.

Silas blinks. Just once. One single movement in his tall, strong body. It says everything and nothing, that blink. He doesn't look away from me. Long gone is the shy man I met with Lindsay seven months ago. He's somber and respectful, our eyes connecting the rest of us, the gaze longer and fuller as seconds pass, my breath quickening, his slowing.

We're reveling in each other. Every breath feels like a new layer, like I'm stripping myself naked from the inside out. The fact that I'm nude under this thin robe, every inch of skin exposed, feels like some sort of disguise.

My inner self needs to undress, layer by layer, piece by piece, until all I am is vulnerable before him, unfurled and flayed, ready for reckoning.

Alice is right.

I need this.

I need *all* of this.

Silas's face turns pink, his breath picking up, his eyes moving to Alice though his body stays rooted. She is focused entirely on me, unaware that she's now the object of his attention. I cannot move, but my eyes can. I steal glances at him, like taking still photos and putting them together in a montage that lets me hold onto that feeling of completion for just a few more aching moments.

"I'm required to remain in the room at all times and to have visual... on the subject," he explains.

"You mean your job requires that you see her at all times?" Alice is clearly amused.

"Yes," he chokes out.

"Then you're in for quite the treat, aren't you, Boy Scout?" Alice grins. "Not only are you forced to look at a lovely naked body, you're getting *paid* to do it."

Silas blushes, his cheeks turning an adorable pink I remember from seven months ago, the first time I met him, when Lindsay and I got together at a coffee shop after she came back from the Island.

That visit with her was so cathartic, so traumatizing, so... hard. We never got a chance to really talk. The coffee meeting migrated to a bar next door and then Tara invaded our space, turning all the attention and focus on her, our reunion an abbreviated affair.

And then, well... we thought we'd have more time.

Instead, we got more pain.

I'm pretty sure that's a feature that is built into life itself, but it feels like a curse. Especially now.

Especially when I see traces of the Silas I knew briefly then. It's an aching reminder of how different life could have been. Is he blushing because he's embarrassed by me?

Or because he's attracted to me?

Power comes to us in mysterious ways. We have all these words to describe power: Empowered. Bold. Strong. Authoritative. Dominant. Fierce. Pushy. Aggressive. Assertive.

Yet power that comes from within, that evolves with insight and blossoms in just the right moment, just when you need it, revealing itself as seconds pass and the scattered pieces inside you all assemble into a mass rally that is loud and proud?

That has no name.

What it has, though, is action.

I drop my robe.

I stand there naked.

And I reclaim myself.

Reclamation is a kind of power. It says *this is mine* once more.

And you cannot take it away.

When I posed for Alice before, in college, she was in charge of a small group of seniors. We met late at night in a tiny studio with big windows, the moon casting its reflected light on my stunned skin. I was a sophomore the first time, told by Alice that my bones were lyrical. How do you say no to someone who exalts your body, compares the lines of your limbs with music?

If that's not power, what is?

It was never sexual. I wasn't aroused by posing. If it were simple arousal, I'd never have done it. That people equate nudity with sex is so reductive. It cheapens both the human form and sex itself. Posing and being captured on canvas is a kind of immortality. Those eyes and hands translate my *now* into a forever. The painting endures. Their vision lives on.

My draped breast, my crossed ankles, my curve of a thigh, my sigh and wistful look become a challenge, a calling, a *mission*.

Art is about more than me. More than my life's horrors and pain.

More than my joy, too.

When I'm posing, I am both free and trapped. I serve both myself and a master so much higher than the known world. I can't move. I can only be observed. I am more than an object but less than a god.

And that in-between is where the creative becomes the holy.

Silas is holding his breath. Mine comes out heavy, thick, rasping, as if I need to be touched by the air, stroked from the inside out. I take the small orchid in its handmade pot painted lilac, deep grooves and small mistakes a mirror to my own blemished skin, my scarred leg from a bicycle fall, my uneven breasts, nipples taut, imperfect as nature intended.

I press my hand against a small table and lean back, moving one knee forward to pose tastefully. I'm not modest. I just know what Alice seeks.

"Good," she calls out. "Chin to the left."

As I turn, I catch Silas's gaze again, eyes locked, my chin up.

I am unafraid.

For the first time in nearly five years, I am truly unafraid.

The next hour passes in an ethereal silence, the room warming over time, the air like a loving mother. Alice always encourages me to feel whatever I feel, to show it in my body, my face, my movements. I've never posed for anyone else. I don't know how other artists do this.

I don't care.

Time has no meaning as I turn inward, finding peace. My breath is all I focus on now, imagining the painting when it's done, wondering which emotions it will evoke in people who look at it. Beauty is subjective. I don't consider myself beautiful. Maybe that's why I said yes to Alice years ago, when she delicately broached the subject.

Being chosen is the highest honor. Having someone see a part of you that you cannot see yourself is a form of love.

And who can say no to that?

Silas moves to one of the big glass windows and leans forward on a wide windowsill, one with small plants in the corner. He's still wearing a suit coat, even in this crazy Texas heat. The pressure of his hands on the wooden sill broadens his shoulders from behind, his back spread wide with muscles I cannot see but know are there. As he breathes slowly, I can see the tension in him.

It's the tension of restraint.

My skin prickles, the sensation starting right below my navel and spreading first to my right thigh, a pleasant feeling that is neither hot nor cold. As more of my skin is consumed by it, my mind goes soft and dreamy, the sharp edges of fear fading to nothing but a blur. I feel like I am floating, weightless, expanding to become part of the world. Each breath I take makes me want to touch Silas. And every breath I push out of my body releases more fear.

When you live in a constant state of vigilance, how do you recharge? The body has limits. It can live for a long time on sheer force of will, but at some point batteries have to recharge. Muscles have to relax. Pleasure has to kick in and be allowed to flourish. We cannot function if we're bathing in stress 24/7. We're not designed for it.

It will drive you insane, to the pit of despair, to a hopelessness that contradicts everything we hold dear about human connection and love.

As I watch Silas staring out the window, his shoulders drop, then he stands, stretching his back. His neck is strong in profile, his chest rising and falling with a deep breath.

Even bodyguards need to reset.

"How are you, dear?" Alice asks.

Silas turns quickly, eyes on me, vigilance activated. Within a second he reviews the room and realizes I'm fine. That Alice is being polite. No danger. No risk.

He can power down again.

But he doesn't look away.

"Do you need a break? The light is still so good. Can you last another twenty minutes?" Alice asks kindly. "Do you need water? To stretch?"

Moving feels like betrayal, but I shake my head.

I cannot look him in the eye. Silas is watching me, his fixed stare simultaneously unnerving and emboldening. This isn't some prurient titillation, an awkward, lascivious look where I'm an object and he's in control, the one who takes and expects his self-gratification to be honored.

This is an equal exchange. He is taking his time. He has no choice.

When you drop your defenses and look at the world as it should be, it takes a very long time to shed all of the false constructs inside you. Finding the truth inside is a journey.

Silas is finding his truth by studying *me*.

My stomach flutters at the thought, my ab muscles curling in just enough to make me take a long, deep breath to re-center. My upper arm brushes against the side of my bare breast. That prickly feeling starts in my right shoulder blade, radiating out to my shoulder, up into my neck, down my arm. I breathe because it's what we do, right? Humans breathe, think, move.

And love.

"That look," Alice says, her voice a thin thread of sound, so quiet, it's almost worshipful. "Hold it."

What look? I wonder, and then Silas's mouth softens, his eyes unfocused. He's looking at my body but he's seeing a part of himself, the inner journey made possible by lowering his defenses. Joy fills me at the thought.

Be real with me, I want to urge.

And let me be real, too.

"Perfect," she says, eyes bouncing between her canvas and me.

In my mind's eye, my body is a straight, centered, wise soul, a glowing core inside. A generator, if you will, that is wise. Born long before my body, the core is more than me, resting quietly, waiting to be called forth as needed. It's crowded out by all of the external chaos that makes up a lived life. Patient, it waits to be discovered, like a long-buried treasure.

Most of us never know it's there.

Silas's gaze peels away the layers that clutter the path to my core self.

Am I imagining this? I don't think so. Doubt creeps in and dissipates fast, like a cloud threatening to rain but at the last minute floating on and spreading out, once more part of the air.

I catch his eye again and all the words come rushing into my throat from the far-flung corners of my body, aching to be spoken.

I want to be a better person with you. I want to be in your orbit, always drawn by forces greater than us, the rumbling hum of physics mixed with the intangible magic of love.

Yes, it's silly. I know. I'm indulging in thoughts and feelings I have no right to possess, but damn it, I don't care.

It's my heart. I can let it run amok for a short while, indulging in fantasy and frivolity, because if I don't, it'll break off its leash. I can't have that. It's a wild animal that needs space or it will do something lethal.

"And... let's break," Alice says, her eyes tucked away by decades, wrinkles making her face a canvas, textured and well used. Her eyelashes are gone, eyebrows sparse, but that long white hair gives her authority, time handing her a kind of beauty I need seventy more years to cultivate.

And I may never possess.

The robe is on the screen, draped carefully. As I move toward it, my calf muscle complains. I take one step and pause, my back to Silas, waiting for blood to flow into the muscle again.

My shoulders ache, so I square them, stretching with a long, slow curve that is yoga-like. Then I reach for the robe and slip it on, the layer veiling me.

Bzzz.

The electronic sound is heretical, interrupting the studio's quiet space. Silas gives Alice an apologetic look, then grabs his phone from his coat pocket. He looks at the message, then at me.

"We've been summoned. They want you at The Grove." He's focused on the screen, typing.

"Now? We just got here!" I protest. "Why?"

"Ridiculous," Alice mutters. "You cannot leave until you've been able to relax and regroup. And eat!" Her weathered, leathery hands go to her cheeks in chagrin. "My goodness, I've completely forgotten to feed you! Where are my manners?"

She walks to a desk where an old-fashioned phone rests, cord and all. It's the kind with finger holes you drag around a rotary. One gnarled, leather-skinned finger slips into a clear hole and drags in a counter-clockwise direction. She lets go, and the dial snaps back. Over and over, she does this as I pray to the smartphones gods and thank them. This is how people used phones when my mom was a kid? No way.

Seven digits later and she's talking with someone. I hear food words like "salmon" and "sauce vierge" and "tenderloin," all of which make my mouth water.

"Drew says Marshall and Senator Bosworth want you back for a big meeting. The car bombing and other research..." That is more information than Silas has ever given me. He's relenting, giving in to some sliver inside that doesn't view me as a scummy traitor.

It's progress.

I'll take what I can get.

"You must stay for a meal," Alice insists, giving Silas a look that dares him to say no.

"Of course," I reply, tightening the sash on my robe.

Silas glowers at his phone. "They're saying they need you in California as quickly as possible."

"Tough shit," Alice barks, clearly fed up. "They can't find Jane to be of much use if she's a starving frayed nerve. You'll remain here for a few hours and eat a proper meal with good conversation." She puts her arm around my shoulders. I lean into her, smelling verbena and lilac, baby powder and some kind of earthy spice, like cardamom.

"You should get dressed," Silas says gruffly, the words an admission that yes, we can stay, but he's in charge.

"Why should she?" Alice replies. "Maybe we're not done painting."

"Paint time or meal time. Pick one. You can't have both," he demands.

Alice squeezes my shoulder. "Jane? You can choose. You don't have to go back. You are your own person."

Silas closes his eyes and takes his three middle fingers, rubbing a spot on his forehead. "You really can't say no. The new information indicates you've been implicated in communications between John, Stellan, and Blaine on a level no one found before."

"I *what*?"

Sadness fills his eyes. Sadness. "That's all I can tell you, and even that's too much. Just know that if you don't come willingly, other agents will come and you'll be taken back in handcuffs."

"Am I under arrest?" My heart thumps in my chest like a backbeat.

"More bullshit," Alice says, going to the fridge to pour more lemonades. I hold up a palm when she grabs the vodka. All my soft, warm feelings are gone, leaving my head swimming. It's the worst of both worlds, the alcohol loosening me at the same time I'm filled with dread.

"Not arrest, but Jane?" He comes close, gently pulling my arm to guide me away from Alice. He leans in, the scent of his aftershave light, intoxicating. "If I don't get you back there, the people who will come and take you won't be as nice."

"Why do you care?" I ask, at first defiant, then strangely pleading.

"I don't know," he whispers. "But I do."

CHAPTER 14

*T*he taste of basil from the sauce vierge on the salmon at Alice's place is still on my tongue as Silas and I walk into the office wing of The Grove. In less than six hours I've gone from posing for Alice to returning for an emergency meeting that puts me right back where I was.

Accused.

This would be so much easier if I knew what people assume I've actually *done*.

You might think I'm about to find out, but that's not how these meetings work. I go in and I'm an object. A thing. A bother. A symbol.

It's the opposite of how Alice views me. Of how I feel when I am posing.

Here, my physical presence is an indictment of their power. In regular life, you know who your friends and enemies are, mostly. Tara, Mandy, and Jenna were supposed to be my friends, and they turned on Lindsay and–by exten- sion–me. They're an exception.

In high-powered meetings with politicians and their "peo- ple," you have no idea who is good, who is bad, and who is driven by some agenda you can't even see.

When I sit in conferences at The Grove, all I know is that

I'm about to be managed, sent somewhere new, turned into a hot potato.

And right now, Silas has me in his hands.

He escorts me to the conference room, but no one is there except for Marshall, who has a tighter-than-usual look on his face. In his hands are the ever-present folders he carries, plus a cell phone. When he and Silas exchange nods, I go cold.

Marshall looks at me clinically. "Jane."

"Marshall."

"Thank you for coming on such short notice." Am I imagining that he's looking me up and down in some sort of robotic fashion? It's not the look you give a woman you're evaluating for sexual interest. It's the same strange inventorying that happens to me whenever I come to one of these meetings.

Usually it's Monica Bosworth who does it with precision, but Marshall might be taking lessons from her. His eyes narrow and he squints, blinking hard as Drew enters the room, followed by Monica.

Oh, boy.

This meeting just got harder.

Drew doesn't sit, handing Marshall a slim envelope. "Exam room set up."

"Exam room?" I squeak, my gut turning to liquid. "What kind of exam room?"

Monica frowns at Drew as if he's created the conflict. "They'll explain," she says.

"Why are you here, Monica?" Drew asks sharply. "You're too busy to have time for this." His tone is perfunctory. She's a problem he's managing.

Like me.

Her tongue migrates to her upper lip, puffing it out slightly as her jaw tenses. As always, the senator's wife is perfect. Not a hair out of place, her makeup expertly applied, the wrinkles hidden to the extent that modern technology can manage. A pale cinnamon lipstick with a slightly darker lipliner outlining her mouth looks like an artist painted it on. At the thought of painting, I feel a half smile creep over my face, the right corner of my mouth rising.

"What's so funny, Jane?" Monica asks, her voice an accusation, acrimonious and taunting.

"Oh–nothing."

"That's right. *Nothing* about this situation is funny," she spits out, looking pointedly at Drew, who ignores her. She hates to be contradicted but she loathes being ignored.

I look away and say nothing, mimicking Drew.

Lindsay walks in.

"Jane," she says quickly, looking at her mother when she says my name. "Mom, are you really going to butt in? You don't need to be here."

"And neither you nor Drew needs to tell me where I should and should not be," Monica says through clenched teeth. "I know full well how to allocate my time, and if I think this is important enough to be present, then it is."

It's suddenly hard to breathe.

Silas pulls Drew aside. I hear him ask, "Why are Monica and Lindsay here?"

"Lindsay's here because of Monica. Trying to rein her in," Drew answers.

"What does everyone here think I have done?" I ask no one, sending the question out into the center of the room.

Marshall clears his throat and answers me. "We have reason to believe you haven't told us the truth, Jane."

Because I haven't. Silas knows more about my informant now, but...

"And that you may be spying via implants."

"Implants?" I look down at my breasts, which are quite small. "You seriously think these are implants?"

Monica rolls her eyes. "Not breast implants. Chips."

"You think my body has *microchips* in it? Like I'm a pet dog? And someone's spying on you with them? That's crazy!"

Monica looks at Lindsay. "Drew implanted Lindsay to track her. That's how she was saved–no thanks to you," she spits out at me. "It's absolutely in the realm of possibility that the people you work for have implanted devices on you. And a new tip says it's more than possible."

For a split second, I wonder if she's right. No, it's not logical. I know I'm not microchipped or implanted or whatever you want to call it. But when you spend so many months being told right is wrong and wrong is right, and when psychological warfare is being used against you in a game you can't understand, it's totally inevitable that you'd doubt your own body.

"You think John and Stellan, or–that they implanted me?"

"Or someone else," she says calmly.

I look around the room, focusing on the men. Why is Monica speaking to me about this? Who made her the spokesperson?

"Did you–do you–what evidence do you have? Who gave you this tip?"

"None. Yet. And you know we can't tell you that."

The word *yet* makes me tighten my gut, an involuntary Kegel closing off my lower body. "Yet?" I remember her words when she first came in.

Exam room.

Marshall sighs and says, "We need to have you submit to a physical exam to search for scars or evidence of implants. It's possible this was done to you without your knowledge."

"I think I'd know if someone inserted something into me!"

"Would you? Were you ever kidnapped, or subdued to the point of being unconscious?" he inquires, eyes sharp.

"What? No!" My eyes dart all over the room, processing memory as fast as possible. "I have told you everything. My mother was lied to, and handed Lindsay up to them without realizing until the last second who was really on the helicopter that took Lindsay away. When she knew it wasn't Mark Paulson, she got a phone call telling her I had been kidnapped. John came to my apartment and calmly explained I needed to be their cell phone mule. They had a complex system of burner phones, designed to prevent being tracked. That's all I did!"

"But they kept you somewhere," Silas prods.

"In Stellan's apartment, for a short time."

"And you swear they didn't hurt you? Touch you? Assault you?" Silas's words are clear. He's asking if they raped me. He already knows the answer–I've testified so many times, telling the story over and over. Why is he asking?

"They didn't. They kept implying it. Said they'd finish what they started four years ago."

Silas's face goes pale.

"Finish?" Lindsay asks in a tone of befuddlement. I realize she's probably only heard bits and pieces of my testimony. Most of it was behind closed doors, in private congressional and intelligence agency sessions.

"That's what they kept saying. I thought at the time they meant that they wanted to do to me what they did to you, back then at the party." I look at her and want to cry. "I didn't know what they were planning at Drew's apartment."

Monica makes a derisive sound of disbelief.

"Lindsay, when I saw you there, I realized how bad it all was. I had no idea my mother put you on that helicopter. I'm so sorry. I really am. And I know you don't believe me, but–"

"We'll see," Monica says, cutting me off. "Once the exam is completed, we'll know more."

"Exam?" We're back to that topic.

"We have a doctor present from one of the intelligence agencies. A specialist in finding implants."

"Specialist?" I squeak.

Marshall sighs. "It's routine. In fact, we're all surprised it wasn't done sooner. Mrs. Bosworth noted the error and–"

I turn and look at Monica. "*You* noted it?"

"When it comes to protecting my family, I am careful to do due diligence. You remain a threat. You are lying and have been lying all along. Your Little Miss Innocent act might fool some people but it isn't fooling me."

"You're so determined to find me guilty of something that you want me to submit to a body search?"

"Technically, you don't need to submit. We have enough

probable cause to find a judge who will..." Marshall's words fade as I realize what he's saying.

They've treated me like an object you move around in a game.

Now they are literally making a claim to my body.

"You have to tell me more than this. It's too flimsy." Alice's defiance is rubbing off on me.

Drew gives me a look with dead eyes. "Fine. I don't have to tell you, but I will if you insist."

"I do."

"We've been given new word that the people behind you were responsible for the car crashes that killed my parents and Mark Paulson's mother and stepfather."

Silas looks down, face a mask.

Monica gives me a twisted smile. "See? Your whole disgusting web is bigger than anyone thought. You're just a pawn in it, a lackey, a game piece. But you can kill the leader by getting enough minions."

"Minion?" I gasp. "I'm no one's minion." Numb blood courses through me. My skin feels like so many balloons being inflated. The accusations are unreal.

Again.

"You're certainly no leader," she says with a horrid cackle that makes me want to run away. "You're just a tool. A sad little tool. And that means we need to figure out how to use you."

"Use me?"

"If we find the implants, we'll confirm your role in it all."

"How does that confirm anything?" I ask. Silas gives me a sharp look, as if I've said something wrong.

"It shows you're complicit," Drew says.

"You just asked me if I'd ever been unconscious around them, that maybe they planted something on me then. How could I be complicit if I never gave consent?" I look around the room, half wild with terror. No one will catch my eye.

"Backpedaling now? How cute," Monica says, moving behind Lindsay, placing a protective hand on her shoulder.

Lindsay's not looking at me, giving Drew a questioning look instead. Her shoulders hunch as Monica touches her.

"I'm not backpedaling," I insist. "I'm trying to use reason and logic here."

"You're trying to play mind games," she replies. "And you're doing it poorly."

"This is a witch hunt," I say, my body separating from my mind. The wedge is small but grows by the minute as the dawning horror of what they're proposing seeps in. "It's like the drowning test for witches in the 1600s. If I sink and die, I'm innocent. If I float, I'm guilty."

Baring my body for Alice to paint a work of art is a far cry from submitting to a naked body search for a team of people determined to find me guilty of crimes I've never committed.

"No one is asking you to kill yourself," Monica counters. The words are out of place, incongruent with what we're talking about.

"Who ever mentioned suicide?"

Her eyes turn sympathetic. "No one, but you know. Your father."

I inhale sharply, the room filled with confused looks. Very few people know that my father committed suicide while my mother was pregnant with me.

So few that it's clear Monica is the only one in the room.

Aside from me.

"Depression, anxiety–they're genetic. They run in families." Why is she talking about this? What on earth is her point?

"Why are you bringing up my father? He has nothing to do with this!" I say, my breath quickening, fists curling into tight balls.

"You father has everything to do with this," she shoots back, eyes little fireballs of blue evil. She shakes her head slightly, as if surprised by her own words, and reels it all back in under control. "I just meant that you seem to have a persecution complex. People often do with family histories like yours."

"You're not making any sense, Mom," Lindsay interrupts.

Silas is watching Monica with cold interest, while Drew sorts through papers in a folder in front of him, but I can see how tightly he's holding his body.

"Drew," I say.

He turns to look at me, impassive but oddly attentive at the same time.

"How solid is this tip that I am somehow connected to the people who killed your parents?" I ask, my voice dropping with pain. Empathy floods me. My mom just died. It's like someone ripped out all my teeth and expects me to still chew. I can only imagine the need for answers if she'd died in a mysterious car accident.

"From the highest levels of government," he says, looking down at the table.

I sigh. "And if I let your doctor do a body check, will you believe me?"

"It will strengthen your case," he says dully. "And discredit the person who tipped us off," he adds. It's an unnecessary comment, but it makes Lindsay squeeze his hand.

Monica rolls her eyes and says to me, "Just do it. Make it easy on everyone, including yourself. Do it for the country."

"The country? I'm doing this because I don't have a choice! Don't try to gaslight me." The longer Monica talks to me, the more I want to push back. Lindsay used to complain about her overbearing mother, and I always thought she was exaggerating a bit.

I was wrong.

Monica reaches for me, Silas shoving himself between us, but she gets my forearm. "Listen here, you conniving little bitch. If anyone is gaslighting, it's you. Lindsay's been through enough because of you. Now we have new evidence that your people might be behind Drew's parents' deaths, and all you care about is putting me in my place?" Her face is red, eyes so narrow, they might as well be closed, and I have the distinct feeling that if we were alone, she'd have no problem strangling me to death.

"I–I'm not! But you can't go around saying that I should–"

"Don't you dare try to tell me what I can and cannot do!" she roars. "You've created an impossible situation for Harry!"

Lindsay looks up, craning her neck. "What does Jane have to do with Daddy?"

"What *doesn't* she have to do with Harry!" Monica explodes. "She's at the center of this whole mess, all the way back. Can't you see that, Lindsay? She's the cancer that has metastasized into every part of your father's career!"

Even Drew looks up, astounded.

"You're giving her a lot of credit for power Jane can't possibly have," he says slowly, frowning.

"How do we know?" Monica stresses. "We can't know until she's been thoroughly investigated. And we have a tip. We need to follow up on it."

"What does this exam involve?" I ask Marshall, deciding to ignore Monica at this point.

"Blood work. We need to run some tests. Looking for biologic agents," he adds vaguely. "And a skin search for implants."

"Can't you just do an MRI or a CAT scan?" Silas interrupts. Monica glares at him.

"Not good enough. Some of the implants are designed to self destruct inside the subject's body if they are subjected to a high-energy scanning technology. Hence the blood work, plus we have a doctor who is a visual specialist," Marshall says matter-of-factly. "It's nothing more than what you'd experience at a dermatologist for a skin cancer check," Marshall assures me.

Monica's chin goes up, her composure back.

"It's a twenty-minute process. If you're really innocent, it should be no problem," she sniffs, giving me a glare. "If you have nothing to hide, why would you argue?"

"For someone who wants to be First Lady, your grasp of constitutional rights leaves much to be desired," I reply, struggling to keep my voice calm. A few minutes ago I was afraid she'd strangle me.

Now I'm worried in reverse.

Drew smothers a smile with his hand, while Lindsay stays

perfectly still, the only hint of a reaction her twitching nostrils.

"Great!" Marshall declares. "It's settled then. Jane, Silas can guide you to the exam room. We'll be here when you get back."

"Assuming the doctor finds nothing," Monica adds. "*When* he finds a chip, you'll be transported elsewhere."

I don't even want to ask where *elsewhere* is.

Silas moves between me and Monica again, deftly getting me out the door and into the hallway, zigging and zagging down turns until we're in front of a plain door. He knocks.

The door opens.

A short man with thinning grey hair answers, wearing a doctor's lab coat, holding a small electronic device in his hand about the size of an iPad mini. He opens the door further and looks at me, one eyebrow going up. Dark brown rheumy eyes take me in. He has no eyelashes, and the whites of his eyes are tinged yellow.

"Jane Borokov, I assume?"

"Are you searching someone else for implants today?" I ask, looking at the clock pointedly. It's late. Then again, when you work for whatever agency this doctor is with, time ceases to matter.

"You expect me to say no." His voice is faintly accented, something from a romance language. I cannot tell whether it's Spanish, French, Portuguese–who knows. Silas motions for me to enter before him, and in the space between us, the doctor starts to close the door, leaving Silas out.

"No. I'm staying," he says, squeezing into the tiny exam room.

"Absolutely not," the doctor says.

"Absolutely yes." Silas's body grows the way it does when he's defending me. "Or she leaves."

"This isn't protocol."

"Depends on whose protocol you're talking about. My orders say I have visual on the client at all times. She's under death-threat watch."

"Or you're a pervert who wants to see her naked."

"Oh, he already has," I quickly explain. "Twice."

"That's not helping, Jane." Silas gives the doctor an unblinking look, saying nothing more.

"Fine. Jane, sit here for the dental exam." He pats the doctor's rolling stool at the end of a standard exam table, the kind you find in any doctor's office.

And then I see the folded stirrups. No worries, though. Marshall said it was just a skin check.

"Dental exam?" I ask.

"Implants can be placed in teeth. Easiest, oldest way to use them to communicate," he explains, though it's clear he's annoyed by being asked.

"Oh. Okay."

"Any crowns? Implanted teeth?"

"No."

"Fillings?"

"No. My mother had perfect teeth, and so do I."

"What about your father?"

"No idea. He died before I was born."

I open my mouth and the doctor pokes around, stabbing my gums, running the sharp metal spike along the edges of all my teeth where they go beneath the gum line. I taste blood quickly.

"Perfectly aligned," he says."Braces?"

"Three years."

"And no cavities?"

"None."

"Well, that makes this faster. Bloodwork next. Do you have one arm that's better?" He moves a tray covered with phlebotomy supplies next to the stool.

I extend my left arm. "Here. I have one good vein," I say, wanting to make this as painless as possible.

The doctor taps it lightly with his glove-covered finger and makes a face of approval. "This will be easy."

And it is, relatively speaking. Eight vials of blood later, we're done. He tapes a wad of gauze over the insertion site and scribbles on the tablet.

He turns away, pointing to a folded sheet at the base of

the exam table. "Remove all your clothes and we can do the next part of the exam."

Undressing for a pose at Alice's is one thing. This–this feels like I'm agreeing to my own abuse. Like I'm offering myself up.

Which I am.

The look on Lindsay's face when Drew said that I might be connected to his parents' deaths made me want to cry, to blabber on and on about how I'm so sorry. To prove to them, once and for all, that I didn't do any of this.

But how do you prove a negative?

My clothes slide off my body as Silas and the doctor–whose name I still don't know and don't want to ask for–turn their backs to me. I undress quickly and move onto the exam table, the paper crinkling beneath my bare ass, the plastic underneath cold on my outer thighs and butt as I hold the sheet up under my armpits, waiting.

"Borokov, huh? Is that Russian?"

"Yes. My mom emigrated when she was young."

"Any family ties back in your motherland?" He presses a hand on my bare shoulder, guiding me back to lie on the table, his face covered by a light-green paper mask, eyes excited.

A cold dread starts to pump through me. "No."

"Does he really have to be in the room?" the doctor snaps as he yanks the sheet off my body, my completely nude form now stretched out on the exam table. My muscles can't relax, so everything feels colder, tighter, more painful.

Vulnerable.

"I do," Silas says, his voice heavy with an emotion that isn't just about duty.

"You're taking up room. It's a tiny exam space."

"Do your best."

I can't explain it, but the doctor gives me the major creeps. Not that it isn't already awkward as hell, being naked in front of Silas. Out of the corner of my eye, I can see him trying to be discreet, looking anywhere but my direction. My nipples harden and one thigh twitches as I think about the fact that Silas is eighteen inches away from me, sitting on a small examination stool, one simple turn giving him a view of my exposed body.

"You're warm, aren't you?" the doctor says, his voice cutting through the handful of seconds where I was transported into my imagination. I shiver, my bladder suddenly pressing, the feeling making me flatten my hips against the paper and vinyl covering the table.

He holds a magnifying glass in one hand.

For the next ten minutes, I am put through a comprehensive body exam, with the doctor searching for a needle in a haystack.

I am the haystack.

He looks everywhere, turning me over, parting my butt cheeks, using the magnifying lens to look at every nook and cranny. He stays on the surface of my skin. I just close my eyes and try to be anywhere but here.

The doctor pokes and prods at every scar, every blemish, eyes scanning my body meticulously, cataloging imperfections.

The stark difference between his gaze and that of Alice painting me is like living in a parallel universe.

As the doctor searches my back, Silas's phone buzzes. He is turned away from me. I open my eyes a crack to see him pull the phone to his ear, taking a call.

"You can talk in the hallway," the doctor says crankily.

"I can't leave the client."

The client.

The doctor's cold latex-covered fingers occasionally touch spots on my skin, his breath hot in erratic patches against my back, my ribs, my buttocks. It's excruciating. Not the touch–the sense of being a specimen. Of needing to "pass" this exam.

Of not knowing why this is *really* happening.

"Mom, I can't–slow down. What?" Silas is speaking as quietly as he can but he's only a few feet away. We can hear it all.

Silas sighs. "Can't talk now. You know what to do. We've talked about it before. She can't compromise my work."

She?

"Look," he says, voice dropping to anger. "It's more of the same. I know–I *know*," he adds, exasperated. "But listen to me. You know what to do. I'll call you when I have a break at work."

Click.

He hangs up on his mother.

I'm relieved to have something other than the exam to think about. What's going on in Silas's life?

Just then, my legs are forcefully parted. I let out a small sound, a protest I didn't consciously mount, one that the rough touch and the creepy vibe elicit.

"We've been told to do a thorough examination," he says. I hear the snap of a glove, then feel fingers on my inner thigh. *High.*

I sit up, fast, and make a growling noise low in my throat, body tightening into a ball, curling all my openings so they are covered.

Except my mouth.

"Whatever it is you think you're about to do to me, *no*. I withdraw all consent for this search."

Suddenly, Silas is between me and the doctor, his wide back dark with his blue suit jacket, the contrast startling.

"You can't withdraw," the doctor says from the other side of Silas. "Consent was never needed. Or asked for," he adds in a disapproving tone, as if I'm the transgressor.

"You heard her," Silas says firmly. "She withdraws consent." His body tenses, holding firm.

"She doesn't have a say in this. It's like any other strip search. We're well within our rights to–"

"She said *no*." Silas's voice is low and deadly, with the kind of authority I've heard in Drew but never this man, who has literally turned himself into a wall.

For me.

"Your boss says yes."

"My boss doesn't know what you're doing to her."

"You really think that?" The doctor's voice is mocking. "I won't stop the exam without permission from your boss."

"And I won't let you touch her again."

"Then we're at an impasse."

Given the doctor is about eight inches shorter than Silas and thirty years older, if this comes to blows, I'm not worried.

My stomach sinks anyhow, because one call to Silas's boss–does he mean Drew?–means I lose.

And Silas has to stand down.

I know how bureaucracies work. I know how this strange, extra-judicial system works, too. I am only standing up for myself because the doctor is about to cross a line.

"I withdraw consent," I say again.

"We may need to do this by force if you don't just accept fate and let me finish," the doctor says.

"Said every rapist in history, ever," I snap. "Now I withdraw consent *and* I'm reporting you to the police! You're threatening–"

Silas acts quickly, his dark suited arm moving to the right, the doctor's lab coat trapped in one big hand. The guy is up against the wall, choking.

Silas's voice is deadly calm.

"You will not threaten her. You will never, ever touch her again. If I hear that you've made that fucked-up force threat to a woman submitting for an exam like this, I'll make sure you're on the radar screen of people in the government you've never heard of–and don't want to. Understood?"

The doctor just makes a gagging sound.

Silas drops him. Ever see a spider skitter away from a small spray of water?

That's exactly what he looks like as he leaves.

"He's right," I say as I grab the thin sheet, covering myself with it. "If you weren't here, he could have just made me do whatever he was about to do. Was he really going to search my… there… for implants? For chips?"

Silas reaches up and hands me a hospital gown without turning around. "It's possible to find them there, yes."

"Why not do a scan?"

"Because bad guys always seem to find a way to be just savvy enough to be ahead of technology. And also because of intimidation."

"Intimidation?"

"As a technique. No one wants a cavity search."

"You knew that was about to happen to me?" I shove my legs hard into my skirt opening and zip up, throwing my arms through my bra loops, snapping fast. I think I'm setting a personal best for quick dressing.

"No. *No*," he says forcefully. "Until I came in here I had no idea what they were doing."

"Drew ordered this?"

"Not Drew."

"Then who? His boss? Oh, my God, did *Harry* order this?"

"I can't tell you who."

"You can protect me from it but you can't name the person who ordered it?"

"Welcome to the security industry."

"It's all about the secrecy, isn't it? Give your clients what they want, protect them at all costs, but use those secrets to position yourself at an advantage." My words come out in a rushed scramble. Fear pushes them through my quivering lips.

He goes quiet.

"Are you decent?" he asks finally.

"No, but I'm dressed."

His little snort of amusement thaws me, slightly. I know he can't divulge information sometimes. It's how this whole world works.

But still—someone ordered a full cavity search on me. Someone high enough up in government to make it happen. Without Silas, I'd be in pain right now.

Or worse.

"Who would do that? I'm a private citizen who is here in protective custody because of the car bomb. No one seriously thinks I've done anything, except for Monica."

Silence.

Oh, no.

"Monica?"

Silence.

I sigh, pacing in the tiny room, narrowing my eyes to shut out the bright, overbearing fluorescent lights above that hover like an annoying alien ship.

"Fine. I get it. You can't say anything." It's easier to be angry with him than to process what just happened.

"No, Jane. I can't."

I walk to the door. Just as I'm reaching for the doorknob, so is he. Our hands collide, his grabbing my elbow to support me.

He doesn't let go when he could. Or when he should.

"I'm sorry you went through that. Are you okay?"

I am holding my breath.

I am holding my breath because Silas is touching me with a gentleness that belies every attitude I thought he had toward me.

He's blocking out the light, his eyes so kind, so sweet. As I look up, I swear he's staring at my lips, which gives me a few seconds to look at him. My skin hurts, like someone is stretching it too hard. The tension makes it unbearably itchy suddenly. Physical memories of the doctor's hand on my inner thigh trigger all my Kegel muscles to clench. I close my eyes, wincing.

"He didn't actually hurt you, did he?" Silas sounds like the thought hadn't occurred to him until now, and that if the doctor did, he is a dead man.

"No. I'm just–I'm just–it's too much," I say, my body taking this tiny little flash of compassion from him and running with it, taking advantage of the momentary lapse in constant vigilance to relax, to process.

To cry.

"Jane," he says, sounding helplessly pissed, still angry at the doctor yet unable to help me. "No one deserves what you've gone through."

"But I do!" I say in a bitter, over-the-top voice. "I'm the worst person ever. Don't you understand, Silas? Everyone thinks they know me. I'm pigeon-holed. I'm screwed whether I'm innocent or not. Sometimes I think it would be easier to just give it up. Tell them they were right all along. Instead of desperately trying to get people to believe my truth, feed them the lie they want. Maybe that's the secret to life: give in sooner than you want to. It makes all the problems go away."

"It doesn't. You just end up with new problems."

A million smartass replies to that comment come flying through my mouth. They stop at my teeth, the tip of my tongue slipping through lips just long enough for him to see. His body drops, like he's let go of a burden across the back of his neck. I feel an intimacy with him that is insane considering what I just went through.

And then I'm in his arms, smelling him, my face pressed gently against his chest. Slowly, with an aching hesitation that must take Herculean effort to overcome, his arms wrap around my shoulders, hands flat against my back, fingers planting themselves firmly in the curve of my waist, offering comfort.

I drink it in, the sensation so unreal that I start to dissociate. If I'm going to separate my mind from my body, shouldn't it be during an assault like I almost experienced from the doctor? Instead, I'm doing this because of an embrace?

Silas's embrace.

"I shouldn't be doing this," he murmurs in my ear.

"No, you shouldn't."

"*We* shouldn't be doing this."

"No, we shouldn't."

He doesn't budge.

Finally he says, "But I am."

"We are."

"I'm sorry, Jane."

"Me too, Silas."

"No. You have nothing to be sorry for. Not to me. Not to anyone." His breath warms my hair and neck, smelling like coffee. The hard edge of his chest holster presses into my breast, reminding me that he's hard core. Dangerous. A trained soldier who can turn on all of the selves inside him designed to kill in order to protect.

He thinks *I'm* the dangerous one?

A stillness settles over us, the air changing. We've moved from comfort to something more, a tantalizing potential that expands as time takes over. Every detail of movement becomes more intense, more important, just *more*. The cloth of his suit jacket scratches against my cheek. His fingers stroke the bones of my shoulder blades, exquisite and satisfying. My hands press him closer to me, his body seeping warmth into mine.

I'm melting.

If I look up, will he kiss me? The attraction is so strong. So intoxicating. I could just pull away and pause time, looking into his eyes to see if he feels this, too.

Silas beats me to it, head tipped down, taking me in with eyes that search mine for answers I can only give using my body as a conduit to the heart.

The same body that was just turned into a rope in a very slick game of tug-of-war.

He bends down and I panic, unsure suddenly, wanting and willing but oh, so uncertain.

When his lips land on the crown of my head, his sigh a breath of promise, I feel two distinct emotions at the same time.

Relief.

And regret.

CHAPTER 15

*M*onica's words won't stop looping through me as we walk back to the conference room. My father killed himself when Mom was pregnant with me. She never wanted to talk about it. I don't even know how he died–just that he did.

Depression, anxiety–they're genetic. They run in families.

Why is she bringing this up now?

As we walk back into the room, Lindsay looks at me, then down at my left arm.

"What's that?"

"The doctor drew enough blood to fill a vampire's backup supply before he tried to give me a pap smear and a free colonoscopy."

"What?"

I look at Monica, who remains impassive. Lindsay's reaction, though, is unfiltered horror.

"Quit exaggerating," Monica says to me, then pulls gently on Lindsay's arm. "And stop talking to her like she isn't a traitorous fiend."

"I don't talk to her like that because she's *not*, Mom."

My heart leaps into my throat, jumping for joy.

And then I get the shakes.

They start in my arms, hands going tingly, my legs unstable. As I sit in a chair at the conference table, I grip the edge with more tension than usual, leaning on it. My feet don't exist any more. My ribcage is stuck in agitation mode, like I've become a washing machine that never quite finishes its spin cycle.

Silas notices immediately and looks at my hands. I pull them into my lap and try to just breathe.

"Jane," Lindsay says quietly. "Are you okay?"

"No."

Silas has pulled Drew aside and is furiously whispering, Drew's blank face going emotional with astonishment, then cold, tight anger.

"That wasn't authorized," Drew says.

"What wasn't authorized?" Lindsay's frown deepens and she moves toward me. "Jane, what just happened in that exam room?"

I can't stop shaking.

She touches my shoulder and feels it, eyes widening. "You're shaking. And pale. Oh, Jesus, someone get her a glass of water. I think she's about to faint."

Silas breaks away from Drew as the room starts to swim. What I see has broken into twenty parallel lines that all turn into waves before my eyes. My teeth chatter. I'm cold.

So cold.

"Here," says a very kind Silas, whose hand is on the back of my neck, his other holding a glass of water. "Breathe slowly and sip."

"I'm fine."

"You're not," he says definitively.

Drew speaks in a low, angry voice with Marshall, who seems shocked.

"Bloodwork and a skin check. Nothing more," he tells Drew as Silas and Lindsay help me.

"Who the hell was that quack, then?" Silas says, his voice becoming louder as I focus, coming back to some sort of baseline.

"You are an icicle," Lindsay says, taking her sweater from

around her shoulders and draping it across mine. "What did that doctor do?"

"He tried to do a full cavity search," I say robotically.

"WHAT?"

Monica walks out of the room, Marshall on her heels. My head is down, so I can see behind me, to my right. They're just outside the doorway, conferring. Whatever Marshall is saying is pissing her off, but he's holding steady.

They return to the room. Silas takes a seat next to me, his hand still on the back of my neck, but then it migrates to my shoulder, like he's holding me up.

"I'll make it brief," Marshall says. "Blood work's been sent to a private lab for tests to be run, including blood markers for known implant reactions and paternity testing."

I gasp. "Paternity?"

"It's routine."

"Not for me!"

Monica is looking at Marshall with a tight, controlled expression that makes me fear for his life. "Paternity? You never said that was part of the deal."

"Given the new rumors we have, it's critical."

"Rumors? Rumors about my father?" I gasp.

"Rumors about who your father might be."

And just like that, I get it. I *get* it.

I know why Monica hates my guts.

Because once, a long time ago, I was teased at school for being illegitimate. For being the love child of my mother and Senator Harwell Bosworth.

It was a half-assed joke someone made in ninth grade, some bullying rich guy named Desmond, who tried to get me to go to a football game with him, overtly telling me he expected a blowjob under the bleachers during halftime. I told him no, and the next day the rumors began.

I'd come home in tears and told my mother, who condemned Desmond and told me in no uncertain terms that guys like that weren't worth the flesh on their bones.

But she hadn't disputed the rumor, I realize.

Does Monica think I'm the senator's love child? Is that

why she mentioned my real father, why she seems so involved in my body check? Why she's so aggressively mean to me?

I wish Mom were alive. I have so many questions and no one to ask.

"I'm sure you ran the paternity tests a long time ago," I protest.

"No," Monica says in a firm, clipped voice. "Your mother put a stop to it. But she can't stop anyone now." Her eyes flit to Marshall, cold and dead.

While I process that gut punch, Lindsay jumps in. "Who do you think her father might be?" she asks, her voice hollow. She's clearly thinking what I'm thinking.

Drew sighs and answers, looking to Marshall not for confirmation but as a warning. "Nolan Corning."

That is *not* the name I was expecting.

"Nolan Corning? You think my mother slept with *him*?" Nolan Corning is the former high-ranking senator who was responsible for the attack on Lindsay nearly five years ago. He did it to discredit Senator Bosworth and eliminate him as a presidential contender. The plan backfired, but it took careful digging and a lot of luck on the part of Drew, Silas, and their friend Mark to nail him.

"We don't think it. We're investigating tips that it might be true."

"Tips from whom?"

Drew goes silent.

"You can't expect me to give and never get back information," I say.

Silence.

"And after what that doctor just tried to do to me with Silas in the room, even I don't trust you," I spit out, livid.

"What about me?" Lindsay says, holding out her arm like she's about to give blood. "How about doing a paternity test on me?"

Monica's smirk fades, her skin turning a shade whiter underneath her makeup.

"That's not funny, Lindsay."

"I wasn't being funny, Mom. Maybe I should have a maternity test."

"Because you're pregnant?" Monica's eyebrows shoot up, overriding whatever Botox she's using. "Because the timing is still terrible, but three months from now–"

"Because it would be a relief to know I'm not *your* daughter," Lindsay smartmouths back to Monica.

"We don't need to draw blood from you, Lindsay," Marshall says. "We have your blood on file. Do you really want a paternity test?"

"I want a maternity test and a paternity test," Lindsay says with a smile, but it fades quickly when she looks at me.

"Done," Marshall says, tapping on his screen.

"This is ridiculous!" Monica declares. "She's being silly," she adds, pointing at Lindsay. "It's a waste of resources and time."

Drew's got an amused little smile on his face, his hand on Lindsay's arm. "You're turning this meeting into a Maury episode."

"Me?" she says, with mock outrage. "If anyone's daddy isn't who we thought he was, it's not my fault. I'm not the woman who slept with the wrong guy." Looking at her mother from under her eyelashes, she dares Monica to challenge her.

"Damn straight," Drew says, his smile deepening. His eyes drift over her belly and he leans in to her, whispering something I can't make out. Lindsay blushes and giggles.

I start to recover. *Really* recover.

Monica storms out, passing the senator at the doorway.

"Monica, I–"

She ignores her husband and soon her footsteps fade out of hearing range.

"What was that about?" the senator asks Marshall, looking around the room with a furrowed brow.

"Nothing important."

"Monica looks angry."

"Like he said, nothing important," Drew reiterates. "If we

gave you a field report every time Monica's angry, you'd be buried in paperwork."

Even Silas cracks a smile at that.

The senator gives Drew a weary sigh. "She may be your mother-in-law, but she's also the future First Lady of the United States of America. You don't want to be on her bad side."

"Too late," Lindsay whispers, looking at everyone in the room as she laughs, her eyes landing on mine for a brief moment of camaraderie.

"Lindsay," he chides.

"But it's true!"

"Anything else I need to know about, Marshall?" the senator asks. He's distracted and irritated.

Silas speaks up. "We need a safehouse for Jane."

"Jane–oh!" The senator looks at me. "I thought you were in Texas at the Mogrett ranch."

"Change of plans, sir," Drew says. "You called her back here for the exam."

"Exam?"

Everyone in the room gives the senator a strange look, including me. "Yes, sir," Marshall says. "The exam for implants on Jane."

"Exam for what? You're not making sense." Senator Bosworth gives me a concerned look. "Implants?"

Silas and Drew share a dark look.

"We received a credible tip that the people Jane allegedly works with may be using implants on her body to gather intel."

He looks shocked, covering it quickly. "Jane. Is that true?"

"No."

"You–you subjected her to a physical exam? Who ordered this? What were the results and what the hell was the purpose?" he demands of the room.

Drew and Marshall immediately look uncomfortable. Senator Bosworth looks at Silas and nods. "Take Jane to the guest house. Get her settled there. Lindsay, you must excuse us. Drew and Marshall and I need a closed session."

Lindsay leaves first, casting Drew a curious look, then me, followed by Silas. We don't say anything until I realize Lindsay is headed in the same direction. She opens the French doors that lead to the stone walkway to the pool. Behind it rests the guest house, a sprawling three-bedroom building larger than most homes.

I'm surprised to find it dark outside, my sense of time shattered by the rush of events. How long has it been since someone tried to fry me in my car back at the coffee shop? Has it really only been a day and a half? Time is elastic.

But the body isn't nearly as much.

A wave of exhaustion hits me, and as Lindsay walks with us, I want to be attentive. I want to talk. She seems ripe and ready for some kind of breakthrough, like she's here because she wants an olive branch, a peace agreement, an accord.

Instead, she opens the front door and just looks at me, worried.

"Sleep," she says. "We'll talk in the morning. The best bed is the one in the first bedroom on the left."

I nod and she turns on her heel, walking away.

Without saying a word to Silas I take her advice, stumbling to the bed, not even kicking off my shoes.

I fall asleep in the guest house, the ocean's waves lulling me to sleep, making promises of peaceful slumber that are just lies.

All lies.

* * *

I AM NAKED, *walking on the beach at night, the full moon shining down on the sand, the water, my body, like a searchlight, the moon making me glow. Luminous and otherworldly, I move like the moon has poured her power into me, all flow and dark heaven.*

I am light.

I am dark.

I am all the shades between.

In the distance I see a couple, hand in hand, my eyes able to make them out in the night, their stroll lazy and unhurried. She's short, he's

159

tall, and their linked hands bind them. Love floats off their bodies like an aura, strong and sure. Ocean salt air laps at my bare skin, anointing me.

I start to jog, then run, then sprint, my joy increasing as I get closer, their faces standing out, sharp and in focus.

Mom.

Dad.

Together.

My sprint is so fast, I take flight, wings sprouting from my shoulder blades as if they'd been there all along. Flying above them, I cry out.

"Stop! Wait!" I shout, my velocity too swift, my arc too high as I pass.

They don't look up.

They don't notice me at all.

My legs thrash, trying to stop, desperate to turn back and find them, but the night envelops me with inky blackness that chills my bones.

It's hard to breathe, the darkness pressing on my breasts, my ribs, invading me from between my legs, making me gasp and choke.

"No, no, no," I beg the unseen force. What had been joyful turns malevolent. It's so fast, I cannot adjust.

"Jane!" Silas calls out from somewhere close, his voice hoarse and panicked, stressed and intense.

"I'm here!" I call back, but the darkness mutes me, eating my words like they are a tasty treat, a spoil of a war I don't even know we're fighting.

"Jane? Jane? Are you here?"

Yes, I try to say, but I cannot, suspended in midair, arms out straight, legs together now, pinned to an invisible cross that seems so familiar. There is no pain. No pleasure. No darkness. No light.

Just a void.

It's all that is left of the world.

It is all that I know.

AND THEN I WAKE UP, the scream trapped in my throat, my neck turned to the right in spasms, the moon trickling just enough light through the window for me to see it was all a dream.

But it feels so real.

Tap tap tap.

I scream for real this time, the sound a strange blend of high and low notes, my heart hammering so hard, it feels like it's on the other side of the bedroom door, knocking.

"Jane?" It's Silas. "Are you safe?"

Am I ever?

No, I want to answer, but the word gets stuck inside me.

Like in the dream.

"Fine," I lie. "Just a nightmare."

He pauses on the other side, the wait long enough for me to know he doesn't believe me.

"Okay. Goodnight."

"Goodnight."

I cry myself back to sleep, trying to recall my father's face from the dream.

I fail.

CHAPTER 16

*B*zzz.

Silas checks his phone. We're in the guest house living room, getting ready for a helicopter to take us back to the landing strip where we can board a plane for Texas. I've managed to drink three cups of coffee with cream and eat two pieces of crème brûlée French toast. Connie, the head chef for the Bosworths, is amazing.

I'm showered, dressed in Lindsay's hand-me-downs, and wondering if I can really talk to her before we head back to Texas. I am about to ask when my phone buzzes.

"It's your phone," Silas announces.

"Me? No one texts me."

Someone obviously is.

I look.

It's Tara. I need to see you.

"Tara? Why the hell would *Tara*, of all people, want to see me?"

Silas takes the phone out of my hand. He's rough, the action fast and aggressive. I reach for it and he pivots.

"It's my phone!" I squeak.

He ignores me.

"How did she get your number? No one knows it. And you're *not* meeting her," he finally declares.

"Says who?"

"Says everyone. Besides, if you're trying to scrub your reputation, being seen with her isn't going to do you any favors."

"Scrub my reputation? You think that's even possible?"

"No."

"Then what do I have to lose?"

"Why would you ever want to spend one second of energy on someone who betrayed you like that?"

"Tara didn't betray *me*. She betrayed Lindsay."

"You're defending her?"

"No. I'm trying to explain why I'm tempted to go see her."

"Go on." He give me a skeptical look.

"I might get more information out of her."

"She's being charged with obstruction of justice and a host of other crimes, is out on her dad's bail money, and you think you can pump her for evidence *we* don't already have?"

"Yes."

"You're confident!" Half-mocking, half-impressed, Silas's all-male laughter fills the air.

"Don't mistake my desperation for confidence."

"You wouldn't be the first person in politics to swap them out." I want to slap the smirk off his face.

"Or the last," I mutter.

He shakes his head. "Drew is going to kill me when he sees this report."

"All the more reason for me to meet her."

"Wasn't she a bitch to you?"

"Not really. She mostly ignored me. I was the tag-along friend."

"The what?" Confusion in his eyes makes me realize how easy guys have it.

"I wasn't really Tara, Jenna, and Mandy's friend. I was Lindsay's friend, and Lindsay brought me along to things."

"Like the party? Five years ago?"

I frown, remembering. "Actually, no. That was a weird anomaly. John called me to invite me, personally."

"And he'd never done that before?"

I shake my head.

"Huh." Silas looks up at me, his long lashes making his blue eyes look striped, speckled, a mosaic appearance that is spellbinding. "You told the investigators that fact?"

"No one ever asked, actually."

"So John had never invited you to a party before?"

"Never. I was thrilled. It felt like I was more part of the 'in crowd,' instead of riding Lindsay's coattails, you know? When you're nineteen and naive, those direct asks have more potency."

He nodded.

"Did he say anything else?"

"He asked me about my favorite drink. Said he wanted to make sure he had plenty on hand."

"And we know he drugged the drinks." Silas's focused reply makes my own mind sharpen.

"I felt weird that night. Got there and pretended to drink."

"Pretended?"

"If I didn't drink, the guys would have badgered me until I did. It was easier to pretend to drink and then dump some of it off in a plant, or in the bathroom sink as the night went on."

"You never had any of the alcohol they gave you?"

"No."

"You realize how suspicious that looks?" He's incredulous.

"Of course I do. But it's true–in fact, I came back and happened to find Lindsay because of my stomach problems. And thank God, too, because the doctors said if I hadn't found her when I did, she might have–"

"Died. I know." He pauses. "Lindsay and Drew drank whatever they provided?"

I nod.

"Lindsay and I liked the same wine coolers. I don't know how they spiked Drew's drink, but they did."

"And the others? They didn't drink the same stuff?"

"No. They were all into wine. Liked to pretend they had palates as sophisticated as their parents'. You know."

"No, I don't know. When I was nineteen, I was clearing out underground bunkers in Afghanistan and trying to save civilian kids from being blown up. Keggers weren't my thing."

"This wasn't exactly a kegger."

"Fine. A 'winer' works just as well," he snaps, using finger quotes.

"You don't have to get caustic about it. We were just college students trying to have fun." I snatch the phone back, my arm rubbing against his chest for a split second. He's freshly showered and shaved, a few pieces of his brown hair wet at the tips. He smells like mint and soap, with a touch of spice added.

I resist the urge to inhale deeply.

He goes dead silent.

Yes, I type in the chat field. *Today, 2pm, Mickey's.*

Mickey's is the same place Lindsay and I went after coffee, just seven months ago. It's where we ran into Mandy that same day, Drew forcing her away in a show of power that helped Lindsay to start trusting him again.

My screen shows dots. She's replying.

Great. See you then. Come alone.

I can't, I type back. *They won't let me.*

Then come as alone as you can, she replies.

She has no idea. Absolutely no idea what that means.

K, I say, as if it matters. As if that single letter means anything more than the pleasantry of acknowledgment.

"You're really doing this?" Aggressive disapproval radiates from him.

"You don't have to ask."

"Of course I do. I'm going with you. I assume this means we need to postpone the plane to Texas?"

"Yes. Alice won't mind. And that's why you don't have to ask, Silas." I turn to confront him head on, a fiery feeling burning through me. My chin goes up, my eyes narrowing, and damn him if he tries to stop me.

"Why?"

"Because you're along for the ride, right? Everywhere I go, you go. Well then, Mr. Tough Guy, we're going to a bar at 2 pm today. I hope you like pool."

I walk away from him and dip into the first bathroom I see, shutting the door with shaking hands. My phone buzzes one more time.

And don't tell anyone I'm seeing you, Tara added, like a knife twist to the heart.

She doesn't want to be associated with me.

And yet she's taking a huge chance like this.

Why? What could be so important? And why does she want to see me, of all people?

After Drew and Silas rescued Lindsay and me from John, Stellan, and Blaine six months ago, the newspapers covered the events properly. Actual, operational facts were very clear: I delivered a phone to John, Stellan, and Blaine. Drew crashed through the wall between his apartment–where Lindsay and I were being held–and his neighbor's apartment. We were all taken at gunpoint to the neighbor's apartment. Drew's rescue attempt came just as they were about to rape Lindsay and she was naked, traumatized, and bleeding.

In the middle of everything, Lindsay even killed Stellan, in a famous video clip where she stabbed him in the penis with a knife, severing an artery.

Those are the facts.

You know what isn't fact?

The often-reported statement that I was part of John, Stellan, and Blaine's team.

That my mother and I colluded with Nolan Corning to bring down Senator Harwell Bosworth.

That I was part of the whole scheme from the very beginning, going back to when I found Lindsay that night of the party five years ago.

That I am Senator Harwell Bosworth's illegitimate daughter.

That I was jealous of Lindsay and did this out of revenge.

That I was the mastermind of it all.

That I am Nolan Corning's secret love child with my mother, a Russian spy.

That I lure small children into sex trafficking, to be sent to an island in Thailand.

I know that last one sounds like the craziest of all the theories, but it's not. Every single one of those "reports" by the media is a lie.

But lies sell newspapers. They increase ad rates. They bring in eyeballs.

If the media discover I'm meeting Tara, they'll eat it up. Covert videos will be shot. Men and women with long tele-photo lenses will hide two blocks away, the right shot worth ten grand.

Ten grand that a tech-savvy website owner can spin into six figures.

We live in a world where truth is relative. Lies can be monetized. Truth? Not so much.

All of this pours through my mind as I turn on the faucet for white noise and stare at my reflection in the mirror until I cease to exist. Seeing Tara isn't about friendship. It's not about appearances. It's about getting one grain closer to the truth.

I can't get anyone to believe the truth.

But collecting more of it keeps me from going insane.

Gone is the Silas who comforted me yesterday. Gone is the guy who defended me. He's back to being aloof, remote, and unfeeling. The perfect man in black. If you're going to do the hard work of government, you need a thick skin. A tough shell.

You need to give no damns.

Or at least, never let anyone know which damns you do give.

Silas knocks on the bathroom door, startling me.

"Occupied," I shout.

"I assume this means you don't want to schedule that meeting with Lindsay?"

"I do."

"She's not available until 2 pm today."

Damn it.

"Ask her for a different time."

"I'm not your secretary."

"It would be so much easier if you were. What's her number?"

"I'm not giving that to you."

"Then what's Drew's number? I'll text him."

"I'm definitely not giving you *that* number."

"Then how do I contact her?"

Silas taps on his phone. "She'll text you."

He walks out of the house, shaking his head. I let him go and don't question anything.

It's 10:54 am, plenty of time before I see Tara. Why can't Lindsay meet me sooner?

My phone suddenly buzzes.

Can I come see u now? I have an opening in my day.

It's Lindsay.

Sure, I tap back. No amount of coffee will give me the energy I need, but too much will turn me into an anxious hummingbird. I pour a glass of water and wait.

Five minutes later, Lindsay's at the door.

And she's alone.

Nervous, I open the door and greet her with a "hi" that she returns. Lindsay is the epitome of the popular girl, all long blonde hair with sun streaks and a face that looks like the sun when she smiles. If you didn't know her history, you would think she was nothing but a beach chick, a spoiled rich girl, vacuous and freewheeling.

She is anything *but*. Shadows move slowly in her eyes, trapped inside an echo chamber where they can only find their way out through time. Healing is only possible when you're given space. Drew carves that space out for her, but time is a kind of space, too.

And no one can make more time. If Drew could, he would, but even he has limits.

"I asked Silas to stay outside," she says pre-emptively. I look toward the nearest window and sure enough, he's there, like a sentry.

"This whole 'must keep eyes on the client' rule is getting old."

"It must be bad if that's your protocol," she says with sympathy.

"So far today, no one has tried to kill me. Came close yesterday with your mother, though."

"Ignore my mother."

"Hard to do that when she turns me into her punching bag." We share a look that makes me relax.

"Welcome to the club." Her sarcasm is as thick as ever.

"How do I unjoin?"

"You avoid. My mom is a garden-variety narcissist. You can't change them. Challenging a narcissist makes them double down. All you can do is avoid, ignore, and be so boring, they don't want to poke you, Jane."

"I see you follow your own advice," I say dryly.

"Running off to Vegas and getting married was Drew's idea. Not mine."

"It worked. She can't control you."

"Doesn't stop her from trying." Lindsay twists the end of a ribbon on her blouse. "I was only half kidding about blood tests proving she's not my mom. I think it would be a relief."

"She loves you, Lindsay." A pang of longing for my own mom threatens to swallow me up. "She wouldn't fight so hard for you if she didn't."

"You think so? I don't know. Sometimes I think I'm just a tool for her to use to get attention."

I give her a sympathetic smile. I don't know what to say to that.

We shrug in unison.

"Look. I know I'm supposed to hate you." Her lip quivers. "And when you showed up at Drew's apartment when John and Blaine were holding me hostage, I was so happy–and then so betrayed."

"I swear, Lindsay–I swear I wasn't in on it with them! Never!" Tears fill my eyes and throat, salt tinging my words. "I swear."

"I want to believe you. I really do. I saw how you reacted

when Blaine tried to–when he was on me on Drew's bed–before Drew busted through the wall and saved me."

"I wanted to stop them, but they–"

She holds up one hand. "I know. I've had six months to think about it. And I think they're all wrong."

"Wrong?"

"I believe you, Jane."

I reach down and pinch the soft skin at my inner elbow. Ouch.

She's real.

And she's serious.

"You do? Why?"

"I was there. I saw how they tied you up, too. That wasn't some fake performance you gave. It was real."

"I can't believe you believe me," I say. "Because no one else does."

"That's not true."

"Drew doesn't. Your mother definitely doesn't."

"She's biased."

"And Drew?"

"Drew's still angry that John and Blaine were ever able to get their hands on me. You know. *Guys.* When your husband protects people for a living and can't protect you, it really fucks with his head. Drew sees villains everywhere. You're caught in the giant net. He's fundamentally logical and will let the evidence sway him."

"Evidence?"

"The implant check came back. You're clean."

"I know." But I'm relieved to know that my body proved me right.

And that no one planted fake evidence on me.

"I know you know, but now they can't use that alleged evidence against you."

"Do you really think evidence matters?" I ask her, flabbergasted. "It's all about perception. No one really looks at evidence. Spin it however you want to make your case–it's spin that matters. Not proof."

"Wow."

"Wow *what?*"

"You used to be so quiet. Even-keeled. Middle-of-the-road Jane. I've never seen you so cynical."

"Try being the social media whipping girl for half a year and see how that feels while you cling to your optimism," I reply, unable–no, *unwilling*–to keep the bitterness out of my tone.

"I do know what it's like." She moves her head to and fro, then adds, "To be fair, I was drugged into oblivion by the staff at the Island, so I don't remember it."

"Lucky you."

Her eyes narrow. "Those four years were anything but lucky."

I hope I don't have to go through three and a half more years of this to be able to understand.

"You're right," I concede. "It's not a suffering contest."

"No. It's not." Her brow relaxes. "And I still have my mom and dad. You don't."

"No. I'm an orphan." A bitter laugh escapes me. "I haven't seen anyone spin the coverage like that yet. 'Crazy Russian Spy Orphan Takes Down White House Contender.'" I pretend I'm reading a headline.

She just shakes her head. "I know I had plenty of headlines like that."

"You're Russian, too?"

We politely laugh.

"Listen," she starts. "We really need to talk. You were my informer. While I was on the Island."

"Yeah, I was. And when we met for the first time in the coffee shop, right after you came home, I wanted to tell you. But I'm not the only one."

"Huh?"

"There was a man who gave me the information to give to you. I could never tell you because if I did, he'd know. I'm sure our conversations were monitored."

"I thought the whole point of the darknet was not to be monitored!"

"These deep state guys can do anything with tech."

She blinks rapidly, digesting that. "Okay... so you were just feeding me bullshit from some guy?"

"Not some guy. And not bullshit. You know what we talked about."

"I do. Now I wonder how much of it was fake."

"None of it. That's what's so scary, now that I know."

"Now that you know *what*?"

"That he's out there. Watching. Paying attention. I thought he was a good guy. On our side. But now..."

"What changed?"

"Me. I don't assume anything any more."

"Even about me?"

"Even about you, Lindsay."

As I say the words, she nods slowly. "That's fair. If I were in your shoes, I wouldn't trust anyone, either."

"I want to, though. I really do. But I can't."

"Are you sure you and Drew aren't twins? Because he said those exact words last night."

I look down. "Pretty sure." The less I say, the better.

She smiles, looking sad. "We've both been through it, haven't we?"

"Yes."

"When I saw you in Drew's apartment—what those guys were doing to us—I..." She chokes up. "I can't talk about it now, but we need to."

"Later, sure." I reach for her hand and squeeze it. "Thank you."

"For what?"

"For treating me like I'm human."

"Everyone deserves that."

"Except for Blaine, Stellan, and John."

"True."

My phone buzzes. It's Tara.

Can you do noon? Change of plans.

Is the bar open at noon? I ask, surprised.

Do alcoholics drink at noon? Yes, it's open, she replies.

I look up at Lindsay.

"Uh, I have an appointment that just got moved to noon."

Some part of me feels guilty for not telling her it's Tara. I should.

But we have a tenuous truce here. I don't want to blow it.

"Understood. You have a busy life."

"I have a *stupid* life. I spend all my time trying to avoid being caught by people who hate my guts. It's really putting a cramp in my Etsy Slow Living hobby."

"Since when do you like Etsy?"

"Since it became the only place on the internet where people don't hunt me down to denigrate me."

"Yay Etsy."

"Exactly. Do you know how soothing it is to order earrings made from recycled belly button lint?"

"I can only imagine."

We laugh.

She leaves and I stand there, wondering why the lie of omission about Tara hurts so much more than my other lies.

I text Silas the new time. I get back a single letter.

K.

K is quickly becoming the *whatever* of the late 2010s.

The short drive to Mickey's takes place like a finger snap, a blink, a skip. It's a fast ride and as we climb out of the SUV a block away, to make our entrance look as normal as possible, I wonder what I'm walking into. Will I be dragged into some new controversy? Is this a set-up, an ambush, a publicity stunt designed to make Tara money or to give her some strange notoriety?

Why would Tara text me about getting together after months of ignoring me?

I must be of some use to her.

If this is a set-up, Silas will mitigate it.

For the first time, I'm grateful I have a security detail when I go out into the world. Oh, how everything changes when your car has been firebombed.

Bars are funny places at the noon hour. I should know. They're great for hiding in plain sight. If I wear no makeup, baggy clothes, and a baseball cap, I can sit in a booth and alternate between alcoholic drinks and plain iced tea, munching appetizers and pretending I'm normal again. Filled with people time forgot, it's unreal how creepy bars are at this time of day.

Alcoholics don't ask a lot of questions. It's refreshing.

I generally don't hang out in bars until later in the day, but I really shouldn't be surprised to find people drinking already. Yet I am.

Tara turns and looks at the sound of the door opening. She gives me a sad smile, but freezes when she sees Silas next to me. He scans the room and seems to stand down, eyes on Tara.

Whatever he's worried is here, isn't.

But what if Tara brings a different kind of danger?

"You brought a bodyguard?" She's upset, accusatory, and she takes one step backwards, toward the door.

"I didn't have a choice, Tara. If you don't like it, I can't help it. They make me."

"They?"

I shrug. "Who knows who 'they' are anymore?" I give her a raw look, hoping she'll understand and not panic. "You know? If anyone understands, it's you."

Bingo.

I said the right thing.

"Oh, God, yes. Except it's not as bad for me as it is for you. I wasn't pulled back in like you were." She reaches for me in a hug. Her entire body vibrates, shaking with fear. It unnerves me, but I hug her, marveling at how cold and thin she is.

"I'm so sorry," she whispers in my ear.

"It's okay."

"No. It's not. But thank you for meeting me. Ever since I saw your mom died, that you were exonerated, and the news story about your car being bombed–that made me finally reach out." She looks around the bar, nervous as a rabbit.

She doesn't want to be seen with me.

Seen by whom?

"Let's sit," I suggest, gesturing to a dark corner where the light won't shine on us. Her expression changes to relief. I take a moment to look at her. On the surface, she and Lindsay look alike. California cool, all legs and blonde hair. That's where the similarities end, though. Tara could be mean, and she's ruthlessly ambitious. She and Lindsay used to be so tight. In high school, I was jealous. Ashamed of my jealousy, but still–I felt it. I wanted to have a true best friend like Lindsay and Tara seemed to be for each other.

I had to settle for being second best. I knew it, too. Lindsay turned to Tara first, and if she wasn't free, then I got attention. That was all in the past, though.

Right? Now I'm the one who has Tara's full attention, and Lindsay is nowhere to be seen.

We slide into a booth. Silas sits at one next to us. A waitress comes over, wiping her hands on a towel, and gives us a weary smile.

"Two cosmos," I order.

"You remember?" Tara perks up.

"Lindsay got me drinking those," I say with a laugh.

"It's good to just talk to a friend," she says, worrying the corner of a cocktail napkin. She looks behind me, nudging her chin up toward the booth where Silas sits. "What's his deal?"

"Private security. Too many people are trying to kill me, so..."

"He's hot. He have a brother?"

"I have no idea."

"Sister," says Silas, his deep voice amused. "I have one sister, and sorry, Tara–she's taken."

"You're supposed to be seen and not heard," I correct him.

"You have me confused with children. Bodyguards should be seen and avoided by bad guys."

"Silas, can you move a few booths away? This really is private."

Just then, the waitress delivers our drinks, winking at Silas as he makes huffing sounds of disapproval but moves one booth away, just out of earshot.

Tara drinks half hers in one long elegant series of swallows. I sip mine.

"So," she says, giving me a strange smile. "How do we start?"

"We?"

"Okay. Me. How do I start?"

"How about at the beginning? Why are we here? Why now? Why reach out to me, Tara?"

"Because this is all going to hell in a handbasket, and I need your help."

"My help? *My* help? Are you kidding me? I can't help anyone! I can't even help myself."

"I know, Jane, and I'm sorry." Her words come spilling out, tripping over each other.

"But why?"

She chugs the rest of her drink and waves at the waitress, who nods.

"It all goes back to the party."

"I'm sure it does."

"Look, we had no idea John, Stellan, and Blaine were like that. None. Lindsay had dated Blaine. We'd all taken them to dances as dates. You know. All but you, I guess."

"I never went out with any of them, but sure. I liked Stellan. Crushed on him, even." I shudder.

"Oh, trust me. We all want bleach showers now to wash off their corrosive stink. Those fuckers."

I stay silent.

"There was no way to predict what they did, right? I just know that John asked Mandy to take us all out for dinner and leave you and Lindsay."

"Me and Lindsay? Leave us there for what?"

My drink roils in my stomach. I'm glad I only sipped.

"What do you think?"

"No," I rasp.

"Yes. I'm sorry. That's our best guess. They said Drew wanted to have some fun and that Blaine thought you were hot, so they wanted time alone with you two."

"I've never heard this before."

"Because we've been ordered never to say it. Never, ever. They'll kill us. Or worse."

"Tara, you have to tell the police!"

"God, no. Are you crazy, Jane?" She looks around in terror, her head moving closer to her shoulders, like a turtle pulling back into a shell. "Even saying it now makes me want to throw up." Her neck tightens, a dry click coming as she swallows. "I don't have a choice."

"Slow down. Tell me the entire story. All the way back to the party."

"We were all there having fun for hours. Water polo was fun, and Mandy was flirting like crazy with Stellan. We decided we were starving and wanted to go get tacos. That's when one of them–I think it was Stellan, but I'm not sure– pulled Mandy aside and told her the three of us should just go and give them an hour or so with you and Lindsay."

"And then?"

"Then you came running out suddenly. We tried to tell you to go back in and get everyone else's order, remember? Mandy was going to ditch you, but you insisted." The judgment in her voice makes me irrationally pissed.

"And then at the taco place, Stellan texted and said we shouldn't come back. To just go home. Party over. We told you, but you insisted on going back, because you'd left something there. So we dropped you off. Your car was there. And then we went to Mandy's.

"Right after we went home, we knew something was wrong because this guy showed up at Mandy's house, where we were crashing for the night. He had a briefcase and a folder with each of our names on it. And one with your name, but it stayed in the briefcase."

"What was his name?"

"No idea. Just a guy with a slight accent."

My arms go numb. "What kind of accent?"

She squinches her face as she remembers. "I don't know. Scottish? Irish? It was like an English accent but different."

"What did he want?"

"To pay us off."

"But your dad has plenty of money," I say. Tara's dad is something like the ninth richest man in the United States.

"To pay us off to go along with pretending Lindsay asked for it, or else."

"Or else what?"

"He'd expose our family secrets."

"That's not paying you off–that's blackmail!"

"Yes."

"And all three of you did it."

"Jane, if you understood–those folders. They had records of horrible things about our parents. Our families. We'd have been ruined."

"So you destroyed Lindsay because you would have been ruined?" I can't keep the disgust out of my voice. "What were the secrets? That someone had an affair? Or your grandfather was a murderer?"

"They threatened to create fake scandals about our families."

"Fake?"

"They–they–" Her voice goes shaky and she swallows the other half of her drink, then sighs loudly. Her voice is tinged with unbridled fury. "They showed us alleged records of downloads from my father's computer, claiming he was downloading child pornography."

"WHAT?"

"He wasn't. He didn't. He *didn't!*" Tara's face flushes a horrible red. "They said they could make it look real. All they had to do was show us that and Mandy and Jenna fell in line."

"Whoa."

"It killed me to do that to Lindsay. *Killed* me. Mandy wasn't as bothered, but Jenna and I were devastated. We got all kinds of unasked-for help after that. Their pay-off wasn't money. It was doors being opened. Mandy got into a competitive master's degree program. Jenna was chosen for a big modeling contract. You know."

"Just like John, Stellan, and Blaine rose up the ranks." Within four years of Lindsay's attack, Blaine was a rising

California politician, Stellan a well-known actor, and John a major league baseball player. Their success was meteoric. Astronomical.

Statistically *impossible*.

"Who has this kind of power?" I asked her, pain radiating out of both of us.

"Someone very powerful and very rich. Someone you don't want to piss off."

The waitress brings Tara's second drink, plus glasses of water for us both. Tara downs her cosmo and sips half the glass of water, running her fingers through her loose curls, sighing.

"What the hell do you expect from me?" I ask, knowing my voice is shrill and not caring. "I can't help you! Besides, John, Stellan, and Blaine are dead. Really dead. I watched them die," I add, putting voice to the fact for the first time in a long while.

"But the people controlling them aren't."

The man with the accent.

"You said the man with the accent was your contact?"

"He was the enforcer. Calm, cool, and so cold, he was creepy. I felt like any minute he'd pull a gun out of his pocket and just shoot me between the eyes."

"He was violent?"

"Not physically. But there was a tension to him. He was devoid of emotion. Chilling." She shudders.

"How did Mandy and Jenna handle it?"

"Mandy was the first to lock it down. She said we had to be united and take all the shit that came our way. This guy was threatening. He wasn't bluffing."

"And all this time, you've never said a word. Why now?"

"Because after Drew and Lindsay killed John, Stellan, and Blaine, the threats started up again. And this time, they were specific."

"What do you mean?"

"They're planning to kill you first, then me, Jenna, and Mandy."

"I know people are after me, but it's because I'm blamed

for what happened to Lindsay. Internet shitlords and trolls want me dead. You're saying more people than that are in line to kill me?"

"What if it wasn't shitlords and trolls who firebombed your car, Jane?" she asks bluntly.

"What information do we have that makes people so evil? What do they have to lose that is so great they're willing to kill for it? I never hurt anyone."

The waitress turns up the lights just then, the dim atmosphere growing brighter as she rolls the dimmer switch slightly.

Tara doesn't answer my question, eyes the color of a pale amber ale studying me, her head tilting. I can tell she's taking in my features–but why?

"You don't have a wild guess?" she asks, clearly knowing more than she's letting on.

"No. I don't." I pause. "But you do, don't you? It's why you're here."

"And because you're the only person in the world who can help," she says, scooching out of the seat. "Listen, I need to pee. I'll be back in a minute."

Reflexively, I start to scooch with her, then stop myself. We used to go to the bathroom in bars in packs. My muscles remember. I don't need to use the facilities and frankly, I could use some alone time to process what she's just said. She waves and walks to the neon restroom sign, her chunky cork heels making her seem taller, more slender, less real and more like a doll, dressed up to be looked at but having no innate function.

Just a toy you play with until it's no fun anymore.

"Reliving old times?" Silas asks, walking toward me, his body a shadow as a bright, low-hanging lamp wreaks havoc with how he looks. As his face comes into focus, I can see he's assessing everything.

"You heard all that?"

"I heard some, and I–"

Bzzz.

He looks at his phone, answering it. "Sir?" he says.

Ah. It's Drew.

Silas moves a safe distance away so he can keep an eye on me but also talk business. As I wait for two different people, I finish off my drink, willing my stomach to stop letting stress get to me. The alcohol needs time to loosen me up, so I don't order a second drink.

The song on the radio changes to a more upbeat tempo, the next four minutes all about bass and clapping. Finally an old rock ballad comes on, and I check my phone.

Tara's been in the bathroom for ten minutes.

I look at Silas, who glances at me and frowns, then says something about "implants" into the phone. I don't really need to pee, but I might as well. If the next conversation with Tara is half as intense as this last one, I'll need to be as comfortable as possible.

I walk past Silas, whose frown keeps deepening. I feel the green neon from the restroom sign change my skin, and I wonder how different life would have been if none of this had ever happened.

CHAPTER 17

$\mathcal{T}$he first detail I notice is the strange pattern in the floor tile.

Uneven, a deep red line like a giant tear drop, fat and thick, cuts into the boring tan linoleum. For a crappy bar, it's a sophisticated touch. As I step on the rounded edge of the red, I slip.

Wait a minute.

That's not decorative tile.

It's *blood*.

My foot slips forward, my other knee bending and slamming hard against the ceramic floor. I scream, sliding a few inches forward, my purse flying out of my hands and turning upside down, showering me with the contents. A tiny tampon lands in the blood, followed by assorted coins, my lipstick, a few receipts, and a breath mint.

My phone slams into the bathroom counter and pings my cheek, the crack of the corner of the phone against my eye socket making me gasp in pain.

My foot hits something big but yielding. Not a toilet.

I look down as I struggle to sit up.

To find Tara laying on the floor, up against the wall, both wrists slit from hand to elbow, blood pouring out of her like someone is pumping it.

"Tara!" I scream, looking at her eyes as she twitches. They're vacant but open, her head at such an odd angle, I'd think someone had snapped it if she weren't moving.

The blood is viscous, unforgiving as I move toward her, half sliding, crawling through it to grab her arm. I press my hand against her wrist, then start screaming "HELP!"

The door to the bathroom opens so fast, I hear it slam into the wall, making a strange cracking sound. "Jane!" Silas comes running into the bathroom but stops cold at the blood on the floor.

"Help me! She's slit her arms!"

He speaks into his earpiece, ordering an ambulance and backup, then drops to his knees, heedless of the blood. "Get pressure on those wounds. Now." Stripping off his suit coat, he lays it along the length of one of Tara's arms and presses, hard.

I take my sweater off from around my waist and do the same. As I press into her, I feel a fast beat coming, slamming hard.

"I feel her pulse," I whisper, relieved, looking at Silas for confirmation, for approval, for salvation.

For everything.

"That's *your* pulse," he says quietly. "I'm not finding hers."

"What do we do? CPR?"

"We do what we're doing now, Jane. Medics will be here any minute."

"Medics?"

"I mean paramedics. They're coming."

I'm frantic, blood in my hair, Silas's coat and legs covered in it, our bodies thrown wholly into pushing against Tara's arms, trying to stem the tide. A five-alarm bell is going off in my head.

"Why would she do this? We were just talking a few minutes ago! She was fine! Scared, but fine."

"*Shhhh*. Focus on the pressure."

"I can't feel a pulse!" Panic rushes in like a swarm of bees. "Oh my God, Silas, she can't bleed out! Tara! Tara!" I straddle her arm, my hurt knee not functioning, screaming with pure, bone-shredding pain. I say her name over and over, as if shouting it will magically stop the bleeding, as if she just needs some common sense to get through.

As if she's not dying beneath me.

Footsteps clack on the tile and stop as Silas barks orders. Then he's standing, pulling at my shoulders, lifting me up under my arms, carefully navigating the crowded restroom. Silas gets me to the main doorway and gives me a stern look, opening his mouth to say something.

Flash!

A bright light makes us both turn as white pinpoints crowd my vision, but I know what just happened.

Paparazzi. Bottom feeders looking for the next sale.

Silas charges the guy, but it's too late. He tosses his camera to someone behind him, who takes off at full speed. Silas plows into the original picture taker, who doesn't even bother fighting back. He goes limp but shouts for someone to take pictures.

Untangling himself from the jerk, Silas quickly stands, then looks at me, his expression changing to dismay.

"Come on," he says, pulling my hand, quickly snaking through the bar to the back. We rush past offices and store-rooms filled with kegs and brightly colored liquor boxes. The smell of rotting garbage fills my nose as we burst into the sunlight outside.

We're in an alley, next to the dumpsters.

The black SUV screeches to a halt. Duff appears out of nowhere. "Get in," he snaps. Silas physically lifts me and throws me in, climbing in behind me, the car ripping out of there backwards, Silas's door still open. We're barreling down the alley in reverse, and all I can do is scream.

And scream

Really scream, Silas on the phone shushing me, talking to Drew in a loud voice over my hoarse, nonsensical sounds.

I can't stop, even if I'm ripping my vocal cords to shreds. Once I stop, the reality sets in.

Tara killed herself.

While I sat there in the booth drinking my cocktail, Tara was despondent, pulling out a sharp blade inside that bathroom and ending her life.

What kind of friend am I? Ex friend, but still. How did I not find her in time? How could she do something so grisly so quickly? What if–

"Jane. *Jane*. JANE!" Silas shouts, his hand on my throat, pressing lightly.

I stop making sounds and stare at him, wide-eyed, not really seeing what was in front of me but instead seeing Tara's body.

"That was Drew. He was calling because the lab courier just died in a single-car accident."

"The who? The what?"

"Lab courier. The person delivering some of your blood."

I stare at my hands, which are rust-colored, covered in coagulating blood. "Whose blood? This isn't mine. It's Tara's." My face goes cold, so cold, my hands starting to tingle. I'm spinning on the inside, completely frozen on the outside, and the taste of copper and something savage is making me start to retch.

I move to open a window. They're locked.

"OPEN A WINDOW!" I scream, furious I can't push the button.

"If Tara's killers are after us, we can't leave an opening for a bullet." Silas's voice is matter-of-fact, too calm and collected.

Too perfect.

"Increase the air," he says to the driver, who complies, the sound from the vents getting louder, a blast of icy air hitting my shins.

"Tara, Tara, oh my God, Tara," I moan, rocking back and forth, groaning her name. I can't stop. I don't want to stop. I look down at my legs and see blood seeping into my shoe, the top of my foot coated in it. I wiggle my toes and feel the viscosity of it.

Silas's phone buzzes. He takes the call.

"Yes. News reports already? Fuck. No problem. What?

186

No. Definitely not. No, Drew. I have proof. Ironclad." I hear Drew say the word "good," then the rest is babble.

Silas finally says, "I'll check out social media later. Right now, we need to get her secured." Drew speaks. Silas looks surprised. "There? You think it's safe? There was paparazzi on the property when we were there before." Drew says a few words. Silas nods. "Okay. Will do."

Click.

"She was just alive! Telling me all about... oh, shit. All about how people were trying to kill her."

"People," Silas repeats.

Something in his tone shakes me out of my crazed state. "You think I did it? You think I killed Tara back there? You were right there, Silas. I was in that bathroom for a few seconds before I started screaming. Do you seriously think I'm that–that I–*fuck you!*" I scream.

"No. I know you didn't do it."

My phone buzzes. I pick it up, swipe, and look at a text.

Oh my God, Jane, what happened? It's Lindsay. She attached a link to a news site.

Stupidly, I click it.

It's a picture of me, covered in blood.

CHAPTER 18

I look like that famous picture from Stephen King's horror novel, from the 1970s movie version, except I'm not on stage in a prom dress. I'm next to Silas, who is mercifully turned away from the camera, broad shoulders tight and big as he moves to rush me away from the fracas.

"I didn't! They're claiming I killed her! But they can't!" My eyes blur, moving so fast, I can't focus. I see the word "Carrie" and the rest of the headline becomes unreadable.

"Give me your phone." Before I can answer, Silas takes it away, shoving it in his jacket pocket.

"Where are we going?"

"To Alice's."

"We can't go there! If someone's trying to kill me, I don't want her to become a target!"

"First of all, we went there before when someone was trying to kill you. Second, she's insisting–called Drew herself a minute ago. And third, you have no choice now. You'll do as I say."

Normally I'd argue, but not this time.

I really will do whatever he says.

"That headline. They think I did it," I cry.

Silas's mouth tightens. "You didn't."

"I know that! You were there and you know it! But–but–

we're running and the police must be looking for witnesses and–"

"It's covered."

"What's covered?"

"Your alibi."

Alibi. The word feels so slimy.

"What alibi? *You're* my alibi!"

"And the footage."

"Footage? What do you mean, footage?"

Before he can answer, I get it. My God. "The bar has cameras in the *bathrooms*?" I give him an incredulous look.

He starts to fidget and looks away. "No."

That shakes me. And then a hot flush of fury pumps my blood.

"Wait a minute. You planted a camera on me?"

"Yes."

"One hand in this mess is trying to do cavity searches on me, and the other hand is planting cameras? You bastard!" I can't scream anymore. All I can do is accuse and judge with a raspy voice.

"No comparison. I never pierced your skin, and it wasn't an implant."

"Where is it?" I look around wildly.

"On your purse. On the buckle. It looks like a tiny chain with a charm on it."

I practically throw my purse on the seat between us and find the chain, which is covered in Tara's blood. He's right– it's a tiny charm with a pinhole lens in it.

And the charm itself?

A button battery.

"You sneaky jerk."

"Go ahead, call me names. I don't care. I did it to protect you."

"Protect me? From who?"

"From whoever just killed Tara."

"Killed? What? She committed suicide!" I know I'm in denial, but I can't help it.

"Jane, do you really think that was a *suicide* back there?"

He's in my face, intense. "Really? Tara's probably right handed. Did you see how clean the right arm's cut was? Both were equally strong and straight, and both went top down."

"Top down?"

"From elbow to wrist. People trying to slit their wrists always go wrist up. Tara didn't kill herself. That was a homicide."

"Oh, no," I groan.

"And whoever killed her is trying to frame you. You know what happens when people are trying to frame you? What the next step is if it doesn't work?"

I don't answer.

"They try to *kill you*. Maybe with a firebomb to the car. Maybe they poison your drink in a bar. Or maybe they ambush you in the women's room and slit your wrists."

"STOP!"

He grabs my upper arms, holding me in place with a grip so tight, I can't believe he doesn't have super powers. His nail beds are a sickly red-rimmed pink, a reminder of blood hastily wiped off. Tara's blood. "I won't stop!" he thunders, his voice filled with pain. "Someone is trying to kill you, and whoever just butchered Tara is suspect number one."

"You know who it is?"

"No idea. But you aren't going to end up in some rundown bar's toilet, bleeding out like a six-point buck on the first day of hunting season."

My stomach rebels, threatening to empty. I look down at my legs and find blood all over them. The arms Silas is grabbing are coated in Tara's blood.

Then I look at him. From the elbows and knees down, he's red, too.

How much blood does the human body hold? I wonder, memory kicking me back to elementary school, when that was a test question and not what you ask yourself after finding a friend performing a one-woman experiment to find out.

Silas's gaze is piercing, intense and frustrated, firm and unyielding. "I do not ever, *ever* want to find you like that. Not with a bullet in you, not with a knife in you, not in a car on fire. Do you understand me, Jane? DO YOU?" he roars, his voice low and loud, as if he can use sound to make the world bend to his command.

"Pretty sure that's a life goal for me, too," I say weakly. He's breathing so fast, like he's just run a marathon, and his eyes are dark, tinged with an emotional panic that deepens as I stare at him. His grip lessens but his fingers remain wrapped around my biceps.

"Do you understand?" he whispers, grabbing my shoulders and pulling me to him, my ear landing over his heart.

It sounds like rain on a tin roof. Tara's blood is all over me. The heat of Silas's body combines with my own panicked self and makes me squirm out of his arms.

"Blood," I gasp. "Blood. Too much blood," I say, keening.

He grasps my hand, holding it in his. "This better?" I look down at our joined hands and realize that yes, it is. I need connection of some kind. Silas senses it, pushes for it.

I nod, then close my eyes.

And immediately see Tara's vacant stare in my memory.

My eyelids fly open and I tip my chin up, looking at the upholstered ceiling of the SUV. "Where are we going?"

"Straight to the airport. We'll shower before or on the plane. They'll have a change of clothes for us."

"A change of–okay." I try to close my eyes again.

I fail.

"Talk to me about anything *but* what just happened," I say. "Please."

"What do you want to talk about?"

"Did you go to college?"

"Yes."

"Where?"

"UC Irvine."

"Is that where you met Drew?"

"No."

"How old are you?"

"How old do you think I am?"

"Older than me." I look at him. "No grey hair. Under thirty." The stupid trivia helps my heart to stop jumping in my chest.

He's amused. "I have friends who are under thirty and have grey hair."

"Really? I don't."

"I'm twenty-eight."

"My guess was close. Twenty-seven."

He just nods and squeezes my hand. This is working. I'm calming down. Then I look down at my body and sit up, fast. I move closer to Silas. He opens his arms, as if to embrace me.

That's not what I'm seeking.

As I angle my head, I get a glimpse of myself in the rear-view mirror.

I start hyperventilating.

I saw the photo online, but as I look in terror and touch my bloody hair with my bloodied hands, it feels like I'm dying. Me. Like this is *my* blood. My slit arms. My vacant eyes.

"*Shhh,*" Silas says, his grip tight on my hand. "Don't look. Wait until we're at the airport and you can shower. It will come off."

"How do you know?"

His stare is steady, words an icepick to my heart. "Because I've been covered in far more blood after an IED explosion. And some of it was mine." He lets go of my hand and bends down to lift his bloody pants leg, the cloth growing stiff as the blood dries. A jagged line of scar stretches up the side of his calf, burrowed under his sock and traveling to his knee. His leg hair doesn't grow on the white, gnarled skin.

"Oh, Silas."

He drops the cloth and looks at me. "I'm fine now. But I wasn't that day. I was lucky. I was the one picking pieces of my friends off my body. But I *had* a body. One that was still alive and breathing. My friends didn't."

The SUV stops in front of a small white building, all the

walls made of metal. We're at a small helipad in an industrial park. I've never been here before.

"What's this?"

"A safe place to use a helicopter. And they have bathrooms. No more problems with the plane and the shower doors," he says.

I grimace, remembering my foible.

"It's safe here," he adds, almost as an afterthought, even though I know it's most definitely not.

It is neither safe nor an afterthought.

I get out of the SUV, flanked on both sides by Silas and Duff. We enter into a concrete-floor building, an open warehouse with an office in the back. As we walk through the glass door, I find a simply decorated space that looks like someone lives here.

"An apartment?" I ask Silas.

"A safehouse."

Ah.

He hands me a small plastic bag. I peer in. Towel, shampoo, some pink underwear. A dress.

Flip-flops.

"Best we could do on short notice. Alice is having some clothes delivered to the ranch for you."

I accept this as my new reality and look around for a bathroom.

"Here," he says, guiding me to the doors. There are two, unmarked.

"I'll be in the bathroom next door. Be quick. We need to move fast. Duff will stand guard."

I nod and go into the bathroom. There's no tub, just a shower. It takes longer than it should for me to figure out how to turn on the water. I shimmy out of my clothes, peeling them off like leeches, shoving them in the garbage, shoes and all.

I get in the shower. The water is ice cold. I haven't given it enough time to warm up.

My skin welcomes the intrusion. The sooner the blood is gone, the sooner I can think again. The drain fills with swirling pink water, small bursts of thicker red making it look like a tie-dye bucket. I start to sob.

That is blood.

Tara's blood.

I leave the shower, dripping all over the floor. I fish through the bag to find the small travel-size bottle of shampoo and soap. No conditioner. A man with short hair must have put this together.

Lathering up, leaving the soap wrapper on the shower floor, I scrub so hard, my skin starts to hurt. I use the bar soap to wash my hair, then switch to shampoo until no more pink water remains. Now the water is warm, turning hot just as I need to rinse my hair again.

I do.

I stand under the burning-hot spray and let my hair feel like it's on fire, the heat hurting my back.

And then I turn off the water and stand there, dazed.

A small mirror above the sink, directly across from me, shows a wet, naked woman who can't quite believe she's here.

It reflects the truth.

Tap tap tap.

"Jane? You ready?"

"No."

"Can you be ready in two minutes? We need to go."

"No."

"No, you can't do it that fast, or–"

"No."

He goes quiet. I grab a towel and start drying off, my hair first, body second.

"No," I whisper as I drop the towel and slip my legs into the pink panties.

"No," I hiss as I toss the simple A-line sundress, a size too big, over my head, instantly covered. The bag has no bra.

"No," I say, louder, as I slide my soles into the flip-flops, jamming a comb through my hair as if my scalp has offended me.

Then I open the door, look at Silas, and say, "No!"

"No–what?"

"This entire day–hell, this year–deserves nothing but *no*."

He nods. "Yes."

And with that he takes me right back outside, through a back door, where a helicopter already has its rotors turning.

We board. I click my seatbelt.

And let the roar of the engine take me away.

By the time we reach the airport, I am good for nothing. Silas has to take me by the hand and navigate, showing me where to go. I can move my feet. That's it.

We board the plane and I take the seat that looks the most comfortable. Silas sits next to me. It's so different from our previous flights. Grabbing a blanket, he waits until I'm clicked in and then drapes it over me.

"Need a pillow?"

I shake my head.

Settling in the seat right next to mine, he puts his seatbelt on. There is no self-conscious posturing of his body, trying not to touch me. We're not intimate. None of this is romantic. I'm in survival mode and his focus is on taking care of me. You don't keep tight physical boundaries when your goal is survival.

You can't.

I jolt when I feel the plane move, my ear brushing against Silas's shoulder. My vision swims, my wet hair moist against my cheek.

I drift off, his hard, solid body a comfort.

One that invades my dreams.

* * *

I'm in the house where the party was, in the hallway upstairs by all the bedrooms. Each door is numbered, one, two, three on the left, four, five, six on the right.

A bright red waterfall of blood is at the end of the hallway.

Copper and fresh meat fill my senses, the odor all-consuming, like I'm eating it. Small animals lick my ankles, obedient, excited pets.

When I look down I can't see them, a black smoke covering everything below my knees.

But I feel them, licking and nipping until the sensation increases, painful bites stabbing my ankles. I have no choice.

I have to pick a door.

I don't want to choose one because the hallway is the safest place. Each choice is a kind of death. Closing off options and entering wholesale into one of them means all the other doors are no longer mine to try.

But the bites intensify until my calf screams with pain and I lift my leg.

To find a tiny animal with red, closing eyes and teeth the size of a steak knife feasting on me.

Behind door number one, the rush of fresh water and cloves makes me take a step forward until a green gas floats around me. I choke. As the mist clears, I see bodies piled on the floor, all of them female, all of them naked.

And all of them with eyes plucked out.

Slamming the door shut, I move forward down the hallway, wading through increasingly bigger animals that I now have to kick away from me.

I smell my own blood.

Door number four is to my right. When I touch the doorknob, an electric bolt sprints through me until my teeth go numb. As I pull away, all the animals scream at once, then stop biting me.

I don't open that door.

Door number two beckons, glowing with sunlight in all the cracks, making promises I hope it can keep. Hope is light, so my eyes try to tell my heart this is the safe place.

Until I open the door to find a man in a white ski mask, holding a bright searchlight pointed at my eyes, his body naked, the animals feasting on his flesh as he moans in ecstasy.

I close door number two. Fast.

"Jane!" my mother calls, somewhere behind a door I've not yet reached, her voice soothing and frantic at the same time.

"Mom!" I scream, opening door number five fast, my face consumed by fire. Hair burning, my head a candle, I turn to door number three and open it–

And a shotgun blasts me, pushing me into the blood waterfall at the end of the hall, where I fall and fall and fall into an endless, eternal abyss.

"Jane!" my mother calls again, only her voice is deeper, more urgent, coaxing me out of the abyss until I startle and scream—

—WAKING UP FROM THE NIGHTMARE, my skin chilled and cheek red.

Silas, not Mom, is calling my name

"What? What happened?" I sit up, completely disoriented, swiping at my ankles with my palms over and over as Silas leans back from me, looking deeply confused.

"You were flailing in your sleep. Kept whispering about blood and being bitten. Were you dreaming about vampires?" Touching my shoulder with a big warm palm, Silas bends into my personal space, his face inches from mine. It's an intimate act, and his warmth feels like a continuation, not a gesture.

Did I fall asleep on him?

"I wish." I shudder and sit up fully, pulling away. My stomach is sour and I feel like my blood has been thickened by cornstarch. "Where are we?"

"Somewhere over New Mexico? I don't know. I'm not a pilot." He gives me a self-effacing smile, as if he's genuinely embarrassed he can't fly a plane.

"Well, I can't perform heart surgery, so we're both inadequate," I say, stretching my arms high as a yawn takes over my body. The only way to get rid of the weird sense of being between reality and dreamland is to shake it off, stretch it out, root myself in the real.

Silas's eyes are all over me, an audience of thousands. I can feel him, even when my eyes are closed. This is no performance. I am not a model for a painting.

I don't care.

This is as real as it gets.

Undefined emotion rushes through my limbs, going where it needs to go, refreshing me enough to shake off the feeling I'm being nibbled to death by sharks and drowning in a river of my own blood.

Silas puts his eyes back in his head and looks away, shifting his weight in his seat so that there is a clear professional boundary between our body spaces.

I unclick my seatbelt and find the bar, grabbing a can of soda. I lift it and raise my eyebrows, trying to catch his attention.

He finally looks at me, shakes his head, and says, "No, thanks." His phone becomes his new object of attention.

"How do you have a signal up here?" I ask as I sit down again, popping open my soda and taking a sip. Cool root beer, my favorite, tickles my tongue.

"Major airlines can do it. You think the government can't? Your connection will be much better on this aircraft, too." His voice is steady, distracted. Whatever emotion I thought I was receiving from him has been tucked away somewhere inside him. Silas is in work mode now.

"I see." I nod and look out the window, letting the sweet drink distract me. A cool sweat starts to chill on my skin. I reach up and brush my short bangs off my forehead. Damp hair greets my fingertips.

That dream was so *real*.

I sip slowly, looking out the window as dusk turns to darkness. When you're this high up over the clouds, the sunsets can be unreal. I've missed the most spectacular part and now just settle for shades of grey, moonlight making thin sections of cotton clouds glow.

Silas's warm fingers brush against my shoulder, one grazing my bare neck. I shiver.

"Jane?"

I close my eyes, the tangy taste of sugar on my lips as I lick them. "Yes?"

"What was your dream about?"

"You really want to know?"

"I wouldn't ask if I didn't."

Tears fill my eyes with a fierce swiftness, as if they're waiting to swarm. My throat goes tight, the bridge of my nose tingling, and I see it all. A montage of every awful moment of my dream pours through me. With a shaking hand, I set my empty soda can on the end table next to my seat and lean back, sighing.

And I tell him.

He nods, looking down at his hands, not from shyness but from the will to listen deeply. When I'm done, he nods slowly.

"It's a pretty obvious dream. Tara's blood, the press nipping at your heels, taking bigger and bigger bites out of you..."

"What's the latest? Have I been blamed for the newest North Korean missile crisis?"

He smiles. "Haven't you heard? You're carrying the love child of Elvis and Kim Jong Il."

The joke catches me completely off guard and I laugh, then belch.

Loudly.

Silas's face breaks into a beautiful smile, pure laughter pouring out of him, booming all the way to my heart.

"Excuse me!" I gasp, embarrassed but laughing. "Root beer."

"Basic biology. You're allowed to be human, you know."

"Tell that to Monica Bosworth."

"I'm trying."

"Are you? Really? Does that mean you believe me?"

"I never said that."

"Then why would you defend me to Monica, of all people?"

"Not defending. Explaining."

"When everything is black or white, right or wrong, explaining *is* defending."

"Just because other people create standards doesn't mean I follow them. Or believe them to be valid," he says, his words laden with meaning.

"But you believe the media when they say I'm complicit?"

"I never said I believe the media. I believe Drew."

Silas isn't pulling punches. A part of me feels horrified, but a deeper sense of grudging respect emerges.

Respect for me.

If Silas didn't respect me, he wouldn't be so blunt. In fact, he wouldn't talk to me at all.

Blunt is a form of improvement.

"Drew doesn't trust me."

"Do you blame him?"

I'm supposed to say no. I know that. Being polite is ingrained in me.

"Yes. Yes, I do," I say simply, giving Silas a sad-eyed look.

"You blame Drew for not trusting you after he went to rescue Lindsay and found her naked, with you in the room, helping her attackers?"

Air gets trapped in my lungs, not leaving, not staying, suspended like I swallowed a cluster of clouds.

"Do you know," I finally whisper, "what Drew found when he came into the room?"

"Lindsay, nearly being raped by–"

"No. I'm not talking about Lindsay. She's important, but–" I choke off my words, realizing I'm racing to line up my evidence to prove to him that I am valid. That I am worth believing.

That I am lovable.

"But?"

"I was next," I whisper. My body turns to wax, my eyes lowering, my chest rising and falling like a bellows pumps air through it. "What they did to Lindsay, they were about to do to me."

"I know. I've read the reports. That's what you say they said. Lindsay–"

"You do *not* know," I say viciously.

He's watching me closely, eyes narrowing, mouth staying rigid.

"You do not know how it felt to have a knife to my throat. You do not know how it smelled in that room, with blood and fear and terror like a demented air freshener from hell. You do not know what it was like to be turned into a human mule, delivering burner phones and messages. You do not know what it was like to pick up Lindsay's naked, bloody body and help her move, to try to protect myself, to protect *her*, to live second by second through the kind of agony that makes your mind try to escape any way it can because it knows your body is about to be shredded to the core."

A long line of mental images, a movie in horrifying slow motion, ripples through my memory, my skin crawling as if John is still touching me, my nose filled with the scent of so much anticipated pain. Silas doesn't look away, his face neutral, eyes watching without obvious emotion, but he's entirely focused on me.

"You don't know, so shut the hell up, Silas, about what you *think* you know about me."

The rest of the ride is nothing but tense silence.

Which is becoming my default.

* * *

I STUMBLE OFF THE PLANE, bleary-eyed. At some point I fell asleep, forehead pressed against one of the small windows. Some nameless driver is on the tarmac with the familiar black SUV. Life feels like déjà vu.

Because it is.

"You feeling okay, Miss Borokov?" the driver asks me with genuine concern as he grabs my elbow before I fall. My stumble is a function of flip-flops I'm not familiar with and exhaustion.

"She's fine," Silas snaps.

"My mouth works," I snap back.

"No kidding," he mutters under his breath.

"I'm *fine*," I say tightly to the driver, just to make a point. Silas rolls his eyes.

It's the closest we can get to a truce.

More tense silence as the driver, whose name I never get, takes us straight to Alice's studio, where she's waiting with vodka, lemonade, and an antipasto platter.

A few bites of cheese and prosciutto-wrapped hearts of

palm later, I'm sipping an ungodly ratio of vodka to lemonade and falling asleep in my own plate.

Silas's phone rings. He looks at it, stands up abruptly, and walks into the other room, speaking in sotto voce. It must be his mother, I guess. There's no way he's that caring with Drew or any other security colleague.

"You look drunk, Jane," Alice says bluntly.

Before I can explain, she holds up a hand. "That's not a judgment. I wouldn't blame you for it."

"I'm so tired," I start to tell her, but instead my words are garbled, turning into salty, blubbering syllables. Awash with emotion, I can't stop.

Alice moves closer to me, patting my back gently, making banal comments designed to fill the space so that there isn't so much pain there.

"This is your haven," she says kindly. "Your place to come and relax."

I snort.

"To the extent that you can," she amends. "I am *not* trying to be flippant."

"Alice, you're constitutionally incapable of not being flippant," I say just before a yawn consumes me, making me stretch and groan. My body feels like noodles in warm water.

"You're feisty when you're tired."

I can't argue, conserving my energy for standing back up. Her salt-and-pepper eyebrows drop down, tight over the bridge of her long angular nose. Concerned hazel eyes meet mine.

I involuntarily touch my own cheek, wondering what it's like to have such deep wrinkles as Alice has on her face. How many decades have to pass before you feel like you're old? Or does she still feel twenty inside, trapped in an old woman's body? Ninety-two is an eternity to me.

For her, it's just her reality.

We move down a quiet tile-floored hallway and both stop suddenly, Alice giving me a light hug and a "shoo!" toward the big bed in my guest room. She's gone before I know it, leaving me in a pastel room with a lilac coverlet on the bed. It smells like a drawer sachet in here.

Mumbled words come through the wall. Silas is on the phone, next door to me. I tiptoe to my open door and stand there, pulling the shell of my ear forward, barely making out his words.

"I know, Mom. I *know*," he hisses, the sound low and tortured. This is clearly a well-worn argument. "Tricia's made another mess we have to clean up, but I won't take Kelly unless–what? She what? No, Mom, I'm working now. In fact, I shouldn't be–"

A very, very loud sound, like a child squealing, comes from his direction.

And then Silas says, "Hey, baby! How's my favorite girl?" in a voice you use with small children you love.

Daughter.

This must be his daughter.

My stomach hurts suddenly, like someone grabbed me below the breastbone and started twisting slowly.

His whole demeanor changes, at least from what I can tell by sound. I'm half charmed, half heartbroken. Tricia must be his wife. Kelly, his daughter.

And I'm nobody.

Quietly, I step back into my room and slowly, painstakingly close the door. I kick off my shoes and, fully dressed, let the cool scented sheets form an embrace, enveloping me in the most powerful balm on the planet.

Sleep.

* * *

THE ABSENCE of a dream is almost as startling as a nightmare.

Waking up with a black hole in my mind is its own disturbance. Since that fateful day six months ago, when Mom was jailed and my hell continued, I've had nightmares–on a spectrum from slightly disturbing to nearly peed in my sleep from terror.

But to wake up with a blank mind is unheard of.

And frightening in its own way, too.

Human beings are wired for flexibility and routine. We need both. Children need roots and wings. Adults need to be grounded and able to fly. I need to be protected and be given freedom.

It's a rare person who gets both.

Muted voices carry from the distance, the distinct sound of Alice laughing. Her cackle carries through the house. A quick look out the window tells me it's either dusk or dawn, the light maintaining the eerie quality of potentially being night or day.

My mouth tastes like dry leaves, my neck has a crick in it, and I need to pee.

The bed is so comfortable, warm and light.

But the bladder calls.

Five minutes later I've taken care of the basics. I shuffle down the hall to discover it's early morning. I've slept for at least ten hours. My stomach growls at the halfway point to the kitchen. Hunger drives me forward, but then I freeze.

Silas and Alice are talking.

"You care about her?" Alice asks him, as if she were interviewing him.

"I'm starting to."

"That's a weaselly answer."

"It's true."

"You think it's just sex?"

"We haven't–" He laughs softly. "If I thought that, I'd never tell you, Ms. Mogrett."

"Good response. That's all I need to know."

"I didn't answer your question."

"Oh, my dear boy, you certainly did." She pauses. "The love of my life was one of my security detail, you know."

"Really?" He doesn't sound surprised.

"Milt Sigmundsson. Hot Scandinavian hero. Six foot six, a wall of a man. Born and raised in Minnesota. Served in WWII and came to DC as an agent during my father's term in office."

"I don't recall his name in your biography."

"Blame my father for that."

"I see."

"No, Silas. You don't. My father sent Milt away from me, forever. Had him stationed in Vietnam in the early stages."

"Did he die there?" Silas's blunt question makes me blink hard. Most men would pussyfoot around the issue.

Not Silas.

"Yes. In my mind, my father killed him. I know it's not technically true, but..."

Silas makes a sympathetic sound.

"War is hell, Alice. I'm sorry he died. Lots of good men and women go to war who don't deserve to die. I've done more tours than most and it's sheer luck that kept me from being one of the dead."

My stomach ties itself into a knot at those words.

"Milt's death isn't the point, though. It's that we spent seven years together. He was assigned to shadow me. You spend that much time with someone, it's hard not to get intimate."

Silas stays silent.

"And I don't mean sexual," she adds in a gravelly voice. "*Intimate.*"

"I know the difference," he says.

"Glad to hear it. Most men in your position don't."

"My position?"

"You're a decorated war hero. You compartmentalize. You close off your feelings in the line of duty. It's why you're so good at what you do. But it doesn't translate well to relationships."

"Now you're my therapist?"

"Once you're ninety-two, son, you're everyone's therapist, whether they like it or not."

I hear him chuckle, then he asks, "What made you start the nudes with Jane?"

"Boredom."

"Come on, Alice. Seriously."

"Because Jane doesn't know how beautiful she really is.

Her innate goodness shines through her skin into the light, like energy. I've never met a person like that since Milt."

"Jane reminds you of him?"

"No. But she reminds me of who I was when I was with him, and that's even more precious."

Silas stays silent.

"You don't believe that hogwash about Jane being part of the conspiracy to hurt Lindsay Bosworth, do you?" It's clear from her tone of voice how Alice feels.

"I don't know."

"Yes, you do." Her voice is caustic now, pure acid. "Why won't you let yourself act like it?"

"It's more complicated than that."

"Life is always simpler than we think. We say it's complicated, but that's just because we don't have the guts to do what we need to do."

"*Hmm*," he says, non-committal.

"It's like sex."

"Oh, brother," he says under his breath.

I smile.

"You either go for it or you don't. And if you do, it's all about courage."

"Sex is about courage?"

"For us women, yes. Always. It takes tremendous bravery to bare yourself in every way possible."

"Jane does that for your paintings."

"If you think that's Jane baring herself in full, you're in for a treat when you finally get your shit together and make a move, young man."

A long sigh escapes him, then shuffling sounds. "I have calls I need to make."

"You have emotions you need to avoid."

"In my line of work, it's the same thing, ma'am."

"You need a new line of work."

"Maybe I'll take up painting."

"Hah!" But I can tell she's genuinely amused. And impressed.

Silas held his own against her.

My stomach growls again and I take one step forward, knowing they heard that. If I step toward them, then maybe they won't realize I've been eavesdropping. Silas quickly looks at me, then away.

Alice points to the kitchen. "We saved some dinner for you. The cook put it in a container you can reheat."

That answers that. It's dinner. I slept most of a *day*.

"I slept that long?"

"You were tired," she says with a laugh.

"How's your daughter?" I ask Silas, suddenly remembering the call I overheard but realizing too late, in the throes of hazy waking up, that I just revealed I was listening to him on the phone last night.

"Daughter?" His eyebrows shoot up like stomp rockets.

"She screamed into the phone last night," I scramble, trying to cover my tracks. "Uh, I could hear her."

"Oh. That. She's fine." Silas holds one finger up to me and points to his phone, as if he has an important call. Alice stands, smoothing the front of her colorful caftan. I'm about to ask Silas more about the little girl, but Alice gives me an inscrutable look that suddenly makes me think it's not so wise to pry.

"You must be hungry," she says to me. "Silas, when your wife wakes up, do you bring her coffee?"

"What? Wife? What?" he asks, his reaction so brutally honest and completely befuddled I can't help laughing.

"You don't have a wife?" Alice asks, definitely prying.

"No."

Alice pats my hand, smirks, and walks away, leaving me with a tense silence that is now painfully awkward as well.

Silas pours me a cup of coffee from a carafe and walks to the fridge, pulling out a small platter of cheeses and olives. On the counter, there's a small plate of crackers. He puts it all together in front of me, urging with a nudge for me to eat.

"She didn't ask me whether I had a husband." One corner of his mouth goes up.

"Do you?"

"No. What about you?"

"You seriously think I could hide a husband from you? From Drew? From anyone in government? Oh, that's right. I forgot to mention him. He's back home refinishing the deck and taking care of our pug puppy. That husband I've been ignoring all this time."

"Good point," he says, plucking a piece of cheese from the plate and popping it in his mouth.

I take a long, shallow sip of my hot coffee and give him what is supposed to be a withering look. He grins back and says, "Hey. I'm sorry about our conversation on the plane. It won't happen again." He seems genuine. Authentic. Silas never struck me as the kind of man–unlike Drew–who would lie easily for the sake of a greater mission.

It's not that Silas wouldn't lie. Any well-trained person in his position would–and should.

It's just that it isn't second nature.

"Why won't it happen again?" I ask, truly curious.

He takes my question as a challenge. "You make it very hard to be nice to you."

I recoil in surprise. "What?"

"You do. I get that you're defensive. Anyone in your shoes would be. But you–"

"I want to know why. Why would you decide to change how you treat me?" I continue, pressing him.

He bristles. "I'm not changing. I was never set on a partic-ular way to begin with."

I make a hooting sounds of mockery. "Right."

"New evidence makes logical people change course," he adds, trying again.

"What new evidence do you have about me?" I ask, eyeing him with suspicion.

"Plenty."

"Documents? Pictures? Records?"

"My own two eyes."

"Those aren't going to help me in the court of public opinion."

"Good thing I don't care about what other people think," he says softly. It has more power than a shout.

"How old is your daughter?" I ask, the question lingering in my head.

"My daughter? I don't have a daughter."

"But you said–"

"You assumed. She's my niece. And she's five." His whole face transforms when he talks about her, every part of him going paternal and sweet, like he can't help himself.

"Five is the best age! Is she into princess stuff?"

"Yes," he says, starting to hum the song "Let It Go" from the movie *Frozen*.

I hum along, too.

"What's her name?" I ask when we're done.

"Kelly. She's my only niece. Mom's only grandchild, and the apple of her eye." This is the first time Silas has offered up information about himself that I haven't asked directly.

It's nice.

"Does she love Candyland? Does she make you let her paint your nails and put your hair in bows?"

Silas reaches up and brushes his fingers through his hair. "I plead the Fifth."

We share a laugh that feels so good. I am groggy from too much sleep but still feel a thrill at the friendliness. I wonder what's making him thaw, but I won't ask more questions about his state. Sounds like talking about Kelly is fair game, though.

"Do you have a picture of her?" I ask.

He's suddenly wary, and I realize my mistake.

"It's okay," I say, holding up my palm. "I get it. Privacy."

"Yes." As if he's having second thoughts, his eyes drift to the right and he frowns slightly. "She looks like you."

"She does?"

"Same shape of eyes." He studies me. "Same full-faced smile. It's a little uncanny."

"Is she your sister or brother's child?"

"I only have one sister."

"And does your sister look like me?"

"No. Not really. Same hair color -- not your dyed hair. That's it."

"Genetics are a roll of the dice."

"I guess so."

I look outside, where the moon is blending with the last streak of pink in the nighttime sky. I nod toward the outdoors and he leans past me, opening the door for us both. I grab my coffee and prepare to walk outside barefoot, not caring.

"When I was a freshman in college, I almost went into early childhood education. I would love to work with little kids."

"Why didn't you?" he asks.

"Money. My mother used to say, 'You have to be well off or marry well to live on a nursery school teacher's salary.'"

"Sounds old-fashioned." Chin tipping down, he looks up at me with a playful, chiding expression.

"She was practical. I liked math, loved coding, so... computer science it was."

"And now?"

"And now? Now I can't get a job scooping dog poop. No one wants me. I'm blacklisted everywhere."

"How do you plan to rebuild?" Silas asks, the question casual.

"I don't know. It's been suggested I change my name. Move to another country. Completely reboot my life. Erase my hard drive and start anew. But... could you do that?"

"How can you not? I see what you go through. I see the stuff we filter so you don't have to read it. I know how many people are actively talking about raping and killing you. The bounties people are offering for nude selfies of you." He peers at me. "Are there any out there?"

"How did we get from me teaching little kids to naked selfies?"

"This is a job about information, Jane." His eyes flash with amusement. "It's a tough job, but someone has to find your naked selfies. For security purposes only, of course."

Is he flirting?

Is Silas Gentian actually *flirting* with me?

Bzzzz.

He looks at his phone, his entire demeanor changing. It's like an icy wind hitting you on a balmy day.

"Work. Need to get back. Talk to you later." Turning on his heel, Silas leaves me, jogging around Alice's studio and toward the main house, his body fit and his pace all business.

And nothing but.

CHAPTER 19

*T*o my surprise, the half-cup of coffee I drank doesn't keep me up. When I return to the house, I find a note from Alice:

I'M OLD.
> *Don't get old.*
> *Off to bed.*
> *See you in the morning.*

IT'S WRITTEN in an old-fashioned hand, the kind people say Millennials can't read, cursive with a practiced steadiness that makes the writing almost a work of art.

By midnight I'm in bed.

At some point, my eyes close and my subconscious drifts off, leaving me with a second dreamless night's sleep.

Maybe–just maybe–my life is improving.

The burst of sunlight that greets me when I wake up is blindingly simple. It's just light. The sun came up. The world didn't end. My problems are just that–problems. *I* am not a problem, though.

The guest wing at Alice's ranch has a lovely kitchen in it,

and as I walk into the living room I smell the telltale scent of perfection.

"Coffee?" I ask, my head pounding from caffeine deprivation.

Silas pulls the nearly full pot from the coffee machine and pours me a mug. "Cream and sugar on that tray," he says, motioning toward the table. A few bagels, some cream cheese, and a small bowl of oranges grace the tabletop.

"Thanks."

"Alice says that's not a proper breakfast, so not to eat too much. We're expected for brunch at eleven."

"This is a big breakfast by my standards. I usually just drink coffee until lunch."

Silas smiles. "Same here. Intermittent fasting?"

I shake my head. I'm not even sure what that means. "Too lazy to cook."

The laugh he offers is much appreciated. So now I get friendly Silas. Nice.

Seriously.

"What's on the agenda for today?" he asks me.

"You tell me. You're in charge."

"I'm not the boss of you."

The air feels different with those words, his intensity out of place, eyes burning for me as he says them slowly. There's a double entendre I don't get, but it instantly drives a pulse between my legs, my skin exquisitely sensitive everywhere, my arm brushing against my nipple and making me struggle not to show my arousal.

We're looking at each other, and I keep thinking he's about to say, "But I want to be." An impulse so strong, I can barely control it washes over me, trying to make me take the next step, push this forward, be bold.

But no.

I can't.

I just... *can't.*

"Jane," he says, his voice so rough, so layered. He takes a step toward me and my hands fly up to my hair as it dawns on me I must be a mess.

"Silas, I–"

He's next to me, his face impassive, eyes full of emotion as we stand, suspended in place, trying to find our way to each other. As seconds roll by, he moves closer.

I can't. I can't bridge the distance between us. I can't take the chance and be rejected.

I just can't.

It would kill me. Like a car bomb, it would burn me to the ground before I even knew what happened.

He moves, though, an answered prayer, a ray of sunshine on a dismal day, a double rainbow in the distance after a storm. We're inches from each other and he touches the back of my hand, his mouth starting to move to ask a question.

Or maybe to come in for a kiss?

Bzzzz.

I jolt, flailing so much I dump my coffee on its side, Silas looking away and digging in his pants pocket quickly. He looks at his text. The expression on his face is so filled with disgust.

All the attraction, the ripe potential in the air between us moments ago, is gone. He's flat again, all business.

What was in that text?

"We need to get back to California. I need to take you to The Grove."

"What? Why?"

"Need-to-know basis."

"Well, I need to know!"

He shakes his head. "Duff will get everything ready."

"This isn't another psycho physical exam they're making me do, is it?"

He ignores me, his attention on his phone.

"Silas?" I go to grab his arm, to tug on his shirt, to make him look at me, but he moves out of range.

His phone is buzzing like crazy.

"No. But we need to go. I have to transfer you to a new team."

"Why? Can't you leave me here with Duff?"

"No."

215

"Why not?"

He doesn't answer.

He just walks away.

Twenty minutes later, Duff's carrying my tiny bag and Alice is hugging me goodbye.

Again.

"I do not understand why I need to go back, Silas. This is really unfair."

He gives a tight-shouldered shrug.

Alice frowns at him, then turns to me. "Something's wrong."

"I know!"

"No. I mean with him. Whatever those texts are, they have nothing to do with you."

"Then why am I being made to go with him? Why can't I stay here?"

"Probably orders. You know how it all works. He has to hand you off to someone with enough seniority or security clearance or–or–or–"

"Or they're all just being assholes," I declare.

"Then there's that," she agrees. Her face changes, going contemplative. "Look, Jane, I had a talk with Silas while you were asleep. He's a good man. It's very hard for me to call him a man, given that he looks like a twelve-year-old to me, but then again, so do you. I've been alive for nearly seven decades longer than you, and everyone seems like a child."

I laugh in spite of myself.

"But he's a good one. Whatever has gone on this past week, it seems to be changing his view of you from the wrong one to a bit closer to the right one. Time is what people need to see the truth. Time with you is showing his true character. But he also has a mission. Men who do what Silas does are married first to the job."

"You're thinking about Milt, aren't you?"

She gives me a saucy look. "You *were* listening in."

"You knew I was there?"

She taps the bone behind her ear. "Hearing aids pick up ambient sounds."

"You little snoop!" I giggle.

"I'm not the snoop. You are!"

"So when you asked Silas about sex, that was–"

"That was an old lady being nosy."

Silas taps on the main door frame. "Time to go. Your bag is packed."

"What bag? I don't own anything." I roll my eyes.

"Come back again," Alice urges. "The door is always open."

One more hug and I'm out the door with Silas, arguing as I try to match his fast pace while we walk around to the main house where the SUV is waiting.

"I don't understand why I couldn't be left there with a different team. Duff is–"

"Not part of our team."

"What? Duff is perfectly fine."

"On what basis do you make that determination? Because he's 'nice'?" Silas uses finger quotes. "Nice people do some of the worst damage."

"You don't trust Duff?"

His face twists with frustrated fury. "Look," he says, grabbing my arm hard and pulling me aside. "Someone killed the driver who was transporting your lab samples. All the samples are gone."

"I know. You told me. I -- "

"The full report came in just now. Drew said it was done in such a professional way that it took more than twelve hours to figure out it was deliberate sabotage."

"*Sabotage?*"

"I shouldn't even be telling you this."

"Why not?" I match his outrage.

He gives me a flat look. "Why do you think?"

"Because you think *I* had something to do with it? You've been with me the entire time, Silas! You monitor my phone, my movements, my everything. I haven't touched a computer since I've been here. I'm under 24/7 surveillance by you–physically! And you still think I'm plotting behind the scenes, in a way that killed a delivery driver so the bloodwork the doctor took yesterday can't be processed?"

He just blinks.

"If I had that kind of power," I say through gritted teeth, "you idiot," added for good measure, "do you really think I would be standing here arguing with you? You'd be dead already."

"I know that." We're at the black SUV, Duff in the driver's seat, the vehicle running already. Silas jerks the back door open but I ignore him, moving around his big body and grabbing the passenger seat door.

I open it, climb in, and slam it for good measure.

"Hi, Duff," I say, smelling his aftershave, the brisk scent of lemon and old wood a nice change from being surrounded by acrimony and deceit.

"Hello, Ms. Borokov. Back to The Grove?"

Silas is in the back seat, his door closing with a quiet, controlled *snick*.

"I have no idea where we're going, Duff." I close my eyes as he pulls away, down the long, lonely driveway toward the airport. "But wherever it is, I'm sure whatever's going on is all my fault."

* * *

WHEN IT'S you plus a person who thinks you can order other people to kill lab couriers, a pilot, and a co-pilot, and that's *it* on a plane, a few hours in the air with nothing to do and no way to sleep feels like being a little kid at the oil change shop, bored out of your mind.

Mid-flight movie? A suspenseful Jason Bourne flick that hits too close to home.

Books? More military thrillers.

Conversation? Let's make that a solid *no*.

Silas sleeps half the time, seated in the other cluster of chairs on the plane, a thick down throw blanket over his shoulders. I'm livid, and I shouldn't care, but I have to admit that he looks so sweet when he's asleep. I'm assuming the vigilant part of him that needs to protect nonstop feels safe falling asleep at thirty-five thousand feet, in a plane filled with just us and the pilots.

And then I stop and think about that for a minute.

If I'm so evil, would he let his guard down like this? If he really thinks I'm some part of a plot where I enacted a plan that led to the murder of a lab courier, would Silas really fall asleep in front of me, leaving himself defenseless? I could kiss him right now, if I wanted to.

Kill. I meant *kill*.

I laugh and shake my head at my own wandering mind. What is wrong with me? First of all, I'm the last person anyone wants to get entangled with, and second, he's the last man I should get involved with.

And third, he's hot.

Wait. That's not a reason to avoid him.

He stirs, makes a funny little sigh, then slowly wakes up, eyes squinting with sleep. Quickly, I move so he can't see me. My pulse leaps forward.

Nearly caught.

"Where are we?" Silas asks, scrubbing his face with his hands, looking around the plane with a strange anger, as if the plane itself has offended him by being the holding place for his nap.

"On a plane."

"I mean, where? How close to California?"

"I don't know. I'm not a pilot," I tease. "But I'm guessing half an hour."

"I slept that long?"

"It seems to be a trend."

Bzzzz.

With a weary sigh I've never seen from him before, Silas lifts his butt off the seat, hips arching, to find his phone in his pants pocket. I look away and take a sip of my lukewarm tea.

He answers the phone for a call. "Gentian. Yeah. What? What do you mean, Drew? She's *what*? Does the senator know? Where else are we supposed to–okay, okay, a hotel, but that needs to be secured in advance, and after what happened with the lab courier, you know we're in—"

Silas stops talking suddenly. I can hear Drew's voice rising, a firm, clipped tone making my stomach clench. Whatever's happened is bad.

"Fine."

He looks at his phone, and as Drew speaks, an extraordinary expression fills Silas's face. It's more than surprise, slightly less than chagrin.

"Got it. Will do." He hangs up on Drew, then taps over to another call on the same phone.

"Mom? Why are you calling on my *work* phone? How did you—" Hysterical crying bubbles out of his phone speaker, his eyes going panicked. He walks over to the other side of the plane. There is no privacy here. He'd have to hide in the bathroom, and even then I could hear everything. The jet is smooth and quiet.

"She's *what*? And where is Kelly?"

My heart goes numb.

"Okay, okay. Kelly's safe. Good. And which precinct?"

Precinct? Why would his five-year-old niece be at a police station?

"The Narcan didn't do it the first—what? *How* many times? Oh, Mom," he says into the phone, his voice a mix of compassion and grief, fear and anger. "Right. I'll be there. You start booking your flight. Use the credit card I gave you for emergencies. This is definitely one." He pauses, voice hitching. "I know. I love you, too. I've got this. Don't worry. It's all going to be okay. It will. I'll get her and we'll make sure she's safe and fine. I've got this. Don't you worry."

Click.

Narcan? That's what you give someone who overdoses on opiates to revive them. Heroin addicts need it, when they overdose. Why is Silas talking about Narcan with his *mother*?

Before I can ask, he immediately taps his screen, utterly focused on movement and action.

"Drew?" he says into the phone. "I have a personal issue I

need to attend to and you'll have to assign her to a new team."

I assume I am "her."

"What do you mean, no? There is no *no* here. I'm not fucking around."

I've never, ever heard Silas speak this way to Drew.

"She what? The senator's new admin did *what*?" Fuming, Silas starts pacing, body language so aggressive, I'm sure he'll punch the wall any second now.

"Not a single guy is available? They're all stuck in decontamination? Fucking hell, Drew. You've got to be kidding me." He takes a short, sparse breath. "I'm sure you don't like it, either. Anyone sick from the powder?"

"What happened?" I whisper.

He ignores me.

"Damn it. I can't. I *can't*. It's about my sister. She finally..." He looks at me, uncertainty coating his face like a mask, then finally he gives in to some sort of inner struggle. "She OD'd. The police have my niece. I need to go get her and establish temporary custody. Now. She's being held with a social worker, and my mom is halfway across the country."

My hand flies to my mouth in shock, his words penetrating my heart in a way that makes me ache for the little girl at the heart of this crisis. I know he's not talking to me, but I can't help but react.

He nods in response to something Drew's said. "Right. No choice. Got it."

Silas ends the call, turning to me with anguish all over him, in his eyes, along the thick ridge of muscle in his shoulders, in every muscle twitch, each reflex.

And then he asks, "Exactly how good *are* you at Candyland?"

CHAPTER 20

*H*ave you ever played Candyland for three hours straight?

It's *liberating*.

For precious hours, my world became spinning and counting, finding my way through gumdrops and chocolate scenery, my ears filled with giggles and gasps, with a little girl who kept looking at me shyly, begging for one more game, as if I'd say no.

I didn't.

I *couldn't*.

Who could say no to this sweet, sweet little princess?

"Your name is Jane. But what's your whole name?" she asks me. Silas has been gone for hours, hastily dropping us off as a social worker and law enforcement officer tried to talk with him after delivering Kelly to his apartment. I know he was arguing with them in the hallway, then moved outside. There's no reason for me to try to find him. His attachment to his niece is fierce, and whatever is going on is critical.

"Jane Rose Borokov."

"No, not all the names. I mean your real name!"

"What do you mean, real name?"

"Is Jane a whole name or a nickname? Silas isn't a nickname. It's his whole name. Kelly is a whole name. Mama says whole names are important."

"What's your mama's name?" I know the answer, but I'm curious.

Kelly scrunches up her face, concentrating. "I know her real name is Patricia, but her nickname is Tricia. She has another nickname, though."

"What's that?"

"Turtle. That's what Uncle Rick calls her."

"Turtle?"

"Yeah. It's not a nice name." Kelly frowns. "It's what he calls her when she goes into the houses and takes too long to come back."

A deep sadness fills me. "Houses?" I ask, knowing before she says it what little Kelly is talking about.

"The houses. You know. Where Mama goes to feel better. Sometimes she feels better by getting money there, and sometimes she gets her medicine there."

Medicine. Right.

"Does she need a lot of medicine?" I ask, prying gently. Any information I can get might help Silas.

"Sometimes. If she feels bad. Uncle Rick needs lots of medicine, too. But he also sells it to people so they will feel better. And if he sells a lot, we go out for ice cream!"

I'm trying not to show her how I really feel. Silas has been hiding this whole mess since he's been working with me. Does Drew know? Does Silas talk to anyone about his sister's addiction? I don't have a sister or a brother but I can only imagine how complicated and heartbreaking having a sibling as an addict would be.

Is.

It's not hypothetical for Silas. It's stone-cold reality.

"Where's Uncle Silas?" she asks for the hundredth time.

I don't lie to her. "He went to the police station to talk to people about making sure you're safe. And you *are* safe," I assure her.

"I know, silly. Grandma's coming while Mama's sick. I'm always safe with Uncle Silas and Grandma."

My heart hurts. She doesn't mention being safe with her mother.

We arrived at the airport in California, took an SUV straight to the police precinct where Kelly was being held by a social worker, and after mountains of paperwork, Silas brought us here, to his apartment. It's simple and boring, all neutral beige and sandstone, like he lives in a furnished model unit in one of those cookie-cutter complexes near major highways.

There is no way he has a wife, or a live-in girlfriend.

Kelly is as charming as Silas described, curious and sweet with dark hair, straight bangs over wispy eyebrows, and red lips like a bow. She was hungry when we got here and immediately ate four hot dogs without buns, a small pile of baby carrots, and drank two huge glasses of milk.

She is also filthy.

The social worker told Silas there was no sign of abuse, or of lice, but that otherwise neglect had put its mark on the little girl. When she smiles, I can see her teeth haven't been brushed in days–weeks?

Her dark hair is matted and squirrelly, one chunk of it uneven compared to the rest. She has an uncertainty in her movements, constantly looking at me covertly, as if expecting to be told no.

When I smile at her or encourage her, she beams.

Her pants are leggings, far too short for her, and her big toe breaks through the top of her worn-down white sneakers. A red long-sleeved shirt with a Disney character on it has layers of stains.

How long has she gone without a change of clothes or a bath? Is this how Silas's family operates? He seems so together, so rational. I knew from college classes that dysfunction comes in many forms, but I've never spent one second of my life like Kelly. Dirty? Sure. From a day of playing hard.

This is the filth of neglect.

"Uncle Silas said I could have more–you know." Kelly looks nervously toward Silas's small galley kitchen, her neck shrinking slightly as she timidly tries to ask for something I don't understand.

"More what, sweetie?"

"Ice cream," she whispers, looking afraid.

"Of course!" I say in an overly happy voice, trying to drive out this fear in her. "Let's get out the big bowls." I'm not really hungry, but I know it'll make it easier for Kelly if I join her.

Two bowls of vanilla ice cream with chocolate sauce poured over it later, we're eating at Silas's small black metal dining table when he walks through the door. He does a double take at the scene before him.

"You made yourselves comfortable," he says, taking in the scattered pieces of Candyland, the stack of cards on the board, the ice cream.

"You said ice cream was okay!" Kelly protests.

"Did you leave any for me?" he asks her in a teasing voice, reaching to ruffle her hair, a strange look passing like a shadow across his face. I can only imagine what her hair feels like.

Our eyes meet.

We both get it.

"How about after the ice cream, you get to take a bubble bath?" I ask. "Princesses take bubble baths, you know," I explain, pretending to be somber and serious. "It's part of the duties of a princess."

"Yay! I love bubble baths!" she says.

Whew.

"JOEY!" she shrieks, the *non sequiter* throwing me for a loop. I follow her gaze to find a small cat, black with a white spot under its neck, peering out at us from under the couch.

"Joey?" I ask Silas as Kelly runs to the cat,who retreats quickly, face disappearing.

"My cat."

"I can see that."

"You're not allergic, are you?" he asks, as if the idea just hit him and it makes this all more complicated.

"No. I'm fine. But of all the names you could pick for a cat, you chose *Joey*?"

"I didn't pick the name," he says, suddenly terse.

"He's a rescue?" I pry, curious.

"She," he corrects me.

"You got a cat from the pound named Joey, and Joey is a *girl*?"

"Something like that," he mutters as he moves to the back of the couch, reaches behind with a practiced hand, and scoops out the little cat. Kelly rushes to pet Joey, who closes her eyes and tolerates it. Joey is an introvert, clearly.

Like all cats.

"I don't have bubble bath," Silas whispers in my ear as Kelly coos over the cat.

"Shampoo can be used in a pinch."

He looks at her head. "I'm not sure I have enough shampoo to clean her hair *and* use for a bubble bath."

I touch his hand, trying to reassure him. "It'll be fine."

He reaches down and takes my hand. "Come talk to me for a minute." Silas gently sets Joey down. Immediately, the cat darts under the couch, much to Kelly's protests.

I follow him into the kitchen and reach for the chocolate sauce, pouring extra on Kelly's ice cream. "Here. Eat this, and Uncle Silas will come back with me in just a minute. We'll be right here." I point across the way to the far corner of the living room.

"No!" She tightens her mouth. "It's ice cream time. Uncle Silas, you need to get your bowl."

"Yes, ma'am," he says, saluting her.

She giggles.

He gives me a look that says we'll talk later, then walks into the kitchen and pulls out the ice cream, looking increasingly interested in his freezer.

"Jane?"

"Yes?"

"How much ice cream did you guys eat? The pint was brand new."

"It's a pint! That's normally only enough for one person. Be glad we saved you any." I stick my tongue out at him.

His laugh warms my heart.

"I'm more of a cookie guy, anyhow."

And there you have it.

Silas just voluntarily told me something personal about himself. A preference. A liking.

A *desire*.

I hear a scraping sound, then Silas joins us with a final scoop of ice cream and a sleeve of cookies, half a box in a plastic tube.

"That's a lot of cookies," I note.

He points to Kelly's bowl. "That's a lot of ice cream."

"Mo iff mah!" Kelly argues.

"She said 'No, it's not.'"

"You speak Ice Cream?" Silas asks in a jaunty, joking tone.

"It was my minor in college. I majored in Sweet 'n Sour, though."

He pops a small chocolate cookie in his mouth and carefully examines Kelly, taking in every detail. I'm sure he's looked her over a hundred times since he picked her up at the police station. He's clearly worried, protective and trying to understand what's happened.

I want to know.

But first things first.

We eat the rest of our sugarbombed treats in silence. Kelly savors every bite, smearing very little on her face. Silas and I are pensive. Time changes when you spend it in the company of a small child.

Especially one you're trying to distract.

"When is Mama coming?" Kelly asks Silas, clearly expecting a time.

He pauses, hand in mid-air before it delivers another cookie to his mouth. This he sets back down as he says, "We're not sure, punkin. She's sick, remember? The doctors need some more time to make her feel better."

"Does that mean I get to stay with you? Please? Can I

have a sleepover here with you?" She frowns. "And Jane? Does Jane live here with you, Uncle Silas?"

If either of us had anything in our mouths at that point, we'd have sprayed it.

Silas turns a furious shade of pink. "Um, no. She doesn't live here, but... she's going to spend the night tonight."

My eyebrows fly high. I am?

"We're gonna have a slumber party!" Kelly whoops, the squeals making me laugh. "We already had ice cream and then we'll have bubble baths and Uncle Silas can get out the nail polish he keeps in his bathroom and we can paint our nails!"

"You have your own nail polish kit?" I ask him with great amusement.

"It's for Kelly."

"Suuuuuure it is. Convenient excuse. Bet you secretly love electric blue toenails."

He rolls his eyes.

"I'm spending the night here?" I ask.

"No other choice. I have to keep Kelly until my mom arrives. Drew said the entire team at The Grove is going through decontamination for hours. This is the best I can do. We have surveillance teams outside in unmarked vehicles. You need to be safe. Kelly needs to be supervised."

"You're not worried the people after me might–you know." I look at Kelly.

"Let's talk about it later," he says in a sing-songy voice, like he's trying not to frighten Kelly.

Good point.

"I'm done!" Kelly announces, then gives Silas a very sly side-eye. "At least, the ice cream side of my stomach is done. The cookie part has some room."

The smile he gives her is so loving, I nearly tear up. "Is it, now? What about the tickle side?"

She shrieks, jumps up, and starts running away, looking over her shoulder to make sure he's actually chasing her. I get the sense this is a well-known game between the two of them. He clearly spends a lot of time with her. Their relationship is natural and strong.

So why on earth is she so neglected?

I hear a bathtub faucet start as Silas makes funny sounds I don't understand.

Is he... giggling?

"Stop tickling!" he bellows. "It's too much! You're a better tickler than I am!"

Curiosity is killing me. I *have* to see this. As I turn down the small hallway and find Silas's bathroom, I'm greeted by the sight of a forty-pound munchkin tickling her giant uncle, who is cringing in mock terror in a corner by the toilet.

"Jane! Help! The tickle monster got me!" he cries out. "The only way to stop the tickle monster is to eat your vegetables!"

"I don't have any vegetables!" I say, playing along.

"Haha! Uncle Silas is in trouble!" Kelly says with glee, her hands like little tickle claws, ready to strike.

I see the tub is nearly full so I turn and grab the knob, cutting off the water. Suddenly Silas's scent consumes me, near my neck and nose, warm hands on the soft spot above my hips and below my ribs, his fingers digging in as I jump with surprise and start giggling, helplessly panting.

"Uncle Silas's turn, Jane! He's the tickle monster now!"

"Stop tickling me!" I gasp.

"She said *stop*, Uncle Silas! You know the rules!" Kelly insists. "If someone doesn't want your hands on them, you stop!"

Oh. Well. I wouldn't put it *that* way, but...

Silas smells so good, his body warm and appealing. Touch is underrated. Going for long stretches without touching another human being is a form of isolation you can't really describe. It has to be experienced and felt directly.

Even being tickled mercilessly is better than nothing.

As I recover, Silas gives me a self-deprecating smile. Kelly carefully steps over the bathtub edge and sinks in under the white shampoo foam. She turns her back to us. I stifle a gasp. Silas's hands curl into balls, fingers tight.

There is a very large fading bruise on Kelly's back.

Eyes closed, Silas struggles to control himself, his quick bottling of emotion almost artistic if it weren't for such a sad, despicable reason.

"Kelly," he asks softly, the back of his head resting against the wall, his eyes closed. "What happened to your back?"

"I fell," she says in a voice so quiet, she might as well be a church mouse.

"Okay," I whisper, needing to say something, to exhale, to breathe, to remind myself she is here with us, safe, and not being hurt like she was in the past. Emotion tornadoes around me until all I can do is link myself to Silas's feelings, tracking him, making sure he's safe, too.

You can fool yourself into thinking the only way to be unsafe is in your body. We have so much more vulnerability on the inside. The wrong person can harm your skin and bones, sure.

But true evil invades your bloodstream.

I grab a small washcloth and hand it to Kelly. "Why don't you wash your body, nice and clean."

"Okay!" she chirps. "Mama taught me to wash like a big girl!"

Silas's brow lowers in pain. The kind that burns from your chest on out.

"Your mama really loves you, huh?" I say reflexively, the words making me choke up. I suddenly miss my mama. So much.

"Yes," she says, looking at Silas. "Hey, Uncle Silas! Don't go to sleep! It's not bedtime yet!"

He opens his eyes slowly and I swear he's trying not to cry.

"No, you're right," he says in a choked voice. His eyes dart to catch mine. "Can you help her wash her hair?" He starts to stand.

"No water in my eyes!" Kelly screeches.

"Don't worry, sweetie," he says, his voice craggy and uneven. "Jane's a good person. She'll be careful."

Jane's a good person.

It's been so long since someone said that to or about me.

"Do you know how to pour the water so it goes on my hair but not in my eyes?" she asks somberly, like I'm being interviewed for a job.

"Yes. I'm an expert." I speak to her but watch Silas as he leaves the tiny room, blinking hard, his face roiling with so many different emotions, but one stands out.

Not anger.

Grief.

Suddenly, Kelly dips under the water, her thumb and index finger plugging her nose, and she comes up sputtering but laughing.

"I did it! Mama told me I could put my face in the water and be okay!" she crows, but too much water is in her eyes and she starts to whine. I grab a dry towel from a rack and blot her face as she wriggles.

"Good job!" I assure her, meanwhile freaking out on the inside. Why is Silas so upset? The mark on Kelly's back is bad. She's clearly been hurt by someone. Silas's sister? "Uncle Rick"? Someone else?

And wouldn't Silas be furious? Why is he so choked up?

Kelly hums to herself as she uses the washcloth to clean herself, blowing on the foamy bubbles and begging for more. I run the faucet and pour a thin stream of shampoo on the running water. We do this for about twenty minutes until finally she trusts me to wash her hair and rinse it the "right way."

"I got some water in my eyes but it didn't hurt!" she says as I hold open a big towel for her to step into. Just then Silas appears, his face a little red, a bottle of hair detangler and a comb in one hand.

"Comb my hair, Uncle Silas?" she asks. He holds the hair items like this is a familiar ritual.

"Of course," he says.

"When's Mama coming for me? I'm spending the night for the sleepover, right?"

Silas looks like he's in the crosshairs of a sniper's shot.

"Uh, Grandma's coming tomorrow, sweetie," he finally

says as he turns her away from him and starts lightly spraying her tangled hair. He's an expert, combing the crazy, straight hair until it shines like a wet seal's coat. "Remember?"

"Tomorrow? So soon?" She claps and grins.

"It's all last minute. A surprise," he adds in the kind of voice you use with little kids.

"Ice cream, a bubble bath, a sleepover, and Grandma! This is great!" she says, beaming.

I look at her face. Dark circles under her eyes but no bruises. She hums a Disney princess song to herself and Silas starts to lead her out of the bathroom.

"I'll help you get dressed," he says.

"I know how!" Kelly protests. "Just give me the clothes."

Silas looks at the dining table at the end of the hall and walks to it, grabbing a bag from a store he must have gone to while he was out. He extracts a pack of new underwear and a cute set of cotton jersey pajamas.

"New? For me?" Kelly asks. "Mama says I only get new stuff for my birthday and Christmas. It's not Christmas, is it?"

Silas is stricken.

"No, no, sweetie. Just some nice, new clothes for you." He hands her the clothes and points to his bedroom. "You go get dressed and come back so we can brush your teeth. I got you a new toothbrush."

Kelly skips down the hallway and goes into Silas's bedroom, cradling her new clothes. The second she's out of earshot, I turn to question Silas, just as his phone buzzes.

He looks at it, mutters something I can't hear, and turns away.

I take a moment to go into the bathroom, take care of my own business, and look at myself in the mirror as I wash my hands. I am shaking, eyes haunted, my own dark circles mirroring little Kelly's. I've obviously been brought into a serious family drama, the personal line crossed in my relationship with Silas.

Relationship? Is that what you call this?

His kiss on the top of my head back at The Grove, after rescuing me from that creepy doctor, runs through me like a racing train. I feel like I'm in the conductor's seat but there are no controls. Just a smooth, flat table covered with nothing, but a panoramic view of what I'm about to crash into.

Something is very, very off right now.

And the second Kelly falls asleep, I'm demanding answers.

I walk down the hallway to find Kelly on top of Silas's neatly made bed, dressed in the clothes Silas handed her. Wet hair curls against her cheek, her eyes closed, the light, rhythmic breathing of a fast-asleep child the only sound in the room.

The light behind me from the hallway suddenly dims. Silas's presence blocks the doorway as I pull up one corner of his comforter and cover her. Instinct makes me bend low and kiss her cheek.

She smiles in slumber.

Tiptoeing out, I carefully shut the door, turning the knob first and letting it click softly. By the time I'm done, Silas is gone from the hall. His apartment is small, so he can't really hide.

I won't let him.

I find him digging around a tiny coat closet by the front door. He turns, a tightly rolled sleeping bag in one hand.

"Oh," he says, looking at the couch. "It's a sleeper. You take the sofabed and I'll crash on the floor next to Kelly in my room. If Joey climbs on the couch at night, I can lock her in the bathroom so she won't disturb you."

"Silas," I say softly.

He's tense, pure adrenaline radiating off him. "Someone else can take over with you around 3 am, so sleeping here is temporary. Drew says once the team goes through decontamination, he can send a guy to–"

"Silas," I repeat, voice firm, trying to shake him out of this weird state.

"It's only for another few hours, and then–"

"SILAS!" I shout, cringing immediately after because I don't want to wake Kelly, but–

His hand covers my mouth instantly, body pressing me against a wall I didn't realize was right behind me. His nose brushes against mine, his eyes wide with emotion.

I can't tell whether it's anger or lust.

I'm not sure I want to know which it is.

"Don't you dare wake her up! Not after what she's been through. Not after what she's about to go through," he says, breath covering my face, anguish in his voice and eyes. We're both breathing hard, me through my nose, Silas through his entire body, which is hot and hard against me. He smells rumpled and tired, wired and ready to defend and oh, so real.

When he peels his hand off my mouth, I don't know what I'm going to say.

We stare at each other, ears perked for Kelly. She doesn't say a word, still asleep. Silas's shoulders drop a few millimeters, tension dropping on a tiny scale, but his body is still walling me off from escape. The weapon on his belt scrapes against my hip, his flat belly against mine, and while he's at an angle, it's really clear how primed for battle his entire broad body really is.

"I'm not the enemy," I whisper.

Any other words might not have mattered. Those *do*.

"No, you're not. You're my client," he replies, but doesn't move back. We're locked in a fused half embrace that Silas started.

How will he finish this?

"Am I?" I ask. "Just a client?"

There. I said it. It's out there now, and his mouth is so close to mine. He's shaking, a short frantic tremor that seems to come from some energy force beneath us. It consumes his entire body, pure energy, all madness in movement.

"No," he says as he backs away. "You're not. Thank you."

Huh?

"I appreciate everything you did for Kelly tonight. It was unprofessional of me to break that line. I should have found a workaround. You've been exposed to way more than you should be, and it's all my family mess. I'm sorry."

This is not what I was hoping to hear.

"I–it was my pleasure! She's sweet and wonderful. Really." I can't not ask, though. "But those bruises. What she said about 'Uncle Rick.' When your sister gets out of the hospital, you'll have to find out what that's all about before she gets to see Kelly again."

Silas staggers to the couch and sits on one end, as if his legs can't hold him up any more. He leans forward, elbows on his knees, head down. His fingers rake his mussed hair.

When he looks up, it's like his eyes reflect a world that is burning.

"That's not going to happen."

"What?" I recoil. "Of course you'll say something. If you don't, I will, and even though I don't know your sister, I–"

"It's. Not. Going. To. Happen," he says through clenched teeth.

"You can't just–"

"Jane," he says in a low stressed voice that sounds like the universe just cracked in half. "It's not going to happen because my sister is dead."

CHAPTER 21

"*O*h!" Puzzle pieces fall into place, *click click click* in my mind as his words sink in. I sit down next to him, perched on the edge of the couch, facing forward.

"Oh, God," I mutter, staring straight ahead, everything going out of focus. "Poor Kelly. You didn't say a word. She doesn't know?" Tears come unbidden, filling my eyes. I don't hide it. I couldn't even if I tried.

"No. Not yet. I thought it was best, until my mom gets here tomorrow."

"Your mom knows?"

"Yes. That was one of the calls earlier today."

"You hid this from me?"

"*You?*"

"Yeah, me. I know we're not friends, but Jesus, Silas. I'm a human being with compassion, you know." Weeping openly, I turn to him and touch his hand. "I am so, so sorry. I'm sorry you lost your sister. I'm sorry Kelly lost her mother. I'm sorry you didn't feel you could talk about it with me. I'm just sorry."

"Stop saying you're sorry. You have nothing to do with my sister's drug addiction and her stupid, stupid relapse."

But he squeezes my hand back.

"You can talk about it with me, you know. I'll listen. I'm here."

"Nothing to talk about. My sister made heroin more important than her kid. Open and shut. Now she's dead and I have to pick up all the pieces. So does my mother. That's what addicts do. They make the dope more important than human beings."

I just nod.

"She made getting high more important than her daughter. Best guess the cops have is that the heroin was contaminated. Fentanyl, some other substance–toxicology reports will take awhile. It's all details, though. Bottom line: my sister, Tricia, is dead and someone has to tell Kelly she's never seeing–" His voice cuts off, then an enormous sound of anguish ripples through him. "–never seeing Mama again."

I move quietly toward him and reach up, sliding the palm of my hand over his jaw, fingers skimming his neck, tips brushing against his hair. He's looking down but lifts his head. Our eyes lock.

His are glistening. The whites are slightly bloodshot, his nostrils flaring, jaw muscles ticking.

His brow is up and as I take in all of the microscopic ways his body is feeling emotion he can't bring himself to express, I realize he is pissed.

Really, really *pissed*.

"Never seeing Mama again," he repeats, standing up and moving away from my touch. He starts to pace, like a big predator churning all the attack instincts into the perfect form. Silas's shoulders swell, his arms curling under yet at his sides, his eyes out of focus as he paces his small, nondescript living room.

"Tricia did it again, damn it. Couldn't hold back. Not even *one bit* for her kid. Nooooo, the drugs were too powerful. And who the fuck is 'Uncle Rick'?" he hisses, the sound like broken glass being dragged over my heart. "Who is he? I'll get Drew to help me find out, but if that fucker laid a finger on Kelly, he's dead."

The way Silas says it makes me shiver.

Because I know he'll do it.

"Silas, we don't know. And right now, you just need–"

"Don't tell me what I need!" he rumbles, the sound somehow more biting because he's saying it low, in a whispered hush that seems to scream. Whipping around, he recedes, body barreling full speed toward his kitchen, fist cocked, elbow coming back. The sound of bone on wood is surprisingly quiet and shattering at the same time as he punches the door jamb quietly, the crunching all the worse for his silent destruction.

"Fuck!" he growls, the sound low and quiet for Kelly's sake, piercing and deep to be in the room and witnessing all his pain trying to come out as he contains it. Savage and real, Silas is unmoored. Unleashed. He grunts as he thrusts his arm back, plowing it over and over into the wood until I see he's leaving smears of blood on the wall.

I don't try to stop him.

I don't think I could, even if I tried.

"Why? Why why why why why," he says, his voice fading as he repeats the word, punching softly over and over. Silas presses his forehead against the wall and bangs it, slowly, the rhythm more important than the impact. I realize how much he's been holding it together, how skilled and eloquent he had to be through our time together with Kelly. How he was broken inside, emotional splinters working their way out of him as he pretended for his niece's sake.

How pain finds a way out, no matter how hard you try to pen it in.

Pain won't be denied. You can defer it. Postpone it. Think you've got it all under control. Just when you reassure yourself you have mastered it, the pain emerges.

Pain dominates.

And when it does, the world submits.

Drops of blood soak his pants leg, just under where his pocket seam resides. His arms are loose at his sides and I come to him now, ready to offer whatever solace I can.

"Silas," I say, the word barely touching my lips and

tongue as I gingerly rest my fingertips on his shoulder. He tenses, then leans against the wall, breathing hard.

A million words rush through my mind as we stand there, Silas's ragged breath its own language. But I say nothing, instead letting him just feel. His bloodied hand rests at his side, making me cringe. The last time I saw so much blood was yesterday, the image of Tara pushed aside quickly, triggering the scent of burning wetness. Before that, it was seven months ago, the day Silas, Drew, and Mark rescued Lindsay and me from our tormenters.

The trauma of both days is palpable.

I don't let go, my fingers connecting us as if we have no choice. Bound to each other by forces beyond us, we're here, together. I'm not just his client. He is not just my security person. There is no "just" here.

I am honored. I am horrified. I am traumatized. I am grieving. The space we're inhabiting right now as Silas steadies his breathing, as his blood smears along an inelegant line on his trousers, as the scent of true expression makes me breathe in deeper–it all feels so sacred.

And oh, so profane.

"Why?" he gasps, then makes a sick, laughing huff. His injured hand comes up and runs through his dark hair as he turns around, staring down at me with eyes that somehow are devoid of emotion and also contain every molecule of feeling in the world. Inky and dilated, his eyes are a window, a black hole, a promise, an abyss.

Jump, those eyes say.

I'll catch you.

I stand on tiptoe, arms at my sides now, and take the leap.

My kiss is meant to be gentle and comforting, to convey that I feel so bad for him and his loss, to try to share in his pain and maybe–just maybe–carry some of the burden of it for a little while. At first he moves back, a tiny recoil of surprise, but before I can react and pull away he's enveloping me, arms crushing me to him, the comforting kiss I started turning rapidly into a passionate exploration that conveys even more of what he's feeling, tapping into what I could see on the surface of his body, revealing the true depths.

My God. It's endless.

Pieces of me come forward and attach to the broken pieces of him, the rush to join a physical sensation as his arms turn to steel bands around me, his heat and touch and scent so all-encompassing. So welcome. So transcendent.

His hands press me against him, shimmying under my shirt, up my back, fingers impossibly strong, palms muscled and heated against my shoulder blades, my ribs, my bones. As I arch my back, leaning into him to breathe in the fire between us, I surrender. All the churning in my mind lessens, the flurry of pain and uncertainty receding like the tides. Silas is my moon, my true North, my divining rod, my center. The trail of touch he leaves along my skin is a thousand years of memory. The sound of his low, deep pleasure–made by *me*–is my compass.

Too much time spent living in my mind, the cage that holds all my screaming thoughts, has meant I've forgotten my body.

But it has not forgotten me.

I reach down and undo his buckle, frantic and in need of more skin, more Silas, more of him. His phone slips out of his back pocket and onto the floor between us, the blue glow showing unread messages, shining up at us. He ignores it.

He focuses on *me*.

We move to the couch, where gravity lets me fall into him. I'm grateful. The laws of physics work for us, propelling me deeper against him, giving me more.

I can't get enough, his groan of relief showing me he feels the same way as I unzip him and stroke the length of him with the palm of my hand, sliding down the long trail of his thigh, taking in his muscled leg, the groove of bone and tendon, the light sandpapery feel of his hair. In the dark, I close my eyes and take in the dusting of tight curls that cover the powerful bulk of him, the same flesh and bone that protects me every hour, every minute, every second we're near each other.

It's intoxicating to be the object of that protection. I've shunned it, resented it, pushed it away, and hated it.

Not now, though. Now I give in to it and let the weight of it blanket me, the warm trusting of his mouth turning me toward all he offers. No longer a client, I'm a lover in his arms. No longer Jane Borokov, a public enemy and object of shame to use as a weapon in the media, I am just Jane, all breasts and gasps and wetness and need, writhing in his lap as he pushes up against me, seeking and seeking and seeking.

I'm here, my mind moans to him in a language that only uses my tongue, my fingers, my nails that dig into broad shoulders designed to move with deep grace to keep danger at bay.

I'm here.

"Jane," he says, as if warning me, as if I don't know what I'm getting myself into, as if I'm in peril. A very different kind of peril. This time, my body isn't being threatened.

It's about to be worshipped.

He doesn't understand that I'm finding the first safe space in months right here, right now, as my hands define him, map him.

Ache for him.

Or maybe he does understand, and that's the secret eluding me. When you spend every waking second in a state of stone-cold panic, the truth becomes a hidden treasure. A secret. Silas's mouth glides across mine, his lips full and giving, his hands taking palmfuls of my willing skin and blending our movement into a fine art.

He cups one breast and kisses me with such fevered power, I stop thinking. All light behind my closed eyes bursts into shades of nothing, words disappearing into colored mists that spread out into the corners of my mind and heart. Slipping under my bra, his fingers make my nipple tighten, a gasp coming from me without volition.

In his hands I am my true self.

I'm so wet for him, those thin pieces of cloth keeping us from joining, my bare belly brushing against his as our shirts ride up. A cold arc of air encircles my waist as Silas uses his open hand to tug at my shirt, signaling what he wants next.

More.

More of me.

He can have it all.

Tap tap tap.

Bzzzzzz.

Simultaneously, someone knocks at the front door and Silas's phone buzzes.

I shriek in surprise, the snap of my bra as Silas snatches his hand away like a rebuke, a punishment, a shaming. I roll away. We both look at the door as Silas automatically buckles his belt, zips up his pants, and tucks everything into place.

Including every single damn emotion he just let me feel.

He picks up his phone and looks at it while striding quickly to the door, opening it swiftly as a man in a suit stands there, hand ready to knock again.

"Blumenthal?" he snaps at the guy, a tall, thin man who seems out of place for a bodyguard, his lean look more marathoner than muscle.

"Yeah. Foster sent me."

"I thought you weren't coming until later," I say in a high, nervous voice, trying to put all the passion we just shared into a box like Silas did. My ability to compartmentalize is at war with the lingering memory of his taste, his hands, his touch, his groan.

Blumenthal frowns. "Foster said this was a priority. Sent the first guy he could." His eyes ping between Silas and me, narrowing.

"It is," Silas replies, clearing his throat. "It's more of a priority than you could ever imagine. Glad you made it early. We're trying to avoid crises."

Suddenly I want to punch walls, too.

Silas looks at me, then Blumenthal. "You know where to take her?"

He nods. "The Grove."

Silas gives him a suspicious look. "The Grove? What? No. Monica Bosworth refuses to let her stay there."

I'm back to being "her" again.

"Change of plans," Blumenthal says with a shrug. "Big meeting in the morning. I'll get her there tonight. Foster says you need to be there at 9 am." His eyes skitter to Silas's bloody hand. Eyebrows go up, but he says nothing more.

Pure terror shoots through my bloodstream, crowding out all of the much nicer sensations that were just there. The Grove? Without Silas? Why? What is Monica Bosworth doing? I race to find something–anything–I can say to stay here for a few seconds longer, to try to reconnect with Silas.

"Silas," I say softly. "What about Kelly?"

"What about her?" he asks gruffly, closed off, shut down.

"When she wakes up, will you tell her I'm sorry I didn't say goodbye?" Tears threaten to take over, my skin tingling with the effort to hold them back. "She's been through so much. I don't want to be another person who disappears on her." A single teardrop, fat and round, breaks the line of my lower lid and lands on my upper lip. I lick it and look at him, imploring.

I might as well have slapped him.

Quickly, microscopically, he drains his emotions off his face and looks neutral again. I get a curt nod. "Right. I'll handle her. My mother is on her way." He gives a tight, polite smile. "I've already inconvenienced you enough. I apologize for the disruption. You don't need to worry."

"I'll feel whatever I want to feel, Silas," I declare. Out of the corner of my eye, I see Joey's little black face peeking out from under the couch, just watching.

Silas' smile tightens to the point of snapping. "You do that, Jane."

And with that, Blumenthal escorts me to a black SUV. Duff is driving.

That night, I sleep in the guest house at The Grove, body reeling from Silas's attention, heart broken from his withdrawal.

I do not dream.

CHAPTER 22

*I*t feels like déjà vu.

All the same people are around the conference table at Senator Bosworth's office. The only ones missing are the senator himself and Silas. His absence makes this so hard. When he's here, I feel like I have a safety net. No one can hurt me.

Not my body, at least.

But Silas isn't here.

Marshall, Marcy, Victoria, Drew, and to my surprise, Duff are all in the room. It appears that Duff is acting in a security capacity, watching the door, eyes straight ahead, zero warmth.

My stomach growls and I reach for my lukewarm coffee, sipping to have something to do with my hands, my mouth, my fear.

A loose plan forms in my mind. It involves going back to Alice's ranch and never, ever leaving.

Haunted by Silas's touch last night, the way his kiss penetrated every part of me, leaving so much undone, untouched, unfinished, it's hard to be present. I need to keep my wits about me. I know this. I need to be on alert, vigilant, and ready for whatever Monica Bosworth has in store for me.

Marshall is standing by the door, chatting with Drew. The two keep looking at me askance.

Whatever is going on is *bad*.

And yet I'm more worried about Silas and Kelly than I am about myself.

Did she wake up sad that I wasn't there? Did Silas have to continue to pretend for her sake until his mom arrived? How did they break it to Kelly? What's next for that beautiful little girl who has already suffered through too much neglect, too many secrets, so many lies?

It's always easier to worry about someone else's problems than your own. Especially when it comes to a child. I would happily play Candyland and eat ice cream with Kelly for the next year. My heart breaks knowing that right now Silas and his mother are comforting a little girl who will never, ever see her mama again.

I inhale sharply, the pain along my heart an aftershock.

Kelly and I have that in common now.

We both lost our mommies.

"Sabotage?" I overhear Drew's tight voice. "We're sure?"

"Confirmed," Marshall says between sips of coffee from an enormous travel mug. "It was planned. We checked the cars before delivery and there was nothing. By the time the car crashed, the fire was too hot. Burned any evidence."

"Chemical sabotage is more sophisticated," Drew replies, crossing his arms over his chest, face increasingly grave. "New materials are coming out faster than we can keep up."

"It sure feels like it," Marshall says.

"We weren't stupid. SOP is to get two vials of everything and send with duplicate couriers. It's rare that it's needed, but what happened in this case is precisely why we do it that way," Drew says to Marshall, who nods, then sips.

"That poor courier," I whisper. They look at me, surprised I'm eavesdropping, but they're talking two feet away from me. How can I not hear?

"She was a field agent. Fourteen years," Drew tells me. He sighs, a long, frustrated sound. "A good woman. Dying for this–" He cuts himself off as Marshall gives him a sharp look, both of them glancing at the folder in Marshall's spare hand.

"The lab work was that important? Worth killing a courier?" I ask.

Both of them suddenly go neutral, stripping all reactivity from their faces.

"We'll talk about that later," Marshall replies. "After we–"

All conversation halts as Monica Bosworth enters the room. She quickly walks to the head of the table and folds herself into the chair Marshall normally takes. The power play is obvious.

Monica does not care about obvious. She's accomplished her goal.

Power it is.

"I don't understand the need for a meeting, Marshall," she announces. "Just send Jane to the Island and keep it simple. You know I didn't want her at The Grove."

The Island?

"We tried to keep it simple, Mrs. Bosworth." He taps the manila folder in his hand, using one finger. "There is a complication."

"What are you talking about?" I ask, looking at Marshall, pointedly avoiding Monica. "Why would I go to the Island?"

Lindsay walks in as I ask the question and stops short, a woman carrying a coffee tray nearly colliding with her back.

"The Island? Why are you talking about the Island?" She frowns at her mother. "You can't make me go back." The staffer smoothly delivers the coffee tray to a buffet table behind Drew, who pivots and pours himself a cup, watching Monica like a hawk the entire time.

"We're not talking about you, Lindsay," Monica announces. She looks at me with a speculative expression. "We're concerned about *Jane's* mental health."

Lindsay and I snort in unison.

"Jane isn't married to Drew," Lindsay mutters. "She has no one to protect her." Sitting in a seat to my left, Lindsay gives Monica a challenging smile. "Is she your target now?"

I close my eyes slowly and bear the pain because she's right.

"Target? You say that as if I'm singling her out unfairly. You know what she did to you!"

"I know what people set her up to do to me, Mom."

"Not this fantasy again, Lindsay. Really." Monica makes a clucking sound intended to shame her daughter. "Some childlike, innocent part of you wants to think your friend couldn't do this to you. But she betrayed you. And look at what happens to people in her path. They die. Even the lab worker delivering those blood samples died while delivering them. How convenient." The last two words are spoken while openly glaring at me.

"Jane isn't responsible," Drew interrupts. "We've confirmed it."

That is the first time he's said a single word in my defense.

Monica sighs, impatient that she's being challenged. "Is this interruption really necessary?" she complains. "We need to move quickly on questions of the Island. The staff needs to prepare for Jane."

"I am not going!" I argue hotly. "I'm not! I refuse! I do not give consent!"

"This isn't like talking your way out of a medical exam, Jane. You can choose the Island or we cut off all protection for you and leave you to the wolves. Given the attempts on your life, I give you a week." Monica's demeanor makes it clear she would prefer it take less than that.

"Monica," Marshall says with firm determination, "we have a different topic that takes precedence."

"Precedence? I only allowed her to stay last night at The Grove because we agreed that the Island would be the best place for her to go to quell her impact on Harry's campaign."

"New information has altered our priorities."

She looks hard at the folder in Marshall's hand. "How significant?"

Marshall's silence speaks volumes.

She begins to stand. "Well, if this isn't going to be a

meeting about the Island, then I have better things to do with my time."

"Stay," Drew says, his voice a staccato point.

"Excuse me?" She's offended.

"Stay, Monica. You'll–well, you might not want to be here for this, but you damn well *need* to be here for this."

Anger turns her face hard. "I don't take orders from you, Drew."

"This isn't an order." He looks at Lindsay, clearly conflicted.

Monica's eyes dart to the folder Marshall holds. "What the hell is in there?" she asks.

Marshall looks like someone just ran over his dog and killed it. "I can answer that right now. We ran the paternity tests. Fortunately, Drew was smart enough to have double vials pulled of all of Jane's blood samples, and we had Lindsay's on file," Marshall explains. He won't make eye contact with Monica.

How weird.

Drew reaches for Lindsay's hand and gives her the strangest smile. It's melancholy and sympathetic, troubled and comforting. She smiles back then falters, seeing the underlying emotions in sharp focus and reacting to them.

She's confused.

So am I. What's going on?

Just then, Silas appears, slipping into the room like a jewel thief. There's no need to be so quiet, so slick. It's jarring.

He sits next to me, on my right, eyes darting to catch Drew's. I want to ask him why he's here, how is Kelly, did his mother arrive–I want to ask him every question in the world, so I can avoid whatever's coming next.

Something is going on. What did they find in my blood? I hear my breath through my nose, the line of sound running behind my ears, like it's wrapping around my head and trying to protect me. I can't get enough air, but I know I'm still breathing. My chest rises and falls, and Lindsay looks at me, brow down, her facial muscles tightening as she picks up on Drew's weirdness.

I glance at Silas.

He's looking at Drew.

"Testing shows that there were no biological agents in Jane, and no implants," Marshall begins.

Lindsay gives me a tiny smile, as if to acknowledge my relief.

I don't feel any.

Because I knew they'd find nothing.

"But one bit of bloodwork is definitely going to be an issue going forward." Marshall's body language is stilted, awkward. Gone is the bureaucratic assurance of a man on a singular mission–to manage Senator Bosworth's public relations issues.

Instead, this is a man facing a serious problem.

"Paternity testing," Marshall starts, clearing his throat, "has revealed..." His voice trails off.

My pulse feels like my heart is treading water in a cage with sharks outside.

"Revealed what?" I ask, my voice high, cracking in half. "My father died when my mom was pregnant with me. I know who–"

Silas reaches into my lap and grabs my hand, squeezing gently. The touch shocks me, an intimate gesture in public.

Oh, God.

Marshall and Monica lock eyes. He looks away first.

And then he opens his mouth to say, "Jane's biological father is Senator Bosworth. It's a match."

My heart becomes my entire body.

I blink, over and over, as if my eyelids can wash the lies off a smeared sheet of glass so I can see clearly. Monica is behind me, pure disgust radiating off her body in waves of heat I can feel. I don't need to turn around and look at her to know how she's reacting.

Lindsay gasps, eyes so big, they look like moons with gemstones in them. "Jane is... Daddy's her–oh!" She looks at her mother, gaping and sputtering like a fish on shore as Drew starts to put his arm around her.

Instead, she jumps up and lunges at me.

I start to stand to get away, because she must be attacking me, angry that I did something wrong, even if I didn't. My mother. Oh, my mother had an affair with Harry Bosworth. It really happened, and now she's dead and I can't ask questions and I'll never know–

Silas moves to protect me, but suddenly Lindsay's arms are around my neck, and she's crying and gasping.

"Sister! I have a sister! I can't believe this!"

I can't either.

"Lindsay," Monica says to the side of us. Her face is as pale as a gallon of cream. "Lindsay, I–"

"The rumors are true, then," Marshall says with a sigh. As Lindsay's sweet perfume fills my nose, her strong arms around my neck, I'm awkwardly suspended, half on my chair arm, half out on the table. Silas stays within inches of us, on guard.

I'm not sure if he's worried about Lindsay, or Monica, or me.

Marshall clears his throat. "Lindsay? Could you please sit down? There's more."

"Sit down? You expect me to sit down when I just found out I have a sister? Are you crazy?"

Marshall gives Monica a look that chills me. I want to flee that look. I want to run away and never get into the crosshairs of that look.

Because that look?

Whatever comes out of Marshall's mouth next is going to break the world.

"God, Mom!" Lindsay says as Drew tries to calm her down. "All these years, the rumors were true! You told me it was all just a ploy for Daddy's enemies to get to him, and that Anya would never do that, and now we find out it's *true*? Does Daddy know? Of course he knows. He was the one who slept with Anya! And Jane, we're sisters! We need to–"

Monica slowly walks over to Lindsay and places two

perfectly manicured fingers over her moving lips, eyes narrow and glistening with unfallen tears.

"*Shh*," she says to her daughter, making Lindsay gulp in surprise.

"I love you, Lindsay," she says fiercely, out of nowhere, making Drew, Silas, and Marshall form identical pained expressions.

My eyes jump to the manila folder in Marshall's hands.

He takes in a shaky breath.

"Blood tests confirm that Jane is, in fact, Harry Bosworth's daughter, Lindsay," he says to her, kindly.

"I know! You just said that!" She gives him an impatient, emotional, giddy look.

Which deflates instantly the second he replies with:

"But you are not."

~*~

WHAT HAPPENS NEXT? *A Shameless Little LIE* is the next book in Meli Raine's Shameless series.

I DID IT. I admit it.

I fell in love with Silas. My bodyguard. My protector.

My new informant.

We're playing a cat-and-mouse game. I'm not sure whether I'm the cat or the mouse, but I can definitely tell I'm in a trap.

A trap with no way out.

I'm not who everyone thought I was. The truth is out there, finally turning the lie about me inside out. I *am* the shameless little lie. It's finally been revealed, and now even more people want to kill me.

As a presidential campaign hangs in the balance, a delicate web of international relations and economic stability at risk, power becomes more important than anything else.

Even my life.

Especially my life. I'm a nothing. A no one. Just a tool, remember?

But tools can be used to open locks. Cracking open the truth and exposing it could change the balance of power. Tip the scales. Make a presidential campaign turn on a dime.

Too bad Silas doesn't believe me when I tell the truth.

And that may make him the biggest tool of all.

ABOUT THE AUTHOR

USA Today bestselling author Meli Raine writes romantic suspense with hot bikers, intense undercover DEA agents, bad boys turned good, and Special Ops heroes -- and the women who love them.

Meli rode her first motorcycle when she was five years old, but she played in the ocean long before that. She lives in New England with her family.

Visit her on Facebook at http://www.facebook.com/meliraine

Join her New Releases and Sales newsletter at: http://eepurl.com/beV0gf

She also writes romantic comedy as Julia Kent, and is half of the co-authoring team for the Diana Seere paranormal shifter romance books.

http://www.meliraine.com
www.meliraine.com
meli@meliraine.com

Printed in Great Britain
by Amazon
.